Who Killed Joe Italiano?

John Bekker Mystery Series

Sunset

Sunrise

First Light

This Side of Midnight

With Six You Get Wally

Who Killed Joe Italiano?

A John Bekker Mystery

Al Lamanda

Encircle Publications, LLC
Farmington, Maine U.S.A.

Chapter One

I usually avoid clichés as much as possible. For a while there, most of them went out of fashion when English underwent a dramatic transformation in the sixties and seventies. New words and phrases came to light; old standbys faded away.

Today, many of those old standbys have made a comeback, thanks in part to talking-heads on cable news. Most of the cable news reporters aren't true journalists in the Edward R. Murrow sense of the word, so they resort to clichés to score their points.

The one that drives me batty the most is commonly used by reporters, news anchors, talk show hosts and sadly, by most politicians. You've heard the phrase a thousand times, so often that it probably doesn't register anymore. It's *at the end of the day*, and when this cliché is used to score a point, it probably means the person using it hasn't got a clue about the particular point they're trying to make. Sadly, almost every politician and newscaster I see on the news today uses this phrase on a regular basis. Even the sports world is not immune to this particular cliché, and I hear it all the time during a ballgame.

However, sometimes a cliché will actually fit a certain situation or set of circumstances.

A few minutes past three in the morning, I came out on the balcony of my fourth-floor hotel room to listen to the ocean at Luquillo Beach. After a particularly nasty case where I was forced to take a physical beating to save the life of a little girl, I jumped into several insurance fraud cases that took ninety days or more to complete.

My daughter Regan decided I needed a vacation and she took

it upon herself to book ten days in sunny Puerto Rico, where the January temperatures reach the mid-eighties and even ninety. She reserved five days at a beach resort called the Ocean View, and the placed lived up to its name.

Four floors, forty rooms in a horseshoe shape, and every room had a balcony that faced the ocean. Tonight was our last night at the beach. Regan had us booked for another five days at a resort on the other side of the island near Old San Juan.

So far, we had visited the rain forest, zip-lined through the trees, swam in the beach every day, took a helicopter ride, and ate a lot of Puerto Rican food in genuine neighborhood restaurants.

From my balcony, I could see the strip of sidewalk across the street where the beach was located. There were street lamps every hundred feet, but while they illuminated the sidewalks, the sand and beach was invisible in the dark, moonless night.

I could hear the waves crashing, though. And the musical sound of a tiny frog native only to Puerto Rico, the coqui frog. It produces a two-syllable song that sounds like *co-key* and when hundreds of them are together, it's loud and goes on all night.

I listened to them for a while and thought about the cigarette I craved, but couldn't have. My daughter has grown a cigarette detector and if she even gets a hint of smoke on me anywhere, she goes ballistic, so I go without.

While I waited for the nicotine urge to pass, a man emerged from the shadows, crossed the street and stood near a street lamp. He was a tall man, maybe in his mid-thirties, dressed in a long-sleeve shirt dark in color, with matching slacks. I thought it odd that on a night where the temperature was around seventy-five degrees with at least eighty percent humidity that he wore long sleeves.

He stood quietly for a few minutes and then pulled a pack of cigarettes from his shirt pocket and lit one with a match. The distance from my balcony to the sidewalk was about three hundred feet and even though he stood under the street lamp, it was too far away and too dark to make out his face.

He smoked until the cigarette was spent, then he stepped on it with his right shoe. When he moved to extinguish the cigarette, light from the streetlamp reflected off his shoe and I could see they were leather loafers.

He stood there for a while longer, just minding his own business.

I should have returned to bed for I planned to be up at five to go running along the beach, which I had done every morning since we arrived. I started in front of our hotel and ran along the beach for thirty minutes until I reached the center of Luquillo, then turned around and ran back. After some pushups, situps and planks held for five minutes at a pop, I was ready for breakfast and met Oz and Regan on the balcony dining room.

I decided to quit watching him and return to bed when he moved suddenly to his left as another man approached from the hotel side of the street, crossed over and came to a stop.

They were separated by about a yard. In the dark, the second man appeared as tall, wore a white shirt designed for the heat, and casual slacks.

Then they turned and walked down to the beach and vanished in the darkness.

After a few seconds, I saw a match ignite and a second cigarette being lit. They were almost nose-to-nose at this point.

The match extinguished and they faded into darkness.

And at that moment, an old cliché ran through my mind, that *nothing good ever happens at three in the morning.*

I closed my eyes for a few seconds, listened to the wave's crash and coqui frogs sing their song, and almost tasted the man's cigarette. When I opened my eyes, all that was left to do was go to bed.

Chapter Two

I woke up again around five-fifteen and after a quick trip to the bathroom; I slipped on my shorts and tee shirt. There is a little, two-cup coffee maker in the room and I brewed two cups, and took one to the balcony.

Along with the glorious Puerto Rican sunrise, I was greeted by two ambulances, four police cars and a small crowd of onlookers held back by several uniformed officers.

The stretch of beach in front of the hotel was used mostly by surfers. The waves were too high and too rough for the casual swimmer and every morning someone came around to flag the water. Most days the flags were red and only the die-hard surfers dared venture out into the waves.

My first thought, as I sat in a chair and sipped coffee in the shade, was that a surfer had an accident and drowned. Mixed in with the on-lookers were several surfers that stood out because of their black body suits.

One of their own died for their cause. A drowning accident on a wave-swept beach happens all the time, even back home where the waves are relatively calm.

So when I left my room and went downstairs for my run, I dismissed it as a simple mishap, an accident common to surfers.

At least that's what I wanted it to be.

Wanting doesn't make it so.

I had to run on the sidewalk for the first hundred yards and then switched over to the sand. I ran close to the waves and their booming noise served as background music. After thirty minutes or so, I arrived at the center of Luquillo Beach. Barely six in the morning, the long stretch of white sand was deserted except for a few guys fishing off a rocky point and a flock of gulls searching for leftover scraps from yesterday.

I stopped for a few minutes to admire the new day and the ocean, then turned around and ran back to the hotel.

About thirty minutes later, I stopped short of the area where the ambulances had been, but were now gone. Most of the crowd had left, except for several police officers, including one in plain clothes that were still milling about.

The plain clothes had the look of detective about him. Most detectives I've met in my lifetime had a look about them, mostly in the eyes, that reeked of curiosity. To be a good detective, a person needed curiosity above and beyond all else. I had that look myself and, to some extent, probably still do.

While I did pushups and planks in the sand, I debated the cause. Should I approach the detective or go about my business and meet Regan and Oz for breakfast?

The detective made the decision for me when he spoke loudly in Spanish and then entered a dark sedan and drove away.

* * *

I met Regan and Oz for breakfast on the balcony at the allotted time of seven thirty.

"What's going on across the street?" Regan asked as we took a table. "There's police wandering around the beach."

"I think a surfer might have drowned," I said. "I saw ambulances earlier when I went for a run."

"Oh no," Regan said.

"It happens, honey," I said. "It's pretty rough waters out there. Most days it's red flags for high waves and strong currents."

"I know," Regan said. "I've seen them."

Oz looked at me as he sipped coffee.

"What?" I asked.

"You didn't happen to go poking that big cop nose where it don't belong?" he said. "Cause we be on vacation."

Oz spoke in soft, truncated sentences and often used slang, but his Morgan Freeman like voice made it sound like Shakespeare.

"No, I didn't, and I don't have a big…" I said.

"We checking out right after we eat," Oz said.

"I know that."

"I'm driving to Old San Juan," Oz said. "You make me car sick."

"How do I make you…?" I said.

"I think what Oz is trying to say is that sometimes you drive like a cop and it makes him dizzy," Regan said. "Me, too. Sometimes."

"Fine. Oz drives," I said.

"They packing up," Oz said.

I looked across the street and the last of the uniformed police were driving away.

"No crime scene tape, no uniforms left behind to guard the area for forensics, it must have been what I thought, an accident," I said.

Oz looked at me some more. He's around seventy-two or -three years-old with coffee-colored skin, graying hair and beard, and soft brown eyes that always have a hint of a twinkle in them.

"Good to know," he said. "If we all be packed, we leave right after breakfast."

We were on the road by nine. Oz drove west on Route 3 that basically, a few twists and turns aside, took us straight to Old San Juan. Traffic was heavy with commuters going to work and tourists.

Our resort hotel was located a mile or so from Old San Juan and overlooked the beach. Fifteen stories, pristine white with two pools, a spa and a gym, the resort was much more modern that the neighborhood we just left.

Regan booked us into three rooms on the twelfth floor, each with a balcony. The ocean view from my room was spectacular. Oz wanted to take a nap before lunch and Regan and I agreed to meet at the larger of the two pools.

Fully dressed with heels, she lays claim to five-foot-three inches tall and appears a little bird of a thing. I suspect she's closer to five-foot-one in bare feet, but it's a point I don't argue.

She has fine features, light brown hair that appears golden in sunlight and intelligent brown eyes.

What's remarkable to me is that in her bikini bathing suit, she has all the curves of a grown woman, which, at nineteen she qualified for. She settled poolside where she read a tour book of the island while I swam a few laps.

Before we left home, my old friend and new lady friend, Sheriff Jane Morgan took Regan to get her nails and hair done. The result was shiny red nails and blondish highlights in her shoulder-length hair.

"Old San Juan seems pretty cool, Dad," Regan said when I emerged from the pool. "Lots of shops, an old fort and tons of places to eat."

"Jewelry stores?" I asked as I took a Chaise lounge chair.

"Something for Jane?"

"Thinking about it."

"Engagement ring?"

"Too soon for that, honey," I said.

"Why? You've known each other since before I was born," Regan said. "And you're not getting any younger. Look at all the grey hairs on your chest and some on your head."

"Grey hair is better than no hair I always say."

"Earrings then," Regan said. "A woman always appreciates earrings."

"That's about what I was thinking," I said. "Maybe you can model a pair for me?"

"Let me look in the book," Regan said.

She studied the book for a bit while I closed my eyes and tried hard not to think about the incident at the beach.

"Dad?" she said after a while.

I opened my eyes.

"Yes?"

"Have you noticed how tired Oz seems these days?"

"Oz is seventy-one or -two now, honey," I said. "It's normal for people of that age to catnap during the day."

"If something happened to him, I couldn't deal with that."

"Don't confuse Oz's need for a nap with something being wrong," I said. "I have the feeling in a few years I'll be doing the same."

"I doubt that."

"He should be awake and ready by now, where should we go for lunch?"

"El Morro," Regan said.

* * *

El Morro is a fort built in 1539 by the Spanish to protect Old San Juan from seaborne invaders. It's a massive structure with six levels, old cannons and watchtowers and even a dungeon for prisoners.

It was hot, close to eighty degrees, and Regan wore shorts and a white tank top. Oz wore summer slacks with this god-awful shirt I picked up for him when I was in Hawaii. I settled for slacks and a Polo shirt.

From El Morro, we walked around downtown Old San Juan until we settled on a restaurant for a late lunch.

Regan dug out her tour book and scanned through it as we ate on a terrace that overlooked a large garden.

"There's a park a few blocks from here I'd like to see," she said. "And a bunch of jewelry stores not far from there."

Parque de las Palomas, the *Park of the Pigeons,* lived up to its name. It's a small, cement park overlooking the bay where, the moment you enter, a thousand pigeons pounce on you in search of food from their cubbyholes in the wall. Regan purchased a bag of food from a vendor and a hundred or more pigeons climbed atop her arms, shoulders and head for a taste.

Oz and I used our cell phones to take pictures and I grabbed a nice shot of Oz with a stray feeder perched on his head.

A few blocks from the park we came to a long street with six or seven large jewelry stores. We hunted and pecked our way through them until we found a store that carried the perfect pair of earrings that set me back five hundred dollars.

"Somebody be happy when we get home," Oz said.

Back to the hotel Regan treated herself to a treatment at the spa while Oz and I longed poolside.

As we sipped ice-cold lemonade, I said, "Regan is concerned about your napping. She thinks something is wrong."

"Something is," Oz said. "It called old age and if you had the sense of a goat, you be napping, too."

"Well, don't nap now because that handsome woman across the pool is eying you with particular interest," I said.

The woman in question was around sixty and looked very much like Eartha Kitt did when she was that age.

"She reminds me of Eartha Kitt," I said.

"Which Eartha Kitt, the gorgeous singer of the forties or the one play Cat Woman on the old Batman show in the sixties?" Oz asked.

"One and the same," I said. "She looks like she wants to talk to you."

"I got no time for female persuasion," Oz said.

"You have nothing but…I don't even know what that means," I said.

"Mean mind your own business," Oz said.

The woman flagged a passing poolside bartender and said a few words to him. He gave her his pad and pen and she scribbled a note.

A moment later the bartender delivered the note to Oz.

"What's it say?" I asked.

"Says to mind you own business and shut up," Oz said.

"If I didn't know better, I would say you're afraid to talk to the lady," I said.

"At my age, I'm afraid to pee in the dark for fear I mistake the sink for the toilet."

"At least you won't miss," I said. "What's the note say?"

"Say am I free for dinner," Oz said. "And I'm not. Regan want to…"

"Regan will be fine in the company of her old man," I said. "Go over there and tell her yes."

"I haven't had dinner with a woman since my wife died," Oz said.

"Twenty years is long enough, don't you think?" I said.

"What we talk about?" Oz asked. "The weather?"

"Simple," I said. "Ask her about herself and let her do all the talking. Just sit there, nod and look wise."

"If she asks about me, I tell her what?"

"The truth," I said. "She looks like the kind of woman that can handle the truth."

Oz looked at me. "If you say you need me on that wall, I slap you."

"Go, or I'll go for you," I said.

"Cause you just so suave with women," Oz said.

"Go or I'll…nobody uses the word suave," I said.

Oz stood up. "Suave sound better than asshole," he said. "Which you is," he said and crossed the pool.

*　*　*

"Where's Oz?" Regan asked when we met in the lobby around seven.

"Oz is engaged for dinner with a lady he met at the pool," I said.

My daughter appeared mildly shocked.

"A woman? Oz? What do you know about her?"

"She looks like Eartha Kitt," I said.

"Who?"

"She was a…"

"You left him alone with a strange woman he just met?"

"Oz is a grown man," I said. "I think he can handle dinner with a woman. Speaking of dinner, where do you want to go?"

"The Kioskos at Luquillo," Regan said. "We were ten minutes away and haven't even been there yet."

I handed Regan the keys to the rental. "You drive," I said. "I don't want to make you car sick and ruin your appetite."

She snatched the keys from my hand. "Don't be a wiseass, Dad. Nobody likes a wiseass."

Regan drove the rental east on Route Three to Luquillo Beach where the Kioskos is located. The kioskos is a long strip mall of restaurants, sixty in all, that is located just a few hundred feet from the beach.

We wandered the mall of restaurants until Regan decided we should try Peruvian. Along with the meal came atmosphere and Peruvian music.

"So about this woman?" Regan asked as we ate.

"What about her?"

"Dad!"

"There's not much I can tell you," I said. "She sent him a note at the pool asking him to dinner."

"And he went?" Regan said.

"Oz has been alone since his wife died twenty years ago," I said. "A female companion for dinner won't kill him."

"Well, who is Eartha Kitt?" Regan asked.

"She was a beautiful black woman singer and movie star in the forties and later was the Cat Woman on the Batman show in the sixties," I said.

"Oz is having dinner with Cat Woman?" Regan said.

"Relax, honey," I said. "At their age, both are spayed and neutered."

"Funny. What should we have for dessert?"

* * *

Around eleven that night, I was watching a western on television. It had been dubbed into Spanish with English subtitles. A soft knock on my door got me out of bed.

"Bekker," Oz said almost breathless.

"Is something…?"

Oz brushed past me and closed the door.

"She wants me to go back to her room," Oz said.

"Who, Eartha Kitt?"

"Yes, of course Eartha…her name be Louisa cause her mama liked the writer so much," Oz said.

"So why are you here with me instead of there with her?"

"Cause she…I mean we… do you have any of those little blue pills?"

"Little blue…you mean Viagra?"

"Jeeze, man, you don't got to shout about it," Oz winced.

"I wasn't…no, I don't, Oz," I said. "It's not something I usually carry around."

Oz sat on the bed. "It be so long since I been with a woman I…"

"Wait a second," I said.

I went to the bathroom and dug through my travel bag for a bottle of L-Arginine and took it to Oz.

"Take five of these," I said.

Oz looked at the bottle. "What's this?"

"It's an amino acid supplement I take before I go running," I said.

"Amino acid? I don't think she's planning on going for no running," Oz said.

"It increases blood flow so you can run longer with more oxygen," I said. "Take five of these and it's like taking one of those little blue pills."

Oz read the bottle. "Yeah? I'll take ten."

"Take the whole bottle," I said. "It's a two-pack."

Chapter Three

The hotel gym opened at five thirty in the morning and I was the first and only patron at that hour.

I didn't mind. I put the wall-mounted television on and watched a fifty-year-old episode *of Gilligan's Island* dubbed in Spanish and did thirty minutes on a Stairmaster for starters. The gym had decent enough equipment and I did a few sets on each and ended with some stretching. By seven, I was on the way back to my room.

Two newspapers were waiting for me outside the room. I took both in with me and tossed them on the bed while I took a shower. I was getting dressed when I glanced at the newspapers.

One was an English version of *USA Today*.

The second was in Spanish. The front page photo caught my eye. I sat on the bed and picked it up. The headline was bold above the photo. My Spanish was weak and I couldn't read the headline or story, but I recognized the photograph.

It was the view from my balcony of the beach with police huddled around a body.

I took the newspaper with me to the lobby and went to the front desk.

"Can you tell me what this says?" I asked a woman behind the desk.

She glanced at the paper and frowned. She had a fairly thick Spanish accent, but her English was perfectly understandable.

"The headline?" she asked.

I nodded.

"It says, *Who Killed Joe Italiano?*"

"Who killed…who is Joe Italiano?" I asked.

"The news said a local businessman. I haven't read the story."

"Is there an English version of the paper?" I asked.

"No, but I can call the paper and have the story translated for you and sent to your room, if you'd like?"

"That would be good. I'll pay whatever it costs."

She smiled. "I'll put it on your bill."

I wandered into the breakfast dining room and took a table for four and ordered coffee. Regan joined me before the cup was empty.

"Where's Oz?" she said as she took a seat.

"I'm sure he'll be along any minute," I said.

And he was. With Louisa on his right arm.

"Dad?" Regan whispered as they walked to the table.

"We have to let him go sometime, honey," I said.

"This thing that look like last Wednesday's meatloaf is John Bekker," Oz said to Louisa when they arrived. "And this beautiful little bird be his daughter Reagan. This be Louisa Annemarie Calhoun."

Louisa smiled at Regan and said, "You are right, she is a lovely young woman."

Oz slid a chair out for Louisa and she gently sat.

"And he is exactly as you said," Louisa said.

"I can just imagine how Oz described me," I said.

With a sheepish grin, Louisa said, "Oz said you most resembled a worn out boxing glove."

I looked at Oz.

Regan looked at Louisa.

"Well, he's no prize, that's for sure," Regan said.

"So," I said. "I think I'll have the pancakes."

Louisa was a charming woman who was also a widow, having lost her husband ten years earlier to cancer. Her two sons were grown with kids of their own and she liked to travel in her spare time, which there wasn't much of. She was, of all things, a NASA mathematician. She, along with a team of engineers and mathematicians, plotted such things as orbits and movements of planets, suns and spacecraft, fuel ratio to distances and things far and away above my head.

She honeymooned in Puerto Rico more than thirty years ago and started taking vacations here a few years back because they always wanted to return but never could find the time.

"Oz invited me to spend the day with you," she said. "I have to fly home tomorrow for a meeting, so if it doesn't put you out…"

"It doesn't and we'd be delighted," I said.

"Oz said that Regan is the tour guide," Louisa said. "So young lady, I am at your disposal."

* * *

We took a boat ride to an island called Monkey Island and snorkeled in shallow waters. The island is home to hundreds of Rhesus monkeys, brought there by scientists in 1938 for the purpose of behavioral study. People are not allowed on the island, but if you stand still in the water, the monkeys will come out and watch you. Don't look the males in the eye as they take it as a challenge and become visibly upset and quite possibly could swim out to you to issue a challenge.

From there we had lunch at a small restaurant in Cayo Santiago. Then it was off to Fajardo where we rented chairs and watched the sunset with the mountains of the rainforest behind us.

We returned to the hotel around eight-thirty, exhausted and hungry, and grabbed a quick bite poolside thanks to room service.

Louisa had a ten am flight and we agreed to meet at seven-thirty for breakfast.

I entered my room and found a folder had been slipped under the door. Before I even opened it, Oz was behind me and ushered himself into the room and closed the door.

"Bekker, can I have that other bottle of L-whatever?" he whispered.

"Arginine and you're going to kill yourself," I said.

"Half then. That way I be only half dead come morning."

I fetched the bottle and tossed it to Oz. "I want whatever is leftover back in the morning."

"Sure," Oz said, opened the door and rushed out.

Alone, I stripped down to my underwear, ran the AC on high, grabbed a Coke from the small fridge beside the television and sat on the bed to read the story inside the folder.

Who Killed Joe Italiano was written by a featured crime writer at the paper named Pablo Pagon.

Joe Italiano is/was a local businessman named Joseph DeSousa and he was a native of New York City. He married a Puerto Rican girl from the Bronx and they purchased a small home in Fajardo thirty years ago.

DeSousa, age listed as sixty, owned or had controlling interests in many businesses on the island. Among them were three beach resort hotels, two real estate companies, two grocery stores, one private cab company and a coffee plantation.

I looked up for a moment to sip some Coke.

"Coffee plantation?" I said aloud.

He was well known for his acts of charity, including financing the restoration of a church and the building of a Little League baseball field. He was often spotted with his wife Maria at church on Sunday.

Besides his wife, DeSousa was survived by his two sons and one daughter and several grandchildren, all of whom lived in New York.

DeSousa also kept a residence in New York and he and Maria divided their time between the two.

Details of his death are unclear at the present time. Authorities stated that his body was found around five in the morning by several early morning surfer. His body had two stab wounds in the chest, but it was unclear if he was stabbed at the beach or elsewhere and moved to the beach and dumped. Motive is unknown.

Police are not granting interviews at this time and his family will be in seclusion until after the funeral services.

Police have requested that anyone with any information to call the state police hotline number immediately and ask for Lieutenant Escalante.

I set the file aside and took another sip of Coke.

"Aw, hell," I said aloud.

Chapter Four

"I be back with the car as soon as she be on the plane," Oz said when we met for breakfast.

"I told him I would take a cab, but he wouldn't hear of it," Louisa said.

"No problem," I said. "We'll just hang out at the pool for a bit."

Regan had really warmed up to Louisa once she realized Oz wasn't going to be kidnapped and held for ransom in a basement somewhere.

With a hug and kiss for Regan and a warm handshake for me, Louisa and Oz departed.

"Okay with you if I grab another treatment at the spa?" Regan asked when we returned to the lobby.

"Sure."

In my room, I called the state police hotline number and asked for someone that spoke English. They all did, and a woman asked the nature of my call.

"Lieutenant Escalante, please," I said.

"In reference to?"

"Joe Italiano."

"Do you have information?"

"I do."

"I'll relay it to him as soon as he gets out of a meeting."

"I'd rather tell him myself," I said. "Have him call me at this number. My name is John Bekker."

I left the number for my cell phone.

* * *

I had the StairMaster in the gym set to level twelve for one hour. There is a little shelf designed to rest a book upon and I placed my cell phone on it.

It rang at minute fifty-seven.

The incoming number showed the state police. I grabbed the phone and stepped off the StairMaster.

"This is John Bekker," I said.

"Mr. Bekker, this is Lieutenant Escalante. You called and said you have some information for me."

Escalante spoke without an accent.

"I do," I said. "Before we talk, I want you to do something for me. I'd like you to call Police Captain Walter Grimes and verify that I am who I say I am. Can you do that?"

"I don't have time for games, Mr. Bekker," Escalante said. "If you…"

"If you don't call Captain Grimes, chances are you won't believe what I have to say to you," I said.

There was a short pause followed by a sigh. "If you're some nut job with a complex, I'll have you locked up. What's the number?"

I gave him the number and reset the StairMaster for another thirty minutes and twenty minutes later, Escalante called back.

"I spoke with Captain Grimes," Escalante said.

"And he said?"

"You sound breathless."

"I've been on a StairMaster for ninety minutes," I said. "I'm still on it."

"StairMaster?"

"What did Walt say?"

"He said you're the best cop he's ever worked with, a prima donna and a pain in the ass," Escalante said.

"He said prima donna?"

"And pain in the ass," Escalante said. "Actually, I think he said major pain in the ass. He also said if I had something that needed solving that the odds of solving it were better with you than without. So, what do you have for me?"

"Remember show and tell from grade school?" I said.

"What?"

"I'm on vacation with my daughter," I said. "Can you meet me at the Ocean View Resort on Luquillo Beach at ten tonight?"

"If you're jerking my…"

"I'm not and bring a few uniforms," I said. "We'll need them."

"Why ten tonight?"

"My show and tell won't work in daylight," I said. "I'll see you at ten."

* * *

I met Regan poolside where almost every chair and chaise lounge was occupied.

"It's almost eleven, where is Oz?" Regan said when I took the vacant chair beside her.

"I suspect stuck in airport traffic," I said. "What's in the tour book for today?"

"We go home in three days, Dad," Regan said. "So we only really have two full days left. I don't think this is something Oz would want to do, but I'd like to try scuba diving. There is a course in Fajardo at the beach this afternoon. They take you out on a boat to a calm bay not far from Monkey Island."

"Sounds fine to me," I said.

Regan looked at me with her cat ate the canary expression. "Am I being selfish?"

"Because you want to learn scuba diving?"

"No, silly. Maybe. I meant with Oz," Regan said. "I practically forced him to move in with us when you bought the house. He looked really happy spending the day with Louisa, I thought maybe…"

"Oz is as much a part of our family as Molly or Buddy or even your cousin Mark," I said. "If he didn't want to be with us he would have stayed at the beach. It did him some good to spend some time with Louisa. He hasn't really talked to a woman since his wife died."

Regan nodded.

"Here he comes now," I said. "Ask him?"

"Ask what?" Oz said when he arrived.

"If you wouldn't mind spending the afternoon on a boat with me watching Regan take scuba diving lesions," I said.

"Only if I partake," Oz said.

Regan sat up in her lounge. "Oz, you're too…"

"Old," Oz said. "You're sometime not too bright father have a saying he used more than once. He said a man is only as old as the woman he feels. Today, little miss, old Oz feel like he eighteen."

"Oh God," Regan said. "The both of you qualify for AARP."

"Don't make us old," Oz said. "Just wise enough to get discounts at the movies."

* * *

"Maybe not so wise," Oz said as I drove back to the hotel after four hours of diving lessons.

Regan got the hang of it right away and after an hour of practice she was diving in ten feet of water. I had snorkeled many times in the past, but never with a tank. It took some adjusting, but I got the hang of it and kept pace with Regan and the instructors.

Oz was the surprise. I didn't even know he could swim, but he could and well. He took to the lessons as quickly as Regan and stayed with her the entire time.

"What's the matter?" I asked.

"I need a nap after this," Oz said.

Regan turned around and looked at him. "What's wrong?" she said.

"I'm pooped, what you think?" Oz said.

"You look sick," Regan said. "Like ash."

"Ash?" Oz said. "You mean my skin?"

"Yes."

"Girl, that's how Oz tans," Oz said with a chuckle.

* * *

The red message light on my phone was blinking when I returned to my room after we had dinner in the hotel restaurant.

I retrieved the message and then called Sheriff Jane Morgan.

"Got my message I see," Jane said.

"I did," I said. "We're at the new place I told you about a few days ago."

"Everything okay?"

"Everything's good. Is something wrong on the home front?"

"Yes," Jane said. "And it pains me to say this to a first class putz like you, but I miss you in a strange dog misses their owner kind of way."

"Which of us is the dog?" I asked.

"I'm too blonde and buxom to be the dog," Jane said.

"You should have taken the time off and come with us," I said.

"Not with budgets due to the county town council," Jane said. "Meeting is tomorrow."

"Maybe we should consider taking a little trip of our own when I get back?" I said.

"Maybe we should," Jane said. "Anyplace in mind?"

"I'll leave that up to you," I said. "It will be my treat."

"I'm worth it, of course, but…"

"Think on it and tell me when I get home," I said. "Right now I have to go to work."

"Work? Bekker, what are you…?"

"Will you be up around midnight?"

"I'll still be in the office."

"I'll call you then."

After a quick shower and change of clothes, I was off to meet with Lieutenant Escalante.

Odd how satisfied I felt about that.

Chapter Five

Ten minutes before ten, I stood in front of the eight-foot-high gates of the Ocean View at Luquillo Beach Hotel and waited for Escalante.

He arrived in a dark sedan five minutes later, followed by two black and whites with Policia written on the sides.

Escalante was around six feet tall, wiry thin with black hair, dark eyes and a pencil-thin moustache.

"Bekker?" he asked.

I nodded.

"Frisk him," Escalante said. "Give me his wallet."

The two uniformed cops gave me a decent enough pat down, removed my wallet and gave it to Escalante. He opened it, held it up to the light of a street lamp and then tossed it back to me.

"So show me and tell me," he said.

"I need to call the desk and have them let us in," I said.

Escalante nodded.

I pulled out my cell phone and dialed the number for the desk. A minute later, the electronic gate slid open.

"I'll need your men to stay here," I said. "And to take this."

I gave one of them an unopened pack of cigarettes, a disposable lighter and a book of matches I picked up at a gas station.

"Do you have a radio?" I asked Escalante.

"Yes."

"Bring it."

Escalante and I went to the office.

"We need to see room 411," I said.

"I recognize you," the woman behind the desk said. "Mr. Bekker, right?"

"That's right," I said. "And this is police Lieutenant Escalante."

She looked at him and I could see distress flash in her eyes.

"It has nothing to do with the hotel," I said.

She nodded. "411 is vacant until tomorrow. I'll let you in."

A few minutes later, we stood on the balcony and looked down on the beach.

"See how the street lamps light up the sidewalk, but a few feet past it is completely dark?" I said.

Escalante nodded. "It's designed that way for people to feel safe on the sidewalk at night," he said.

"The news story said he was stabbed in the chest, but didn't give details," I said. "I say he was stabbed on the right side near the ribs."

Escalante looked at me.

"That's right, isn't it?" I said.

"It is."

"The ME put the time of death at around three-thirty in the morning?" I asked.

"He did."

"Around three, I came out to the balcony for some fresh air," I said.

"Did you see anyone on the street at the time?"

"No. Call your men and have the one with the cigarettes cross the street and stand under the street lamp directly in line with this balcony," I said.

Escalante removed his radio from his belt and spoke to the officers in Spanish.

We watched one of them cross the street.

"This man was about six feet tall, slim and wore a dark-colored, long sleeve shirt and leather shoes," I said. "Joe Italiano, as he was called, came from the right side of the fence out of our view and then crossed the street and met the first man. Tell the other officer to do that and have him face him from our left."

Escalante spoke in Spanish to the second officer and he crossed the street and stood in front of the officer with the cigarettes.

"See how the officer I gave the cigarettes to is a mirror image of the other one?" I said. "If he reached out with his left hand he would touch the other officer's right."

"Yes, I see that," Escalante said.

"Tell them to hold their positions and walk onto the beach until we no longer can see them," I said.

Escalante told them in Spanish and when they disappeared into darkness, he told them to stop.

"That's how it went down at three in the morning," I said. "First long sleeves, then Joe Italiano. They said a few words then went onto the beach."

"Where you can't see them from here," Escalante said.

"Tell your man to light a cigarette using the lighter, holding the lighter in his right hand and cupping it in his left," I said.

Escalante told him in Spanish on the radio.

We watched and there was just a tiny glow of light that quickly faded.

"That's how a right handed person lights a cigarette," I said. "Now tell him to do it again but in reverse."

Escalante told him.

The light from the lighter was bright enough to illuminate the smoker's face and the other officer opposite him.

"Now tell him to do it again using the match," I said. "Lighting the match with his left hand, cupping with the right."

Escalante told him and we watched as the officer lit the match, cupped and held it to the cigarette.

"What did you see?" I asked.

"I saw the same thing," Escalante said.

"No, you didn't," I said. "With a lighter you get instant flame that's constant. With a match you get a spark and slow ignition. Tell him to use a match again."

We watched as the match did a spark and slow burn.

"He used a match," I said. "Twice. He smoked one cigarette when he was alone under the street lamp, and then another on the beach. He's a left handed smoker who uses matches."

Escalante looked at me.

"I'm not about to tell a fellow police detective how to do his job, but if it was me, I might do a search for two cigarette butts and a book of matches on the beach," I said. "Maybe look for a butt on the sidewalk or street and a matching brand near the crime scene. DNA can be lifted from cigarette butts if they haven't been destroyed. Maybe get a forensics crew out there tonight with million watt candle power searchlights and pick up every butt inside a thirty square foot perimeter of the crime scene, matches, too."

"Is there anything else you wouldn't want to tell me to do?" Escalante asked.

"Do you drink coffee, Lieutenant Escalante?" I asked.

* * *

A few blocks from the hotel is a burger joint called Surf's Up. We ate there a few nights ago after the trip to the rain forest. It was open until one. We took a table on the porch facing the ocean and ordered coffee.

"That's an impressive observation about lighting the cigarette left-handed," Escalante said.

"I smoked for a long time," I said. "I know how a right-handed person lights a cigarette."

"Maybe so, but only a really well-trained cop would notice," Escalante said.

"Robbery ruled out?" I asked.

"As far as we can tell, nothing is missing from his body," Escalante said. "Wedding ring, gold Rolex watch, wallet with eleven hundred dollars all intact."

"Have you talked to his family, friends, employees yet?" I asked.

"I have six detectives conducting interviews," Escalante said. "Including his business appointments, computers and phone conversations. I'm handling the family, but so far all I've talked to is Mrs. DeSousa."

"His finances?"

"Every shred will be put under a microscope."

"Enemies?"

"No known, but it's almost impossible to have his kind of money and not have any," Escalante said.

"His charity work?"

Escalante took a sip of his coffee, and then set the cup down. "That, too, although I can't see killing a man in cold blood because he built a hospital."

"Maybe not, but maybe a competitor wanted the land where he built the little league baseball field," I said. "You never know."

Escalante sighed. "I quit, too. Now would be a good time to light up."

"It would," I agreed.

"How long were you on the job?"

"Sixteen years."

"Private?"

"A few."

"I'm going on twenty-two," Escalante said as he picked up his cup. "Fourteen as a detective, four as Lieutenant."

"How long have you been divorced?" I asked.

Escalante was about to take a sip, paused and looked at me. "Three years. How did you know?"

"You were rubbing the ring finger of your left hand," I said. "Either you have arthritis in that one joint or you're playing with the ring that used to be there but no longer is."

"Captain Grimes was right about you," Escalante said.

"Prima donna, good cop or pain in the ass?" I said.

"That the odds of solving a problem are better with you than without."

"Shall we walk back and see if forensics found anything?" I asked.

"Sure."

I left a tip and we walked along the sidewalk. We could see the powerful searchlights the forensics people were using on the beach some four blocks away.

"You're wearing short-sleeves, as am I and the uniformed officers," I said. "What would you say the temperature is right now?"

"Seventy-seven when I arrived," Escalante said.

"About what it was when I came out on the balcony, but with higher humidity," I said. "I know people get acclimatized, but would you wear long sleeves on a night like this?"

"I would not, but some here might. He could have come from an evening of night clubbing, or expected it to be cooler by the ocean," Escalante said.

"Maybe."

"But you don't think so?"

"Did you ever meet DeSousa?"

"Several times," Escalante said. "Once at a police fundraiser. He donated one hundred thousand to our equipment fund."

"And?"

"And nothing. He shook my hand along with a hundred others."

"Did he own firearms?" I asked.

There was a slight hesitation, and then Escalante said, "Yes. He had a permit and owns several."

"But none with him?"

"No."

"Odd. Three in the morning, a meeting at the beach in the dark, you own a gun and don't have one with you for protection," I said.

We reached the crime scene where six forensics officers were still combing the beach for evidence.

"I'm assuming the nickname Joe Italiano comes from the natives?" I said.

"Yes, but the funny thing is DeSousa is Portuguese," Escalante said. "DeSousa sounds Italian and a few locals started calling him that thirty years ago and it stuck."

"His wife is?"

"Puerto Rican, although born in the Bronx," Escalante said. "So was DeSousa."

"Lieutenant, we covered every square inch and picked up

more than thirty butts, some loose change, a button and five used condoms," a forensics officer said in English.

"Any of the butts match brands?" Escalante asked.

"Several."

"Take them in for processing," Escalante said.

"The button, too," I said. "See if it can be matched to a particular brand of shirt."

The forensics officer looked at Escalante and Escalante nodded.

"Okay," the forensics officer said and returned to his crew.

"When we left for Puerto Rico it was fifty-three degrees," I said. "Not cold enough for a coat, but I wore a long-sleeve shirt. Maybe the perp flew in from somewhere colder to meet DeSousa and didn't have time to change his shirt. Cigarette lighters are off the no-fly list, but maybe he didn't know that and picked up a book of matches at the airport. I might check flights and see who flew in and out on overnight flights and see if they had checked luggage and had hotel and rental car reservations."

Escalante smiled at me. "Anything else you might or might not do?"

"What kind of knife was used?"

"The ME said it was a long knife with a serrated edge," Escalante said.

"Sounds like a bread knife found in kitchens everywhere," I said. "An odd choice of weapon, isn't it?"

"It is."

"Can't bring it on a plane, but you can buy one anywhere," I said.

Escalante nodded.

"Maybe he buried it on the beach or tossed it in some weeds on the way out," I said. "A metal detector would be handy."

"It would," Escalante agreed.

"DeSousa's car was found where?" I asked.

"Around the corner," Escalante said. "A black Town Car."

"It's been gone over?"

"Still in the process. It's pretty clean though."

"I go home in two days," I said.

"I'll need you to come to the station and fill out a statement," Escalante said. "So far, you're my only witness."

"I'll stop by tomorrow sometime," I said. "Thanks for the coffee,"

* * *

It was after one am when I returned to my hotel room. I wasn't tired and knew sleep was off the table for a while.

I grabbed a Coke from the fridge and found some stationery and a pen in the desk. I sat, sipped and stared at a blank piece of paper.

Why three in the morning?

Legitimate business meetings take place during normal business hours.

Why park around the corner when parking is allowed in the street in front of the beach?

I took a sip of Coke and thought about that.

DeSousa parked around the corner so he could hide in the dark and watch the sidewalk for whoever he was meeting.

Maybe he thought the man wouldn't show?

Why no bodyguards?

A man as wealthy as DeSousa running around at three in the morning alone and unarmed didn't make sense.

I sipped some Coke and thought for a moment.

I grabbed my cell phone and dialed the hotline number. A woman with a thick Spanish accent answered the call.

"Lieutenant Escalante," I said. "Tell him it's John Bekker."

"I'll need to call him," she said. "Can he call you back?"

"Yes."

I took the Coke and phone out to the balcony. Ten minutes later, Escalante called.

"Autopsy of DeSousa?"

"The second stab wound pierced his heart," Escalante said. "It's what killed him."

"Have the ME measure the distance from the entrance wound to the heart," I said. "A standard bread knife has a blade eight inches long."

"Sounds about right."

"Toxicology?"

"In the works."

"It has to have occurred to you that the stabber is a drug dealer," I said. "That DeSousa was looking to score."

"He could snap his fingers and a dozen flunkies would bring him whatever he wanted," Escalante said.

"Unless he wanted absolutely no one to know about it," I said.

"True. Well, we'll have the report in a few days. Anything else?"

"Yeah, sleep."

"Not an option for me right now," Escalante said.

I hung up and returned to the desk.

I read my notes.

What jumped out at me was the dark side of the moon.

Chapter Six

"We go home tomorrow," Regan said.

We were having breakfast poolside. The morning air was relatively cool with a hint of what was to come later in the day.

"So let's take a vote on what we do today," Regan suggested.

"I like to maybe check out those jewelry stores in Old San Juan," Oz said.

I looked at him.

Regan all but burst into laughter.

"What?" Oz said. "I could use a new watch."

"With Louisa's name on it?" I said.

"It's okay, Oz, we understand," Regan said.

Oz glared at me. "Looking at something, fool?"

"As long as were going to Old San Juan, there are some historic churches I'd like to see," Regan said. "Dad?"

"The bioluminescent bay after dark," I said.

"Agreed," Regan said. "Jewelry store is up first."

"I need a small favor," I said. "Between Old San Juan and bioluminescent bay, I have to stop off at the state police station for a few minutes."

Regan and Oz looked at me.

"Just for a few minutes," I said.

"Why?" Regan asked.

"I need to give a statement to a Lieutenant Escalante," I said.

"Why?"

"I witnessed a crime, a murder."

"Dad!" Regan snapped.

"And we off," Oz said.

"Ten minutes, that's all it takes," I said.

"How did you…never mind, I don't want to know," Regan said. "Ten minutes."

"That's all it takes," I said.

"I'm going to my room to change," Regan said.

Once Regan was gone from the table, Oz took a quiet sip of coffee and then said, "You lie with such a straight face it sickening."

"I witnessed a murder, what am I supposed to do?" I said.

"I ain't talking 'bout that," Oz said. "Course you gotta say what you witnessed. I'm talking bout telling her ten minutes when you damn well know it be hours."

"Have you ever felt my daughter's temper?" I asked.

"Be like that movie *Wrath of Kahn*," Oz said.

"I figure it's better to have her mad at me for just part of the day than all day," I said.

"Your problem be you much smarter than you look," Oz said.

"I always thought of it as an asset," I said.

"If you leave off the e and the t," Oz said. "You got it right."

* * *

I looked at men's watches while Oz and Regan picked out a bracelet for Louisa.

"Dad, what do you think?" Regan asked.

I left the watch counter and walked to her. She extended her left wrist to show me the gold bracelet with diamond chips she and Oz picked out.

I looked at Oz. "Finally cracked open the piggybank," I said.

"They'll ship it from here," Regan said. "As soon as Oz signs the card."

"Well, sign the card, we have churches to see," I said.

"Oz doesn't know what to say," Regan said.

"Oh for…say anything," I said.

"How would you like a gift that say anything on it?" Oz said.

"Write this, Oz. All women like to hear this," Regan said. "*My dearest Louisa. Thinking of you.* Sign it, *fondly, Oz.*"

"That be good," Oz smiled. "That be real good."

"It shows you care without being overly sloppy," Regan said.

"Listen to Little Miss Hallmark here and sign the card," I said.

"Is it okay I pay for it first?" Oz asked.

* * *

Between visits to four-hundred-year-old churches, we squeezed in lunch at a restaurant that overlooked the bay and Fort el Morro.

Then we made a quick stop at Pigeon Park so Regan could feed the pigeons again followed by two more churches and a walk along blue cobblestone streets.

From there I drove to the state police station near Old San Juan. I called Escalante earlier and told him to expect me around three.

"We'll wait for you here," Regan said as I left the car.

I nodded and entered the stationhouse.

"Do you speak English?" I asked the sergeant at the desk.

"Yes," he said.

"Could you tell Lieutenant Escalante that John Bekker is here to see him," I said.

He nodded and picked up the phone.

Five minutes later, a uniformed officer came down a flight of stairs, walked to me and said in English. "Mr. Bekker, I'll take you to the Lieutenant."

Escalante's office was tucked in back on the second floor. His name was stenciled in gold lettering on a frosted glass door.

The officer knocked and opened the door. "Lieutenant, Mr. Bekker," he said in English.

I wasn't expecting to see Maria DeSousa in the office with Escalante. She was seated in a chair facing Escalante's desk and turned when I entered the office. She was a handsome woman around fifty-five, with coal black hair and dark eyes reddened from crying and puffy from lack of sleep.

She stood up and was around five foot four or so and maybe a hundred and twenty pounds. She wore a sleeveless black dress with a black fishnet shoulder wrap.

"You are Bekker, the man who last saw my husband alive?" she said without a trace of an accent.

"Yes," I said.

"Mrs. DeSousa, this is John Bekker," Escalante said. "He's here to give a statement."

"Lieutenant Escalante called me this morning," Maria said. "He told me about you, what you said and did. He said you were a great police officer and detective in the States. I would like you to help him find my husband's murderer."

I looked past her at Escalante and his face was expressionless.

"Mrs. DeSousa, I am truly sorry for your loss," I said. "I understand what it is like to lose your spouse. However, I'm on vacation with my daughter and we go home tomorrow morning. I am sorry, but I won't be around."

"The Lieutenant said you are now a private detective," Maria said. "I would like to hire you to assist him in finding the man who killed my husband."

"I have clients waiting back home," I said. "I am sorry."

Maria's eyes blazed with anger and she marched past me and stormed out of the office and slammed the door.

"She's emotional right now," Escalante said. "I'll speak with her later."

"I understand," I said. "I'll write that statement now."

* * *

Escalante saw me out and walked with me to my car. When we reached the front steps of the stationhouse, I could barely believe my eyes.

Regan and Maria DeSousa were hugging in front of the car. Oz looked at me and shrugged.

"I see you met my daughter," I said.

"And this nice gentleman Oz," Maria said.

"Oz and I will go home tomorrow, but you have to stay and find out who murdered Maria's husband," Regan said. "I'll explain to Jane."

"You'll explain to…" I said.

Regan looked at Maria. "Okay?"

Maria smiled and wiped away a tear. "Thank you," she said.

Regan winked. "He'll always do as I say out of guilt. It's like having a super power."

Oz grinned and looked away.

I looked at Escalante.

"I can clear it with the captain," he said.

I sighed. "I'll call Jane myself," I said to Regan. "But you take the blame."

"I'm your daughter and young and innocent and that makes me blameless," Regan said.

"This girl gonna go far," Oz said.

I looked at Maria DeSousa "I can stop by and meet with the Lieutenant after I take them to the airport," I said. "Around ten-thirty."

"I will be here," Maria said.

* * *

We were eating ice cream cones at the bay where the boat launches for the bioluminescence tour. The park adjacent to the bay was filled with food vendors, native arts and crafts and rides for kids.

The boat left at six-thirty, calculating sunset at seven.

"Don't worry about Jane, Dad, I'll explain it to her," Regan said.

"Exactly how did you meet Mrs. DeSousa?" I asked.

"Well," Regan said in between licks on her quickly melting cone. "She said that she was looking out the window and saw our car arrive. She saw you get out and then me and Oz. When she came out alone, she knew we were with you and she introduced herself."

"And she convinced you to tell me to stay how?"

"She said her husband was a very important man to Puerto Rico,"

35

Regan said. "He gave millions to charity and somebody murdered him. She said that you were the last person to see him alive and could be a great help to the police. She said that in addition to paying your fee she would make a large donation to any charity you choose. Hope Springs Eternal could use a nice donation, don't you think?"

I looked at Oz. Vanilla ice cream was in his beard. "The kid own you, Bekker," he said.

"Big talk from a man with ice cream in his beard," I said.

"It's time to line up for the boat," Regan said.

The boat ride was a gentle trip through a narrow channel into a lagoon. By the time we entered the lagoon, the sun was down and darkness was settling in. An instructor onboard told us about the live algae in the water that caused it to light up when agitated. We each received a long stick that when placed into the dark water and stirred, agitated the algae and it glowed brightly. The moment you held the stick still, the algae quieted down and the bright glow vanished.

Quite a trick for just some algae.

* * *

Our final dinner together was spent at the Kioskos in a Puerto Rican steak house. We were back at the hotel by ten-thirty.

I called Jane from my room.

"Hey Bekker, need a ride from the airport?" Jane said, cheerfully when she answered the phone.

"Regan and Oz might," I said.

There was a short pause. Then, "Something happened. What?"

"Let me grab a Coke," I said and snatched one from the fridge.

By the time the can was empty, Jane was up to speed. "For crying out loud, Bekker," she said.

"It was an accident," I said. "Nothing planned."

"And you're there to save the day," she said.

"You're a cop, Jane, you know how it goes," I said.

"I do know and I'm mad anyway," Jane said. "And I must sound a lot like your old girlfriend Janet to you right now. I'm sorry. I should know better."

"How much vacation time do you have?"

"Enough to take off for six months and oh no you don't," Jane said. "I'm not taking vacation days to fly there and play Pink Panther learns Spanish with you."

"What's the temperature there right now?"

"Fifty-one and raining."

"It's seventy-seven and clear enough to see every star in the sky," I said. "In fact, I might take a dip in the pool right now."

I heard Jane inhale and then sigh.

"Are you smoking?" I asked.

"None of you damn business," Jane said. "In fact, fuck you," she said and hung up the phone.

Ten seconds later, the phone rang.

"I'll see what I can do," Jane said.

"I got you a very nice present," I said.

"Expensive?"

"Yes."

"Good. I'm worth it."

"I know."

"That's good you know. It cuts down on me having to remind you. I'll see what I can do tomorrow. Now talk dirty to me and say goodnight."

A while later, I called Regan's room.

"I'm going for a swim," I said. "Want to join the old man?"

"It's creepy how you can survive on so little sleep," Regan said.

"You can sleep on the plane," I said. "Meet you in ten minutes."

Chapter Seven

I walked Regan and Oz to the line for passenger screening.

"This is as far as I go," I said.

"How long do you think you'll be?" Regan asked.

"Hard to say," I said. "A week, maybe more. Jane is picking you up, so leave my car at the airport."

Regan gave me a tight hug and a soft kiss on the cheek. "Don't do anything stupid like getting beat up or shot," she said.

"Promise," I said.

Regan nodded and walked to the counter with her boarding pass and driver's license at the ready.

I looked at Oz. "I know you'll…"

"Go on out of here before you step on your tongue and say something stupid," Oz said. "Which, come to think of it, be nothing unusual for you."

"I'll see you in a week or so," I said.

"Don't be concerned 'bout that young deputy sheriff she be dating, he a gentlemen and she got a good head on her shoulders," Oz said.

"I wasn't concerned about it until just now," I said.

Oz gave me a wink and a smile, turned and walked behind Regan.

* * *

Escalante was in his office when I arrived at the state police station.

"What do you want to do first?" I asked.

"Had breakfast?"

"Actually, no."

"I know a place not far that has great donuts," Escalante said. "We'll take my car."

On a blue cobblestone side street, we sat under an umbrella and drank excellent espresso coffee and munched on donuts every bit as good as Pat's Donuts back home.

"Let's talk it out, see what sticks and what doesn't," I said.

Escalante bit into a strawberry cream donut and washed it down with a sip of espresso. "Go," he said.

"We know that I witnessed an unidentified man wearing a long-sleeve shirt light a cigarette left-handed at a few minutes past three in the morning from my fourth-floor balcony," I said. "We know that I also witnessed a second man now known as Joe DeSousa arrive between five and ten past three. I didn't have my watch, but I know how long it takes to smoke the average cigarette. We know that they left the sidewalk and went to the beach where it was too dark for me to see them from the balcony. Go."

"Early morning surfers find the body of Joe DeSousa around five-twenty in the morning," Escalante said. "The ME places the time of death at around three-thirty. Cause of death is two stab wounds made by a long serrated knife that may or may not be a common kitchen knife. The wounds appear to be made by a left-handed person. Go."

"DeSousa's car was found parked down a side street instead of under a street lamp along the sidewalk, where, I believe he sat and waited for Mr. Left-handed to show without being seen," I said.

"Good point," Escalante said.

"We know that DeSousa is rich and powerful, owns guns and can well afford a driver, yet went alone and unarmed," I said. "Why?"

Escalante looked at me and nodded.

"We don't know if the two men were friends, enemies or even knew each other," I said. "We don't know the nature of the meeting or why it was necessary to hold it at three in the morning on a deserted beach. We don't know if Maria Escalante knew at the time that her husband wasn't home, but I'm guessing no."

"Agreed."

"So let's look at what we do have," I said. "Go."

"We have thirty-one cigarette butts, five used condoms and one button," Escalante said. "I feel pretty safe saying the condoms aren't a factor."

"Agreed," I said.

"We have the lab analyzing the butts and button for DNA," Escalante said. "DeSousa's car has been checked and it's clean."

"Did the lab analyze the blood on DeSousa's clothing for separate blood types?" I asked. "It's possible the perp was wounded in a struggle before DeSousa was killed."

Escalante looked at me.

"Have them do it if they haven't done it on their own," I said.

Escalante nodded.

"You have DeSousa's appointment books and computer, both home and office," I said. "Any results as yet?"

"His books are on my desk," Escalante said. "Too soon for the computer."

"We don't know what his last day on earth was like, we need to speak to Maria DeSousa about that," I said. "Among other things. Are your people running down his charity donations and such?"

Escalante nodded.

"Phone records, finances and the like?"

"It will take a crew of eight men weeks to sort it all out."

"Want another cup?" I asked.

Escalante nodded and I waved a waitress and held up two fingers.

"We have a lot of lists to make," I said.

"We do," Escalante agreed.

"Who is working the airlines for passengers flying alone and possibly with no checked luggage, coming and going inside of three days?" I asked.

"Do you have any idea how many people fly to and from this rock every week?" Escalante asked.

"Alone, without checked luggage and returning the next day," I said. "And from a cold or cool climate."

"Which is only half the world right now," Escalante said. "Which is why people come here right now."

"Look at the bright side, we've just eliminated half the world," I said.

The waitress arrived with two large cups of espresso.

"Mrs. DeSousa said she would be at your office today," I said.

"I called her and told her we'd be stopping by around noon and not to bother," Escalante said.

"It's going to get rough on her," I said.

"I know," Escalante said. "The captain stressed the point to me this morning that while he wants as thorough an investigation as possible, he doesn't want her harassed. Joe DeSousa was an important man to Puerto Rico. His deed and charity will continue through Maria and if her boat is rocked too harshly, she could pull up stakes."

"She didn't strike me as defenseless," I said.

"No."

"Police captains have a way of becoming politicians," I said.

"Like your friend Captain Grimes."

"We started out together in the academy," I said. "He's a good man, a good cop and a lousy politician."

Escalante nodded.

"The questions have to be asked," I said.

"I know."

"The other night when I was in my hotel room, I asked myself what is DeSousa's dark side," I said. "No one is perfect no matter how many acts of charity he performs. In many instances, the acts of charity compensate for the dark side of a person's personality."

"DeSousa is a local legend," Escalante said. "Living here thirty years, although for the past twenty years he has spent summer months in New York. Still, if dirt on him existed, it would have come out by now."

"Do you know what the Harvest Moon is?" I asked.

"The fall moon, the brightest moon of the year," Escalante said.

"That's right, the brightest moon of the year," I said. "And even it has a dark side even if you can't see it."

Escalante nodded.

"Point taken."

"So let's go back to your office and check for updates and then go see Maria DeSousa," I said.

* * *

"Although Puerto Rico is an American territory, we're not a state and our resources are poor," Escalante said from behind his desk. "Lab work on the cigarette butts and button could take weeks, even months."

"I understand," I said.

"Even gathering and sorting through airlines ticket lists will be a daunting task for my men."

"We could use some help," I said.

"We could."

I pulled out my cell phone. "Maybe I can get us some," I said and dialed the number for the FBI in Washington.

"Very few people have my direct line," Paul Lawrence said. "So when I see your cell number, I know it's one of two things. You need a favor or you're dead. Since you're not dead, it must mean a favor."

"And it's a whopper," I said.

"Oh good, I haven't had lunch yet," Paul said. "Super-size the fries and soda if you don't mind."

"How are you these days?" I asked.

"Looking forward to the day I can go fishing and never look back. You?"

"I'm in Puerto Rico on vacation," I said.

"Nice. It's thirty-one degrees with light snow here."

"Around eighty with some clouds," I said.

"Boo freaking hoo," Paul said. "So what do you need this time?"

"DNA on some cigarette butts and a run down on a button," I said.

"Because?"

"A very important man was murdered and resources are limited," I said.

"I thought you said you're on vacation."

"Was. I'm now officially helping the state police."

"What's the significance?"

"The suspect is a smoker. I'm looking for two butts with the same DNA," I said. "And the button might have come from his shirt."

"Overnight it to me, I'll see what I can do," Paul said.

"Anybody there drink rum?" I asked.

"This is Washington," Paul said. "They drink anything they can get their hands on so long as somebody else pays."

"I'll send six bottles of Don Q," I said. "Can't get it in the states."

"Send the rum to my house. I'll distribute it to the boys."

"I might call upon your generosity again before this is through," I said.

"What else is new," Paul said. "I'll call you with the ifs, buts and maybes in a few days."

I hung up and looked at Escalante. He was watching me with mild curiosity. "So you just call up the FBI when you need a favor just like that," he said.

"Paul and I go way back," I said. "Call your guys and have him pack up the stuff. Where can I get Don Q?"

"On this rock, only everywhere," Escalante said.

"Check on your guys handling the airlines status, then let's head over to Maria DeSousa's home after we check his appointment books," I said.

There were two sets of books. One for business, the other for casual. DeSousa was apparently an old-fashioned type who relied more on writing things down than an iPad or laptop.

The business book was new. It started in January.

"Where is last year's book?" I asked.

"Maria didn't have it," Escalante said. "She said she would search his home office for it today."

"Your men got this book from his home office, why didn't they find it then?"

"He may have a storage area they missed?"

I nodded.

We read the month of January. There were appointments for

meetings for all of his businesses, fourteen in all. Several charity meetings and board of directors meetings on three companies for which he sat on the board, but had no financial interest in.

"Have your men check each board member of the companies DeSousa sat on," I said. "Board members make powerful enemies."

That was it for January.

"We need last year's book," I said.

DeSousa's personal appointment book was the eighteen-month kind and it was fully intact. It ran from January of last year to June of this year. The months of June through September were spent in New York, according to the appointments for dinner parties and other such events.

During the past thirty days, DeSousa hosted three barbeques at his home and one birthday party for Maria's fifty-fifth. They attended two charity events in San Juan and Old San Juan and four little league games at the field he built. They hosted a championship party at their home for the winner of the little league winter world series.

"What's this?" I asked and held my finger on December 3rd.

"NPR," Escalante said. "I don't know."

"National Public Radio?" I said. "Maybe he donated money or gave an interview?"

"Maria would know."

"Let's go ask her," I said.

* * *

The DeSousa home was located in the hills of Fajardo. Fajardo is not a wealthy town by any means, but it does have a beautiful beach and bay and hard-working, friendly people.

When Joe purchased the plot of land in the hills and built the home, it had six rooms and a small, above ground pool. That was nearly thirty years ago. Today it has fourteen rooms, a cement pool and patio, and a four-car garage.

"The man could live anywhere on this rock, but he chooses to stay in a poor town," Escalante said on the drive over.

"Like Warren Buffet the billionaire who lives in the home he purchased forty years ago in Nebraska," I said.

A Ford Bronco, a Taurus and a late-model Buick were parked in the cul-de-sac driveway when Escalante pulled in and parked behind the Buick.

"The Town Car still impounded?" I asked.

"Pending the lab report," Escalante.

A man came out the front door and approached us.

"That's Xavier, the oldest son," Escalante said. "Next is Ricardo or Richard, and Rose, the only daughter, is the youngest."

"My mother is in the garden," Xavier said. "We're about to have lunch. Please join us."

* * *

The backyard garden was a quarter acre of lush flowers and neatly mowed lawn. A fountain with a statue of the Virgin Mary was centered on the lawn. A table with twelve chairs was protected from the sun by a long, retractable awning.

Maria wasn't in black, probably because the heat and humidity was too intense to wear black. She wore a simple white sundress with sandals.

Xavier, Richard and Rose also wore bright, casual clothing. The only person in dark colors was the live-in maid/chef/housekeeper, a woman named Gloria Rodriguez, who had been in DeSousa's employ for twenty years.

Talk at the table was limited. Small-talk about Maria's children in New York, the coffee crop, a few charity events and such.

Business came later after dessert and coffee were consumed. The coffee came fresh from DeSousa's mills and was maybe the best tasting brew I've ever had.

After lunch, Escalante and I met with Maria in the spacious living room. The house was not air-conditioned. A constant breeze from the mountain air-cooled every room and ceiling fans on reverse kept the cooler air circulating downward.

Maria sat in a comfortable chair that I suspected was DeSousa's favorite. Xavier, Richard and Rose occupied the large sofa. Escalante and I took the love-seat type sofa opposite the large sofa. A glass coffee table was between us.

Gloria served fresh coffee on a silver tray and left the tray on the glass table.

"We have some hard questions to ask," I said.

"What does that mean?" Xavier asked.

"It means that you won't like some of them," I said. "But they need to be asked. Every question has a purpose and that purpose is to find who killed your father. Okay?"

Xavier nodded.

I looked at Maria.

"Let's get the tough ones out of the way first," I said.

She nodded.

Escalante had out his small notebook and pen.

"I need to know about your husband's vices," I said.

"Vices?" Maria said.

"Did he gamble, drink a lot, drugs of any sort," I said. "And women."

Richard was instantly on his feet, fury in his eyes.

"Sit down," Maria commanded.

Richard glared at her, but slowly sank down to the sofa.

Maria looked at me. "Joe never gambled, occasionally took a drink of Don Q with coconut milk and the only drugs I'm aware of were prescribed for minor arthritis in his knees and that was only sometimes when it was damp. As for women, in our entire marriage, we never slept apart. No man is a saint, but after thirty years of marriage a woman knows her husband."

"How well did you know your husband?" I asked.

Richard was on his feet again. "She just told you," he snapped.

"Sit down, Richard," Maria said.

"Who is the cop here, Lieutenant?" Richard said.

"We both are," Escalante said. "Now please sit down."

Seething, Richard took a seat.

"What do you mean by that question, Mr. Bekker?" Maria asked.

"Everybody is somebody else at times," I said. "You said Joe didn't gamble."

"That is correct," Maria said.

"How did you meet?"

"In the Bronx," Maria said. "I was from a Spanish neighborhood. Joe came from the Portuguese section. We met at a dance at Bronx Park Hall, something that used to take place quite often thirty-five years ago. I thought he was Puerto Rican and was surprised to learn he wasn't. Funny thing is I didn't speak a word of Spanish and didn't learn until we moved here and it was necessary. Same with Joe."

"What was he doing for work when you met?"

"There used to be a large coffee factory in the Bronx then," Maria said. "He worked as a roaster. That's where he learned the coffee business."

"So when you moved here you really had very little?"

"Yes."

"So Joe built a small empire all on his own?"

"Also yes."

"So each time he used his own money or borrowed from a bank to start a business, he took a big gamble," I said. "A much bigger gamble than say buying a lottery ticket. Wouldn't you agree?"

Maria smiled at me. "I would."

"Would you also agree that there may be things about Joe that he might have kept secret from you, things that you weren't aware of?" I asked.

Maria nodded. "I would have to agree that might be true."

"So, let me ask you this," I said. "Did you know he had gone out the night he was killed?"

"What does that have to do with anything?" Richard snapped as he once again jumped to his feet.

"No disrespect to your father, Richard, and I have the feeling he might even approve, but if you open your mouth again without me asking, I will spank you and send you to your room," I said. "Clear?"

Next to Richard, Rose stifled a laugh.

"Richard, sit down and shut up," Xavier said.

Fuming, Richard sat.

"To answer your question, Mr. Bekker, I did not know," Maria said.

"Because?" I asked.

"I have a herniated disc in my back," she said. "The fourth one. I require surgery and have been putting it off for quite some time. My doctor prescribed Valium to relieve the pressure in the muscles when it gets out of hand. I took two the night of…that night and nothing short of a train wreck in the bedroom was going to waken me."

"How often do you need the Valium"

"At first just a few times a month," Maria said. "Now maybe three times a week."

"So there were three times a week when you couldn't account for Joe's actions or whereabouts," I said.

Maria nodded. "This is true," she said.

"So let's work through that day," I said. "Tell me about it as best you can remember."

Maria sighed and nodded. "We had breakfast in the backyard as we like to do on cool mornings. Joe had to run some errands for me and…"

"What kind of errands?" I said.

"He went to the pharmacy to pick up my Valium."

"What pharmacy?"

"The Walgreens."

"What else?"

"Let me think," Maria said. "Oh yes, to the dry cleaners to pick up a few dresses of mine and then the market for a few items Gloria wanted for the kitchen."

"I'd like the name of the dry cleaners and market."

"Of course," Maria said.

"What time did Joe leave and return?"

"He left about ten and was home around twelve-thirty."

"And then?"

"We had lunch around one-thirty."

"Did Joe see or call anybody before lunch?"

"No, but Hector came by around three-thirty for a meeting."

"Who is Hector?"

"The foreman at the coffee plantation, Hector Santiago."

"How long has Hector been with the plantation?"

"At least ten years."

"Do you know what the meeting was about?"

"Production, that's all I know."

"Perhaps I can help," Xavier said. "I work for my father as executive vice president of marketing and sales out of New York. We had a conference call that lasted about one hour."

"About what?"

"We distribute to a dozen major cities on the East Coast," Xavier said. "Demand is high for our coffee and not just among the Hispanic community because it's excellent coffee. We would like to expand to the Midwest and West Coast, but in order to do that we need to grow more beans. More beans means more land. My father wanted to explore the possibility of buying additional land and adding another roaster."

"What time did the call start and end?"

"Four to five I would say," Xavier said.

I looked at Maria. "What time did Hector leave?"

"I'm not sure. Five-fifteen, I think."

"And then?"

"He stayed in his office until six," Maria said. "Then we had dinner around six-thirty with Gloria."

"Where does she live?"

"She has a small apartment in the basement with a separate entrance."

"What time did you take a Valium?"

"We watched a movie. Right after that I took two. That had to be ten o'clock or so, I think."

"What movie?"

"Oh. One that we missed a few years ago when it came out," Maria said. "The one with Sandra Bullock in space."

"Gravity."

"Yes. We streamed in on Netflix."

"Then you went to bed?"

"Yes."

"So you have no idea what time your husband left the house or why?"

"No."

"None of your children were in the house at the time?"

"No."

"Gloria?"

"Yes, but I'm sure she was asleep. She's usually in the kitchen by six-forty-five, so she turns in early."

"We have his appointment book for business for this year and his personal book that covers eighteen months, but the business book for last year is missing," I said. "I don't think the Lieutenant's men would have missed it."

"Um, I wasn't thinking clearly the other night," Maria said. "It's probably with our accountant Javier Ramirez. Joe always gave it to him for tax purposes."

"We'll need his address," I said.

"Of course."

"Would you like to take a break, Mrs. DeSousa?" I asked.

"Xavier, please tell Gloria to serve coffee and cake in the kitchen," Maria said.

* * *

Maria and Rose went to the bathroom, leaving Escalante, Xavier and Richard in the kitchen. Gloria set plates and coffee cups at the table. The kitchen was large with a spacious chef's island, a table and chairs and a long marble counter filled with appliances.

"My mother is tired," Xavier said.

"And you're making it worse," Richard said. "Not to mention my father isn't dead a week yet."

"Richard, please," Xavier said.

"Fuck please," Richard snapped. "We don't even have dad's body yet and this asshole and his questions…"

"Now is not the time for this, Richard," Xavier said.

Richard glared at me. "If this asshole didn't have a badge," he said.

"That's enough, Richard," Xavier said. "Are you so stupid that you can't see these men are here to help?"

"Appointment books and coffee production, you call that helping," Richard said. "They should be out looking for dad's killer, not pestering mom with this bullshit."

"What do you do for work, Richard?" I asked.

"What does that have to do with anything?" Richard said.

"I was wondering who would be dumb enough to hire someone as stupid as you," I said. "Now I understand you're upset over your father's murder, but if you want to help us you need to grow up and act like a man."

Behind Richard, Gloria watched me with mild amusement.

"If this wasn't my mother's house, I'd let you have one good," Richard said.

"For God's sake, Richard," Xavier said. "Mr. Bekker looks like he could fold you in half and stick you in his wallet."

Gloria chortled a laugh.

Richard spun around and glared at her. "Is something funny?"

"Here comes Mom," Xavier said. "Now shut up."

We took seats and Gloria served coffee from the DeSousa plantation and a wonderful Puerto Rican spice cake she baked earlier in the day.

"Mrs. DeSousa, you look very tired," I said. "Maybe you'd like to continue another day?"

"No, I'm fine, and please call me Maria."

* * *

I took seconds of the coffee to the living room when we resumed. So did Escalante.

"Please stop us whenever you feel too tired or stressed to continue," Escalante said.

Maria nodded.

"We removed two handguns and one shotgun from your husband's closet," Escalante said. "None have been fired in a long time. Are you aware of any other firearms he may have owned?"

"No," Maria said. "He never even carried them that I'm aware of. They just sat in his closet for years."

"May I say something?" Xavier said.

"Sure."

"My father told me that when I was just a child that he purchased the firearms for protection," Xavier said. "He was worried about possible home invasion. We were the only family in town that had more than average. Later, he installed a home alarm system that contacted the police if it had been triggered. I doubt he ever fired any of the weapons."

"I saw the keypad beside the front door, is the service still in use?"

Maria nodded.

"So for Joe to leave the house after it's been set he has to turn it off, is that correct?"

"Yes. There is a code that allows you thirty seconds to exit."

I looked at Escalante. "A call to get the reports should give us the exact time he left the house that night."

"What is so important about that?" Richard said. "Maybe he couldn't sleep and went for a drive, ever think of that?"

"He did go for a drive," I said.

I looked at Maria. She appeared worn out and pale.

"Just a few more questions for today, okay?"

She nodded.

"Did Joe have a will?" I asked.

"A will? Yes. It's a mutual will," Maria said.

"What does it say?"

"It's on file at our lawyer's office," Maria said. "It says that if I survive Joe, I inherit everything and in turn, our children inherit everything in equal parts."

"We'll need your lawyer's name," I said.

"Of course," Maria said.

"We found the initials NPR in Joe's appointment book," I said. "Does that mean anything to you?"

"No, I'm afraid it doesn't," Maria said.

"I'll stop for today, but I'd like to ask you to do something for me," I said. "I'd like you to think about all the left-handed people you know and make a list. I'd also like you to think about any potential enemies Joe might have made over the years and make a list. Okay?"

"I'll do my best," Maria said.

"Before we go, we'd like to see Joe's office and talk to Gloria," I said.

"Xavier, take them to the office," Maria said. "I'm going to take a nap for a while."

* * *

DeSousa's office was a converted bedroom. Xavier identified it as the room he grew up in until the age of thirteen.

It housed a large oak desk, leather chair, two file cabinets, a flat screen monitor where the computer had been and dozens of photographs on the wall of his children and his grandchildren in various stages.

Two windows faced the ocean. The view was magnificent and the ocean breeze cooled the room.

I stood and looked around for a while to get the feel of the man.

"Do you want me to open the cabinets?" Xavier asked.

"No. Let's go see Gloria," I said.

* * *

Gloria served coffee in the kitchen of her basement apartment.

"You've worked for the DeSousa family for twenty years?" I said.

"That is correct," Gloria said. "Close to twenty-one now."

"Mind a few personal questions?"

"No."

"Are you married?"

"No."

"Divorced?"

"No. In my twenties, I had ovarian cancer," Gloria said. "They removed my ovaries. I figured if I couldn't have children, I had little use for a husband under foot."

"You must be very familiar with the family after twenty years," I said.

"I would say so."

"How would you describe them?" I asked.

Gloria sipped some coffee, then said, "Joe was a very hard working man. I can't think of one day when he was not involved with something at one of his businesses or a charity event."

"How was his temperament?" I asked.

"You mean did he have a temper?"

"Yes."

"He could be stern with a business problem, but I never saw him angry with the kids when they were young or with Maria," Gloria said. "And Richard was a handful."

"I can imagine," I said. "What about Rose?"

"Quiet. Pretty. Much like she is today."

"Did you know he left the house the night he was killed?"

"No."

"Because?"

"I usually go to bed at eleven," Gloria said. "I'm up at five-thirty every morning, so I turn in early."

"Could you hear a car from your apartment?"

"It faces the back. The garage is in front. Maybe if I was awake and with all the windows open. Maybe. But you see I have an air conditioner in the bedroom because it faces the back and gets no breeze."

"Are you aware of other instances where Mr. DeSousa might have gone out late on his own?"

Gloria frowned for a moment. "I don't...I would have to think about that. I know that there were many times when he came home late from meetings, but not going out."

"What about Maria?" I asked.

"She is very kind and caring, but she was the…what is the word… discipline. Joe would let the boys get away with anything, but Maria would put them in their place, especially with Richard."

"On the day he was killed, he ran errands," I said. "One was for you."

"Yes, at the market near the drugstore," Gloria said. "I usually go myself, but it was just a few items and he was going out anyway."

"Thank you, Gloria," I said. "I'm sure we'll talk again."

* * *

"What do you do, Rose?" Escalante asked.

We were at the backyard table enjoying the lofty breeze blowing down from the mountains.

"Do? You mean work?" she asked.

"Yes," Escalante said.

"I have two years left to get my master's degree in business."

"Impressive," Escalante said. "Where do you study and live?"

"NYU, and I share an apartment on West Ninth Street," Rose said. "And yes, my father foots all the bills. He didn't want me getting sidetracked with having to work."

"When you graduate, do you plan to stay in New York?" Escalante asked.

Rose shook her head. "The plan was to return to PR and take over for my father. He would have been sixty-three by then and we discussed it many times. He was looking forward to that day."

"How does Xavier feel about that?" Escalante asked.

"It was his suggestion," Rose said. "You see, Xavier has a wife and two young children and a house in Hartsdale. He doesn't want to move them to Puerto Rico and he is very happy managing the coffee distribution in the states."

"And Richard, what does he do?" Escalante asked.

"Other than being a rude pain in the ass, I really don't know," Rose said. "Something in the financial district with stocks."

55

"I take it you don't see each other much," Escalante said.

"Hardly ever," Rose said. "We run in different circles."

"Where does he live?"

"West Eighty-First Street, the Charter Arms."

"Expensive?"

"At least a million for his five room condo overlooking Central Park."

"Rose, you must have met many of your father's business associates," Escalante said. "Any of them left-handed?"

Rose shrugged. "I really don't know. Who notices such things? Wait, my cousin Ruben is left-handed. He lives in the Bronx with my aunt. He's thirteen and pitches in little league. That's how I know he's left-handed. They call him southpaw or something."

"I think we can eliminate him as a suspect," Escalante said.

"Are you going to find who killed my father?" Rose asked.

"Yes," Escalante said.

* * *

"What do you do, Richard?" I asked.

"That's none of your fucking business," Richard said.

"We can make it our business," I said.

"How and why?"

"The why is because you may know someone who wanted to murder your father," I said. "The how is with a search warrant of your Manhattan pad."

"Search it," Richard said.

"Oh, we will," I said. "And we will confiscate your home computers and just about everything you own as we look for clues. It could take months, right Lieutenant?"

"As long as a year," Escalante said.

Richard glared at me. Finally he sighed. "I work for Porter and Price Investments."

"As what, a stock broker?" I asked.

"Two years as a trader before I got my license," Richard said. "I'm in my third year as a broker. I want to make mergers and acquisitions before I'm thirty."

"No desire to follow in your father's footsteps?" I asked.

"None. Unlike my brother, I am my own man," Richard said. "And I can't stress enough how much I hate this stupid useless island that should be the land of milk and honey, but isn't."

"Why?" I asked.

"Where are you staying?"

"One of your father's hotels."

"Nice, isn't it?"

"Very."

"Drive three blocks from it down any side street and people are living in tin huts with leaky roofs," Richard said. "We have all the natural resources and the protection of the United States and yet nearly seventy-five percent of the people live in poverty or close to it. This hundred-mile-long rock is seventy billion in debt, thanks to welfare, drugs, crime and unemployment. So why the fuck would I want to live here?"

"To make it a better place," I said. "That's how it works. If everyone runs away from the problems, they never get fixed."

"My father has been trying to do that for thirty years and what did it get him?" Richard said. "I can walk ten blocks from this million dollar house and show you entire families living in one-room shacks."

"And I can walk fifteen minutes north of that Central Park West palace you live in and show you entire families living in burned out buildings on 110th Street, that isn't the point," I said. "You either turn-tail and run or you try to make a difference."

"Do you know what they say on Wall Street about trying?" Richard asked.

"No."

"The word try is just another way of saying fail."

"Okay, so don't fail when I ask you if you know of any enemies who would want your father dead," I said.

Richard looked at me.

"Despite what I just said, my father was a good man and he believed in everything he did," Richard said. "What he gave to charity you couldn't make in a lifetime."

"Even the Pope has enemies," I said.

Richard sighed. "I got nothing," he said.

* * *

"My mother is resting comfortably," Xavier said.

We were in the kitchen at the table.

"Hartsdale is a nice community," I said.

"Yes, it is. How did you…?"

"Rose," I said.

"Of course."

"So now what?" I asked.

"I don't know what you mean."

"The idea was for Rose to earn her master's and then take over for your father so he could retire," I said. "She's at least two years away from that. Who runs the show until then?"

"I haven't…we haven't discussed it yet," Xavier said. "Mother and I. She's terrific at charity work, but she never got involved in the business end of things. I suppose I can take charge and commute on a regular basis until Rose is ready to take command."

"Richard hates living here, how do you feel about it?"

"I'd love to live here year-round," Xavier said. "Get away from the cold and snow. And some day we will, my wife and me, but for now our kids are in a good school and their education is a priority for us. When they are grown we probably will buy a house somewhere close by my mother."

"Any idea who might want you father dead?" I asked.

"God no," Xavier said. "I've been asking myself that question since I first heard the news. And all day today since you first asked my mother."

"No enemies, people he didn't like who didn't like him?"

"I'm sure there are people who didn't like him in business, but enough to murder him? Unlikely."

"Yet murdered he was and by a knife-wielding, left-handed man at three in the morning on a deserted beach," I said. "How do you explain that?"

Xavier sighed. "I can't."

* * *

"Enough for one day," I said to Xavier, Rose and Richard. "We have more than we can process at the moment. Please tell your mother we'll be in touch real soon."

Xavier walked us to Escalante's car.

"Anything we can do," he said just before we drove away.

* * *

We drove to the Walgreens, the dry cleaners, and the food market and clocked the mileage. It was just short of fourteen miles.

We sat in the parking lot of the grocery store for twenty minutes to allow for shopping time.

"Say thirty minutes drive each way and another thirty for shopping," I said. "That leaves an hour of Joe's time unaccounted for."

"Which could have been taken up by talking to people he knew along the way?" Escalante said.

"Granted," I said. "Let's get back to your office."

It was close to dinnertime when we reached Escalante's office. Several messages were waiting for him when we entered.

"The lab confirmed two different blood types on DeSousa's shirt," he said. "A-negative for Joe, B-positive for the attacker. Neither is rare, but at least we know Joe didn't go down without a fight."

"The other message?"

"The lab reports nothing suspicious on his hard drive," Escalante said. "He rarely, if ever, used it for business. Mostly family photos and personal emails, things like that."

"Have them try to recover deleted emails and folders," I said. "Just because you delete them doesn't mean they can't be recovered."

Escalante called his lab. When he hung up, I said, "Follow me to my hotel. I'm buying dinner."

Chapter Eight

“This is one of DeSousa's hotels?” Escalante said. We were poolside, eating steaks.

“It is,” I said.

“The place you stayed at in Luquillo, why the switch?”

“My daughter's idea,” I said. “The whole trip, actually. I worked three difficult cases over three months. She thought I was a bit worn out and surprised me with the vacation.”

“How old is she?”

“Nineteen going on twelve.”

Escalante looked at me.

“Long story,” I said. “Do you have kids?”

“Three,” Escalante said. “Between nine and thirteen.”

We finished our steaks and ordered dessert.

“That analogy you made about people having a dark side like the Harvest Moon, it really is true you know,” Escalante said.

A waiter brought us coffee and cake.

I sliced into a coconut cake and washed it down with a sip of coffee.

“So what's your dark side?” I asked.

“Cop to cop?”

“Sure.”

“Midlife crisis when I turned forty,” Escalante said. “The waistline was a little bigger, my hair was a little bit less and life seemed to be passing me by. I did something really stupid and had an affair with a twenty-two-year-old airline stewardess. My wife found out and you can guess the rest. She's a very strict Catholic and I committed a cardinal sin in her eyes. I suppose I did. The odd thing is I didn't find the girl the least bit attractive. It was all about my fear of growing older."

"Any chance of reconciliation?" I asked.

"I haven't suffered enough yet to suit my wife, but at least we talk now."

I ate another piece of cake and took a sip of coffee.

"I miss my kids," Escalante said. "And I miss my wife and being a family. That's my dark side, what about you?"

"I guess it's fourteen years now," I said. "I was working special crimes and was involved in an organized crime task force. I got too close to a mobster and he ordered a hit on me. I wasn't home. My wife was killed and my daughter, just five at the time, witnessed it. She spent ten years at a clinic for traumatized children and I crawled inside a bottle of Scotch and spent a decade drowning my sorrows. I'm sober two years and my daughter, while she had made enormous progress, balances her fragile mental state like a bird on a wire in a strong wind."

Escalante stared at me.

"Shit," he said.

"Yeah."

"The nineteen going on twelve?"

"Yeah."

"Well, I guess we have some work to do tomorrow."

"We do."

"How long do you plan to stay?"

"I'm not sure," I said. "Let's see where the evidence takes us."

"I'll be in the office by nine," Escalante said.

"I'll be there."

* * *

I stripped down to my shorts, grabbed a Coke from the fridge and checked the messages on my phone.

Regan called and then Jane.

I called Regan first.

"Everybody safe and sound?" I asked when she picked up.

"Oz is snoozing and I'm playing Game of War with Mark," Regan said. "Aunt Janet said he could stay over. Molly and Buddy are in the backyard fighting."

"So everything is normal?"

"As normal as it gets around here," Regan said. "I go back to work tomorrow. Father Thomas and Sister Mary Martin want to up my hours to thirty a week."

"Can you handle thirty?"

"I guess I'll find out since I said yes."

"Don't overdo it."

"Look whose talking."

"Staying to help was your idea."

"I just said what you were thinking."

"Let's call this one a tie," I said.

"Deal. So how long do you think you'll be there?"

"Don't know. There's a lot of stuff to process. At least a week."

"Better call Jane."

"She's next up."

"Gotta go, Mark is kicking my butt," Regan said.

"Bye, honey."

I hung up, sipped some Coke and dialed Jane's home number.

"I'm in the tub up to my ears in bubble bath with six scented candles for a soothing ambiance," she said when she answered the phone. "And you are, hopefully, alone and lonely. At least you better be."

"I am, but I don't have to be if you'd hop on a plane and keep me company," I said.

"I would except for one thing," Jane said. "We had a shooting at the regional high school today."

"A...Jesus, was anybody hurt?"

"No, thankfully," Jane said. "Witnesses claim a dark blue Accord drove by around nine-thirty this morning and opened fire with a 9MM handgun and fired fifteen rounds into the building. Several windows were broken, but thankfully no one was hurt. Tomorrow is Saturday and I'll have two cars on site until Monday. Then I'll have four during school opening and two the rest of the day."

"Are you running down blue Accords?"

"Course. If this asshole is in state, we'll get him."

"Is Walt assisting?"

"He is, and some manpower from the state police. How is your little shindig going?"

"Ifs, buts and maybes, with a dash of clueless, and a pinch of who-the-hell-knows rolled into one."

"Sounds like a plan," Jane said. "Oh, my deputy is calling. Gotta go. Call me tomorrow."

"I will."

After hanging up with Jane, I lazed on the bed and thought for a while. I tried to make sense of things and put them into some kind of perspective order.

There is an unaccounted hour for the day DeSousa was murdered. It could be something or it could be nothing, but it's an hour that needs to be looked into.

The left-handed man used a knife that appeared to be a common kitchen knife. Before or during the time DeSousa was stabbed, he managed to cut or inflict a wound on the left-handed man because two types of blood were found on DeSousa's shirt.

The left-handed man wore long sleeves and smoked using matches.

DeSousa's business all seemed to be healthy and financially stable.

DeSousa was a church-going, very charitable man seemingly void of the common vices that plagued many marriages.

But things aren't always what they seem.

DeSousa was a well-liked, well-respected man with few if any real enemies.

But who but him knew what lurked on his dark side of the moon?

Maria DeSousa has a bad back and often took Valium to relieve spasms. She took a dose around ten in the evening so by ten-thirty she was loopy and ready to sleep.

Gloria goes to bed at eleven and her basement apartment faces the rear.

Four unaccounted hours of time, from eleven to three in the morning.

DeSousa's children were in New York the night of his murder. The lone visitor to the house was Hector, the coffee plantation manager. After a conference call with Xavier, he left around five-fifteen. DeSousa was alone in his office from five-fifteen until six-thirty when Gloria served dinner.

More time unaccounted for.

I grabbed some hotel stationey and a pen and made some notes.

Phone records incoming and outgoing on DeSousa's hard-line and cell phones.

Deleted emails.

Accountant for date book.

Check with Paul on DNA and button.

Check airlines passenger lists.

Check with lawyer for will.

Speak with Hector about the meeting with DeSousa.

I set the paper aside and rested my head on the pillow. On the surface, there was no reason for Joe DeSousa's murder.

On the surface.

DeSousa went to the beach at three in the morning for a reason. Discover that reason and motive comes to light.

There are only so many motives when it comes to murder.

Money.

Sex.

Power.

Revenge.

The obscure, such as guarding a secret.

Insanity.

Money? Joe DeSousa was a wealthy man. He didn't need money, but perhaps the murderer did. I made another note.

Possibility of DeSousa pulling out of a deal?

Sex? DeSousa wouldn't be the first saint that was a secret sinner.

Possibility of a secret love affair? Murderer could be a jealous husband/boyfriend?

Power? DeSousa had power on the island, perhaps he wanted more? The plan was to retire and turn over the reins to his daughter, but he would be only sixty-three and what does a man do with his time going forward?

Check possibility of DeSousa's political ambitions.

Revenge is a great motivator. History is littered with greats plots of revenge against kings and emperors.

Possibility DeSousa was murdered for revenge?

Protecting a secret was another great reason for murderer. Many a political enemy was murdered throughout history to guard a secret against exposure.

What skeletons hid in the DeSousa closet?

Insanity? Always a great defense, rarely true.

The man who killed DeSousa appeared cool, calm and collected. However, many an insane person displayed the same outward traits.

However remote, insanity couldn't be crossed off the list.

I felt my eyes grow heavy, and closed them.

The next thing I knew it was morning.

Chapter Nine

After a seventy-five minute workout in the hotel gym, I showered, dressed, and met Escalante in his office at nine in the morning.

"Had breakfast?" I asked when Escalante opened his office door.

"No."

"Let's go," I said. "I saw this diner called Juan in a Million I'd like to try."

Juan's held twenty-five tables and twenty-four of them were occupied when we arrived. We ordered scrambled eggs with home fries and soft taco shells, juice with ice, and coffee. We loaded the shells with eggs and hot sauce and cooled things down with the icy-cold juice.

I gave Escalante my notes from last night.

"So many details and loose ends," he said.

"I've never had a case where there weren't," I said.

"Xavier DeSousa called this morning," Escalante said. "The family wants to know when the body will be released."

"Is there a reason to hold it?"

"No, not at this point."

"You have the full coroner's report and photographs?"

Escalante nodded. "They want the body sent to a funeral home in San Juan. I told them I'd make the arrangements."

"Let's go to the park," I said.

* * *

We sat on a bench in the park that led to Fort el Morro and sipped coffee from takeout containers.

The temperature was mid-seventies with a beautiful ocean breeze. Tourists by the hundreds wandered the grounds and fort, much like I did just a week ago.

"What do you like for motive?" I asked.

"Motive? It's difficult to say," Escalante said. "It wasn't a pro killing. Even on this rock, guns are easy to come by and a silencer could be made or bought. And why would a pro agree to meet on a beach at three in the morning?"

"So we can rule out a professional hit," I said. "But not an amateur one."

"Amateur, no, but again, even a rank amateur can find a gun in Puerto Rico," Escalante said.

"I rule out passion and revenge," I said. "Ever see the victim of a crime of passion? There is far more damage to the victim than just two stab wounds. The medical report indicates that DeSousa took several minutes to die after the second wound. In a true crime of passion, he would have been stabbed fifty times and had his face kicked to mush. The guy stabs DeSousa twice, knows the second wound is fatal but not immediate and leaves the scene before DeSousa's lights go out."

"He panicked," Escalante said.

"I think so," I said. "Why else wouldn't he stick around to make sure the job was done? It reeks of scared amateur."

Escalante sipped coffee and nodded. "Still think the perp is not local?"

"It doesn't make sense to me he would dress for a night of dancing for a meeting on the beach," I said. "Ever go to the beach? It's messy. You wear things you don't care about in case they get filled with sand and salt water. I know about that. I've lived on a beach for a decade. Everything is always salty, wet and covered in sand."

Escalante nodded.

In the distance, I could see dark clouds gathering above the rain forest.

"It was amateur hour, alright," I said. "The kitchen knife in itself tells me so. The clothes and leaving DeSousa alive back it up."

"Puerto Rico has a population of almost four million," Escalante said. "But we average ten million visitors a year, mostly through the Luis Muñoz in San Juan. The week DeSousa was killed, a hundred thousand or more flew onto this rock, not to mention thousands more on cruise ships. It's a small needle in a large haystack to find one man flying alone, even if the airlines are doing the looking."

"Most cruise ships have a curfew, so it's doubtful he would be off the ship at three in the morning," I said.

"Who do you want to see first, the lawyer or accountant?" Escalante asked.

"Who is closer?"

* * *

David Ortiz, Jr. kept the books for DeSousa for fifteen years or more. His office was in downtown San Juan on the sixth floor of a renovated office building. The etched lettering on a frosted glass door read CPA and Tax Specialist. The view from the window behind his desk was of the bay where cruise ships dock. Some sailboats dotted the waters in the background.

Ortiz Jr. was about sixty, with silver hair and moustache, and a fine voice fit for radio. He dark eyes spoke of intelligence.

"I'm still in shock over Joe's death," he said. "How are Maria and the family?"

"About what you'd expect in a situation like this," Escalante said.

Ortiz Jr. nodded. "You said in your call that you needed his appointment book?"

"Yes. I was told that you review it for tax reasons," Escalante said.

"I do. It's in Joe's file for this year's tax preparation," Ortiz Jr. said. "I'll get it for you."

"Make it the last three years," I said.

Ortiz Jr. looked at me. "Alright," he said.

He picked up the phone on his desk, punched in a number and spoke to somebody in Spanish.

"Won't be but a moment," he said after he hung up.

"Thank you," Escalante said. "We'll return them to you as soon as we're done."

"Mrs. DeSousa told us that you review the book for possible tax deductions?" I said.

"And I generally find a dozen or so every year that Joe didn't think were eligible," Ortiz Jr. said.

"How did he do last year?" I asked.

"All told under one umbrella of his corporation, about sixty-five million," Ortiz said. "After all is said and done, he cleared one million seven hundred thousand for himself and donated four million six hundred thousand to charity."

"The rest goes to?"

"Running his corporation," Ortiz Jr. said. "Payroll, expenses, taxes, upkeep, and crop supplies and so on."

"Could he keep more for himself?" I asked.

"Sure, if he wanted," Ortiz Jr. said. "We had that very conversation many times. He just wasn't that interested in his personal wealth compared to the wealth of the companies he built."

"If he were to sell his entire corporation, what would it fetch?" I asked.

Ortiz Jr. thought for a moment. "Easily five hundred thousand."

"And his own personal wealth?"

"Around forty million in personal assets," Ortiz Jr. said. "At least three quarters of that in cash. He also had an insurance policy for ten million."

"Thank you for your time," Escalante said.

* * *

Peter Cueto was your typical non-trial lawyer in that he was a real smoothie.

Silk suit and shirt, perfectly cut dark hair, fine features and manicured fingernails, he reminded men of Frank Kagan, former lawyer to mobster Eddie Crist.

"How may I be of service?" he asked with just a touch of accent.

"We need to see Joe DeSousa's will," Escalante said. "And before you start with any bullshit about privileged information, I have a warrant."

"No need for a warrant," Cueto said. "Right after you called, I pulled the document. It's right there on my desk. The English version. I can provide the Spanish one as well if you wish."

Escalante picked up the folder and opened it. "This is forty pages long," he said.

"Forty-three exactly," Cueto said.

"In simple English, what does it say?" I asked.

"Don't let the page count fool you, it is fairly simple," Cueto said. "In the event of his death and Mrs. DeSousa survives him, she is to inherit controlling interest in everything that he owned. Roughly fifty-one percent. The remaining forty-nine percent is to be divided equally among his three children. It also says that ten percent of the profits of the corporation are to go to charity annually. The charities are listed. All personal wealth in the form of cash, insurance policies and personal land holdings go to Maria and then later are passed on to his surviving children."

"Anything about his daughter taking over for him?" I asked.

"Not in the will," Cueto said. "He wanted to transfer power to her upon the completion of her master's degree. Those are separate documents."

"Any idea why he wanted to retire?" I asked.

"We discussed it. All he would say about it was that it was time," Cueto said.

"Anything left to a non-relative?" I asked.

"One hundred thousand to the housekeeper Gloria," Ortiz Jr. said.

I nodded. "Has he or his corporation ever been audited?"

"Only every three years like clockwork."

"Why?"

"It's standard for a medium to large corporation to undergo such an audit on a regular basis," Ortiz Jr. said. "We've never failed to get a passing grade from the IRS."

"Does Gloria know about the money?"

"No. She'll find out when we read the will publicly next week."

"We need a copy of this," Escalante said.

"That is your copy," Ortiz Jr. said. "The original is in my safe."

* * *

Escalante's cell phone rang as we were returning to his car.

"It's my captain," he said, and answered the call.

Escalante spoke in Spanish for a few minutes and then turned to me and said in English, "Captain wants to see me. Us."

"No problem."

* * *

Captain Hanley Flores reminded me of Walt Grimes in a way. Both were tall men, ramrod straight, around the same age and with a sense of authority about them.

Flores spoke perfect English and with little to no accent.

Escalante expected Flores to ask for a progress report.

Instead he said, "The governor is waiting on us."

"The governor?" Escalante said.

"Yes. Right now."

* * *

Governor Santiago Ortega was two years into his second four-year term. Surprisingly, he was just fifty-two years old. He was around six-feet-tall, with salt and pepper hair, fine features and a moustache that bordered on walrus.

He also spoke with little to no accent.

"You are the police detective from the states assisting Lieutenant Escalante?" Ortega asked when we took chairs at the conference table in his large office.

"I am, sir," I said.

An assistant to the governor served coffee and then left the office.

"It is Bekker with a C or K?" Ortega asked.

"Two K's," I said.

"Dutch?"

"Norse."

"You look like you'd have little trouble fitting in with your Viking ancestors," Ortega said.

He sipped coffee.

"Tell me everything," he said.

I looked at Escalante and nodded. He spoke for about an hour. Occasionally, Ortega scribbled a note of a legal pad, but didn't interrupt.

"Thank you for the report," Ortega said when Escalante concluded. "And please keep confidential what I am about to tell you."

"Of course," Flores said.

"Joe DeSousa was a close and personal friend of mine," Ortega said. "And he was the best man I know. My second term as governor is up in two years. Joe and I were planning to launch a campaign to get him elected as my successor."

Escalante and I exchanged glances.

"Question, Mr. Bekker?" Ortega asked.

"That explains his desire to turn his company over to his daughter," I said.

"I suppose it does, although no one besides Joe and me was aware of these plans," Ortega said. "Even his wife was kept in the dark about any of this."

"May I ask why?" I asked.

"Several reasons, actually," Ortega said. "The first is he wasn't sure how Maria would react to the news. His wife was the most important thing in his life. The second is he wanted to make sure his company was in capable hands before he relinquished control. His charity work was very dear to him. Our plan was to slowly take his family under our wing and test their responses. I'm sure with the company on solid ground they would have supported his decision."

"Was there anyone else who might have known about this?" I asked.

"It's doubtful," Ortega said. "These plans were never discussed outside of this office and we were always alone when we met. What is your thought process on this?"

"If someone found out what he was planning and considered Joe an enemy, murder might be a good way of ending those plans," I said.

"I suppose it would," Ortega said.

"What do you think his chances of winning would have been?" I asked.

"Excellent," Ortega said. "This beautiful island is going through some difficult times. Joe knew how to create jobs and wealth. People here know that. He would have won handily over any opposition."

"Governor, I would like to tell his family of this so I can gauge their reaction," I said. "One of them might have accidently found out and spilled the beans to the wrong person."

"I suppose there is no sense in keeping it secret any longer," Ortega said.

"Thank you, Governor," I said.

"How long do you plan to stay and assist Lieutenant Escalante with this?" Ortega asked.

"Until something breaks or I become a pain in the ass," I said.

Ortega stared at me for a few seconds and then he broke into a smile. "You and the Lieutenant come to dinner tonight. Seven-thirty and no need to dress formally."

I looked at Escalante.

"We'll be there, Governor," he said.

* * *

Flores bit into a big, juicy burger, chewed, swallowed and dabbed his chin with a napkin.

"Solve this and you'll be made captain in homicide," he said to Escalante.

We were in a small outdoor café in Old San Juan called The Rice and Beans.

"We need to see DeSousa's personal doctor," I said to Flores. "That's where we were going when you called."

"Do you think he was ill?" Flores asked.

"We know he had minor arthritis in his knees," I said. "There could be something we don't know about, but primarily I'm interested in his mental state."

Flores nodded and took another bite of his burger.

"I think I'd like to try the coconut cream pie," I said.

"It's seven-fifty a slice," Flores said.

"I'm on expense account, it's on me," I said.

"In that case," Flores said.

I had to grin. Flores reminded me of Walt in more ways than one.

* * *

Doctor Carlos Machado couldn't see us until after his last appointment at four-thirty. He was in his mid to late sixties with a crown of white hair, and he wore rimless glasses. He spoke with a slight accent that could have been Caribbean. We met in his office. He sat at his desk and we took chairs opposite it.

"I have to say I'm still in shock over Joe's death," Machado said. "I assume that's what you wanted to talk to me about."

"We're interested in his health," Escalante said. "And before you give us any of that jazz about doctor/patient confidentiality, the patient is dead and we have a warrant."

"No need for a warrant," Machado said. "As you said, he is dead and I'd like you to find out who murdered him as much as you do."

"So, how was his health?" Escalante asked.

"For a sixty-year-old man, he was in excellent health," Machado said. "His vital signs were good; his cholesterol levels were normal, his blood work normal and his blood pressure inside the accepted range for his age."

"He had arthritis in his knees," Escalante said. "His wife mentioned that."

"Minor. Nothing serious. I have a worse case of it than he did."

"When did you last see him?" Escalante asked.

"About two weeks ago at a charity event in San Juan."

"As a patient."

"Oh. For his annual physical on his last birthday," Machado said. "Seven months ago, I believe."

"A lot can happen to a sixty-year-old man in seven months," I said.

"Sure, but when I saw him two weeks ago at the event, he appeared healthy and normal," Machado said. "A doctor can look at a long-time patient's eyes and know what's going on behind them. His next physical was just three months away, plenty of time to catch anything that may have developed."

"How was his mental state?" I asked.

"I'm not a psychiatrist."

"But you are a doctor and can tell when a patient you've known for years undergoes a personality change," I said.

Machado sighed. "Joe is…was the type of individual I refer to as a cat."

"Cat?" Escalante said.

"Ever own a cat, Lieutenant?"

"My kids do."

"Cats are masters of masking their pain," Machado said. "A cat could be riddled with cancer and greet you at the door as if nothing was wrong. You scratch their ears and they purr and on the inside cancer is eating them alive. That was Joe's personality. If something was bothering him, you'd never know by his mood or actions."

"So you don't know?" Escalante said.

"Correct."

"Did he have a doctor in New York?" I asked. "He spent at least four to five months there every year, so I imagine that he would."

"Yes, he did," Machado said. "And we share reports with each other whenever Joe came to see one of us."

"When did he last see his New York doctor?" I asked.

Machado turned to his computer and did some typing. "Let's see," he said. "A week before he returned to Puerto Rico in November. His knees were bothering him. He was given a prescription for arthritis."

"Did he use it much in warm weather?" I asked.

"Actually, no. It was the cold that bothered his knees," Machado.

"The name and number of his New York doctor," I said.

"I'll write it down for you," Machado said.

* * *

Escalante dropped me off at the hotel for a quick shower and change of clothing. Ortega said not to dress formally. I picked out lightweight, tan slacks, a teal Polo shirt and black loafers.

I was in the lobby by seven. A few minutes past, Escalante picked me up in his unmarked cruiser.

He wore tan slacks and a button-down, white short-sleeve shirt.

We arrived at the governor's residence at seven twenty-five.

The governor wore slacks and a blue short-sleeve shirt. The air-conditioning was on high and it was a welcome relief to the high humidity.

"My wife is visiting her sister in Miami," Ortega said. "Along with our two daughters. Normally she watches my diet like a hawk, so when she's away I take advantage."

The statehouse chef served shank steak that came rolled and held in place with string. The middle was stuffed with red and yellow peppers, and mushrooms, and seasoned with spices and hot sauce. With it, the chef served half-inch-thick steak fries and dirty rice.

"Save room for dessert," Ortega said. "My chef makes a hell of a pastry."

And he did. Dessert was apple strudel served warm with freshly made whipped cream that was so good I had seconds.

Over coffee, Ortega got down to business.

"I require a favor from you, Lieutenant," Ortega said. "And you as well, Mr. Bekker. You see, the DeSousa family is very important to

Puerto Rico. In addition to the jobs and taxes they supply, the charity work benefits many people and causes."

I ate the last bit of strudel and whipped cream and looked at Ortega.

"When you catch a break in this investigation, I would like to be made aware of it before it goes public," Ortega said. "Embarrassment to Maria DeSousa and her family at this time could heighten the damage they have already suffered and that wouldn't be good."

"Excuse me, Governor, but are you suggesting that we keep certain facts from the public?" Escalante asked.

"What I am suggesting is that if there are certain, embarrassing details that don't need to go public in order to bring to justice the man responsible for Joe's murder, I would appreciate it as your governor," Ortega said.

"And if we can't?" Escalante asked.

"That's why I need to know first," Ortega said. "So I can prepare a statement to neutralize or at least minimize the damage to the DeSousa family."

Escalante nodded. "Of course we don't want to cause any undue pain to the DeSousa family, Governor. What you're asking is what I would do anyway."

Ortega nodded and then looked at me.

"Anymore of these strudels?" I said.

* * *

Escalante was fuming on the drive back. He gripped the wheel so tightly that even in the dark I could see that his knuckles were white.

"Ortega is nothing but another politician," he said.

"Of course he's a politician," I said. "That's how he became governor. In this case though, he's also a close friend of the family and I believe he's sincere when he says he wants to protect them."

"I suppose," Escalante said. "It just rubs me wrong is all."

We arrived at my hotel.

"We'll talk to the family tomorrow after we check in for updates," I said.

Escalante nodded. "Nine o'clock?"

"We'll do breakfast first," I said.

After Escalante dropped me off, I went to the hotel parking lot for the rental car. I stopped at a Walgreens for a sixteen-ounce cup of cappuccino and then drove to Luquillo Beach.

Chapter Ten

I parked on the side street opposite the beach and sipped the cappuccino. The street lamps illuminated the sidewalks and a few people took advantage of the cooler breeze coming off the ocean to walk their dogs.

Around eleven, the sidewalks were deserted and my cappuccino gone. I left the rental and crossed the street and stood beside the streetlamp where the killer smoked his first cigarette.

Except for the short-sleeve shirt, we were dressed similarly. The night was also similar in that it was around seventy-five degrees with high humidity that the ocean breeze brought little relief from.

Just standing there, I began to sweat. After fifteen minutes, about the same time it took for DeSousa to show up, the back of my shirt was drenched and my face was covered in sweat.

I walked down to the beach to the area where the body had been found. About thirty feet. I looked back at the hotel and the balconies without lights on were nearly invisible. They wouldn't have been able to see me in the dark.

To my right, black waves crashed on the beach.

It was overcast and the moon wasn't up.

DeSousa and the killer squared off. The killer lit another cigarette and in the time it took for the match to ignite and light the cigarette, both men were visible to me. Maybe three to four seconds.

Things went dark again.

The meeting between the two may have started out amicable, if not friendly. Something changed the tone. The killer pulled the kitchen knife from behind the small of his back and stabbed DeSousa.

The wound wasn't fatal.

DeSousa fought back and somehow managed to cut the killer before the killer delivered the second wound that pierced DeSousa's heart.

The killer, still in possession of the knife, fled the beach, leaving DeSousa to die slowly on the sand.

I walked down to the ocean and listened to the crashing waves for a bit as I rolled the scenario around in my mind.

Pieces of the puzzle were missing.

Something didn't fit.

And I knew I wouldn't figure it out tonight, so I returned to the rental and drove back to my hotel.

* * *

"Any progress on your shooter?" I asked Jane when she answered her cell phone.

"He hasn't struck again, so I guess that's progress," she said.

"Any blue Accords on the hot sheets?"

"None."

"Stolen 9MM handguns?"

"Not a one."

"Ask the state police to cross-check with the DMV any 9MM gun owners with Accord owners," I said. "The shooter might be really stupid and you might get lucky."

"I thought you'd be whispering sweet…that's not a bad idea," Jane said.

"So maybe if you get lucky, you can hop a plane to PR so I can get lucky?" I said.

"Speaking of luck, are you behaving yourself?"

"What's luck got to do with…?"

"There are a lot of beautiful, scantily-clad women on those beaches," Jane said.

"And I wish one of them was you," I said.

"That's bonus points," Jane said. "Let me run with your suggestion tomorrow and I'll see if I need a new bathing suit."

We chatted for a few more minutes and after hanging up, I checked the time and it was close to midnight, too late to call Regan.

I stripped down and took a cool shower, then blasted the air conditioner to rid the room of humidity.

I sprawled out on the bed with a can of Coke and went back to the beach.

The question in my mind was what lit the fuse? Was the only purpose of the meeting to kill DeSousa? If so, DeSousa had to know or at least suspect his attacker meant him harm.

Why not arm himself? He owned guns, why not bring one? Better yet, why not hire bodyguards? Money wasn't a problem for DeSousa, so why no bodyguards?

The answer was simple. Joe DeSousa had something to hide.

Find what that something was and you find his murderer.

I replayed the scene on the beach over in my mind.

They went down to the beach where it was dark. The point of the meeting was probably conversation on DeSousa's part. Something triggered the smoker and he pulled the kitchen knife and stabbed DeSousa.

DeSousa fought back and…and what? Got hold of the knife and cut the smoker?

Then the smoker somehow regained possession of the knife and stabbed DeSousa a second time causing the fatal wound?

That didn't make sense. A knife fight is a quick, brutal and ugly thing. Maybe if the first cut had been minor, DeSousa would have had time to react, but it was a piercing stab to the ribs.

If you've ever had a bruised or broken rib, it totally incapacitates you to the point you can't even breathe.

So how did DeSousa, a sixty-year-old man with no fighting experience manage to inflict damage to the smoker before succumbing to the second wound?

Anger increased adrenaline and made a man capable of things far above his normal. That's how heroes in war are born. DeSousa would have had to be in a total rage that night.

I closed my eyes and visualized what I witnessed.

The smoker appeared calm and collected as he waited and smoked a cigarette. No nervous twitch, tapping of the foot or swinging of the arms. He didn't look around as he smoked. He just stood there and waited as if he was sure DeSousa would show.

When DeSousa arrived, he appeared calm and unafraid to enter the dark beach.

Something sparked the fight. A word, a gesture, a look or movement.

I opened my eyes and sat up, then went to the window. It was late, but a few people were poolside having drinks.

I thought about the fight. If I were on the beach that night, could I defend myself against a surprise attack with a knife? In broad daylight, yes. I was trained to do so and have done so many times in the past.

In near total darkness where you never saw the attack coming was a completely different scenario.

So how did DeSousa…?

"Yes, of course," I said aloud.

Chapter Eleven

Escalante picked me up at the hotel and we decided to hit Juan in a Million again for breakfast.

We ordered the three-pepper omelet with sides of home fries, sausage, bacon and toast. The omelet itself was stuffed with diced green, yellow and red peppers. The toast was thick slices of crusty whole wheat bread lathered with fresh strawberry jam. I was up at five-thirty and spent seventy-five minutes in the hotel gym, so I was running on fumes and was hungry.

"I went to the office first," Escalante said. "My guys report more than three thousand men flew into and out of this rock two days before and two days after DeSousa's murder without checked luggage."

"Business travelers?"

"Mostly," Escalante said. "Nowadays you can cram a week's worth of stuff into an oversize carry-on bag and shove it into an overhead and save fifty bucks on checking luggage. Despite tourism, the biggest income to this rock is industry. That brings business travelers by the tens of thousands."

"They have a printout of passengers?"

Escalante nodded.

"The body released yet?"

"This afternoon."

"I'd like to see it before we talk to the family," I said. "I have a theory."

Escalante looked at me. "Alright," he said.

* * *

The ME at the morgue led us to the section where DeSousa's body was stored.

"I thought we were moving him out today?" he asked.

"We are," Escalante said. "The funeral home should be here this afternoon for the body."

We reached the bank of slots and the ME pulled out the sleeve where DeSousa's body was held. He removed the sheet.

I looked at the body of Joe DeSousa. The two stab wounds on the right side of his chest were close enough for me to see that both stab wounds happened in quick succession. One followed by the other. If the two stabbings had time between them, they wouldn't be so closely grouped. DeSousa would have moved, dropped to one knee, made an attempt to escape and the second wound wouldn't be so close to the first.

"The smoker…" I said.

"The smoker?" Escalante said.

"Sounds silly calling him the killer," I said. "Look at the wounds closely and tell me what you think."

Escalante and the ME studied the wounds.

"The second one is what killed him," the ME said.

"Anything else?" I asked.

"The first one didn't kill him," the ME said.

"See how close together the two wounds are," I said. "That means he stabbed quickly and DeSousa didn't have time to react. Boom-boom. Had there been reaction time, the second wound wouldn't be so close to the first."

The ME and Escalante studied the wounds again.

"Agreed," Escalante said.

"So what does this mean?" the ME asked.

"DeSousa's shirt had the blood of the smoker on it," I said. "How did it get there?"

Escalante looked at me. I saw understanding in his eyes. "DeSousa had his own knife and struck the first blow," he said.

The ME stared at me.

"It's one way," I said. "Look at his face and hands, there are no defensive wounds that a person gets when trying to defend himself from a knife attack. No cuts on the hands, wrists and forearms that happen when defending yourself. It was pitch-black and the only way to ward off a knife is to absorb some cuts. The other way is after the smoker stabbed DeSousa twice and before he fell, he managed to get a lucky stab at the smoker with his own knife."

"So where is DeSousa's knife?" Escalante said.

"The smoker took it, or one of the surfers did, or it's still buried in the sand," I said. "We probably won't know until we find the smoker."

* * *

While Escalante drove us to the DeSousa home, I used my cell phone to call Walt.

"John Bekker for Captain Grimes," I told the desk sergeant.

Escalante glanced at me.

"How is the royal pain in my ass enjoying his stay in Puerto Rico?" Walt asked when he picked up.

"The royal pain in the ass needs a favor," I said.

"That's what makes you royal," Walt said.

"Get ahold of your fellow stars and bars in New York and pull the arrest record on Joseph DeSousa," I said. "Juvenile mostly. See if he has any gang related activity maybe related to the use of a knife."

Escalante almost drove us off the road.

"Possession of or use of a knife in gang fights," I said. "No shortage of them in the Bronx back then."

"And for this tidbit I get?"

"Two bottles of Don Q rum."

"No good. I got to pay off Venus for her time."

"Four bottles."

"I'll call you later."

I hung up and tucked my phone away.

"That's pretty far-fetched and potentially damaging to the DeSousa family," Escalante said.

"Not really. Not if you step back and look at it from an impartial distance," I said. "Would the average sixty-year-old man agree to meet a stranger alone on a deserted beach at three in the morning? DeSousa legally owned guns, but it looks like he brought a knife even though he didn't know if the smoker had a gun of his own. It tells me DeSousa wasn't uncomfortable in a one-on-one, mano a mano situation. We have to examine the possibility that the smoker wasn't there to kill Joe DeSousa, but the other way around."

"Jesus Christ," Escalante said.

"That's one giant bitter pill," I said.

"But why?" Escalante said.

"That's our job to find out," I said.

* * *

Rose served coffee in the kitchen along with a large plate of pastries and cookies.

"I baked the cookies and pastries just this morning," Rose said. "For something to do, I suppose."

Maria DeSousa sat at the head of the table with Xavier and Richard on her left and right. Rose sat next to me with Escalante on her right.

"We've uncovered some information that you may or may not be aware of," I said. "I'm betting it's may not or you would have mentioned it earlier."

Maria stared at me.

Escalante cleared his throat. "We have it on a reliable source that your husband and father was going to run for governor," he said.

There were a few moments of stunned silence.

Then Maria said, "My Joe? Run for governor?"

"That's ridiculous," Richard said.

"The source is Governor Ortega," Escalante said. "I assure you it's accurate."

"Why didn't he tell us?" Xavier asked. "We're his family. We had the right to know this."

"Yes, of course," Rose said. "Ortega's term is up in two years. That's why Dad wanted to retire and turn the business over to us, so he could run for office."

"Okay, so Dad was thinking of running for governor, so what?" Richard said. "That would have been two plus years in the future. How does that have anything to do with who killed him?"

"He may have had a political enemy who didn't want him as governor," Escalante said. "Which makes the question, 'did he have any enemies at all?' that much more important."

"What were Joe's political beliefs?" I asked.

"He…both of us actually… are members of the New Progressive Party," Maria said.

"I'm afraid I'm not up on the politics of Puerto Rico," I said.

"The New Progressive Party wants statehood for Puerto Rico," Escalante said. "The Popular Democrat Party wants things to stay as they are."

"Joe believed that becoming a state could only benefit Puerto Rico the way statehood benefitted Hawaii," Maria said. "I believe that as well."

I reached for a cookie and took a bite. "Excellent," I said.

"Thank you," Rose said.

"You don't really believe somebody killed my father over politics?" Richard asked.

"Who killed Lincoln? Who killed Kennedy? What started World War One?" I asked.

"Sure, but PR is a hundred-mile-long island with less than four million people," Richard said. "Nobody is going to start a war over this rock."

"How do you think the U.S. got this rock?" I said. "The bottom line is we now have a new dimansion to look at and we need you, all of you, to help us."

"Mr. Escalante is right," Maria said. "We need to help in every way we can. I ask, though, if whatever you require from us can wait until after the funeral?"

"Yes, of course," Escalante said.

"Thank you," Maria said.

"When is the viewing and funeral?" Escalante asked.

"The viewing will be in two days," Maria said. "The funeral in three. The announcement will be in tomorrow's newspapers."

"Thank you," I said.

* * *

"I wish I still smoked," Escalante said as he started his car.

I rested my head against the seat. "I wish I still drank," I said.

Escalante put the car in gear. "Office?" he asked.

"Office," I said.

Chapter Twelve

"So what do we know that we need to know more of?" I asked and took a sip of coffee.

We were in Escalante's office. I was at the window looking out. Escalante sat behind his desk.

"DeSousa's political connections," Escalante said.

"His enemies," I said.

"His background growing up in New York," Escalante said.

"Where's the appointment book Ortiz gave us?" I asked.

For two hours we poured over the book and made lists of appointments and names to verify. More work for Escalante's staff of detectives is what it amounted to and that's about it.

"What else do we need to know?" I asked, returning to the window.

"What was DeSousa doing during those missing hours?" Escalante said.

"Who wants Puerto Rico to remain a holding and not become a state?" I said.

Escalante looked at me. "We need to see…"

"The governor," I said.

* * *

Ortega kept us waiting thirty-five minutes before he could see us. The waiting room was large and comfortable, with a flat-screen television and a library of books and magazines.

Finally, an aide called us to his office.

"Nice to see you again, Lieutenant, Mr. Bekker," Ortega said. "Would you like something cold to drink?"

"Sure," Escalante said.

"Bring us some fresh lemonade," Ortega told the aide.

The aide nodded and left the office.

"Please have a seat," Ortega said.

We took chairs opposite the desk.

"So you have something to report?" Ortega asked.

"You're a member of the New Progressive Party?" I asked.

"That's correct."

"The other party is the Popular Democrat Party?" I asked.

"Yes. There is also the third, much smaller Puerto Rican Independence Party."

"I take it they want Puerto Rico to become an independent nation?" I asked.

"A ridiculous notion in this dangerous age," Ortega said. "Without the protection of the U.S., we would be invaded by a host of nations looking for a strategic stronghold in the Caribbean. Puerto Ricans would no longer be U.S. citizens and free to move to the States at will. Think of how many athletes and entertainers started here and moved there. The Independent Party received less than three percent of the vote last election for those very reasons. Now what is driving these questions?"

"You're for statehood?" I asked.

"Yes."

"The Popular Democrats are against?"

"Yes."

"You failed to sway the people to vote for statehood?"

"I did."

"Could Joe have pulled it off?"

"If anybody could, it would be Joe."

"That makes your enemies Joe's enemies," I said.

"What are you…yes it does, doesn't it?" Ortega said.

"Ever get any death threats, governor?" I asked.

The aide returned with a pitcher of lemonade and three glasses.

Each glass was filled with plastic ice cubes that contained frozen gel. The plastic cubes kept the drinks cold without melting and watering down the lemonade.

I took a sip. It was ice cold, sweet and delicious.

"Yes, I have," Ortega said.

"How many?"

"They were mostly cranks who want Puerto Rico to become an independent country."

"How many?" I asked again.

"Three hundred the first term, maybe two hundred during the second to date."

Escalante looked at me.

"Protective Services has checked out every one of them," Ortega said. "Like I said, they are mostly cranks."

"Protective Services are your secret service?" I asked.

"Yes. They are part of what you would call the state police."

"I know who runs that division," Escalante said. "We'll talk to them later today."

"Do you really think some misguided crank is responsible for Mr. DeSousa's murder?" Ortega asked.

"I think whoever killed DeSousa had a reason," I said. "Our job is to follow the evidence and clues until we uncover that reason. That means we have to look at everything, crank or not."

"Of course," Ortega said.

"We'll talk to the secret service division, but off the top of your head, do you remember any threats that were taken seriously?" Escalante asked.

"There were a few," Ortega said. "I know some individuals were arrested. You'd have to get the particulars from the secret service."

"We will," Escalante said.

"Governor, in those meetings with DeSousa, were enemies and opponents ever discussed?" I asked.

"Sure, but never in the context of murder," Ortega said. "Opponents who want to undermine my campaign and Joe's future campaign, mud throwers and smear merchants, reporters with political axes to grind, but never anything closely related to murder."

"After we check with the secret service, I'd like to meet with you again and see if any names we highlight ring a bell," I said.

"Whatever I can do to help," Ortega said.

* * *

We picked up the passengers list from Escalante's detectives and reviewed it in his office at the conference table.

Nearly three thousand names. We divided the list into two parts.

"The smoker was between thirty-five and fifty," I said. "Cross off every male under and over and every female."

Two hours later we had narrowed the list to eleven hundred.

"Let's take a break," Escalante said. "I want to see if Protection returned my call."

Escalante went to his desk and called the detectives squad room. He spoke for a few minutes, hung up and returned to the conference table.

"Captain Sanchez is free at five this afternoon," Escalante said. "The Protection Division is in a different building."

I looked at my watch. "It's getting late," I said. "Call him back and see if he's free for dinner. My treat. Say around seven."

Escalante made the call and then returned to the conference table.

"He's free," he said.

"Good," I said. "So let's narrow the list one more time. Let's concentrate for now on males flying in from a cold climate. I doubt you'd wear long sleeves flying in from Miami, Austin or San Diego where the weather is just as warm."

By six-fifteen we narrowed the list to four hundred and seventeen names.

"Tomorrow we check who rented cars and who are frequent travelers to Puerto Rico," I said.

"Where do you want to go for dinner?" Escalante asked.

Chapter Thirteen

David Sanchez was a large, beefy-type guy in his mid-fifties. He looked the sort who would have volunteered to run beside the governor's car in a parade in his younger days. He wore his sandy hair in a crew-cut and had deep brown eyes that took everything in as he spoke.

I took him and Escalante to my hotel where we had dinner poolside in the early evening shade.

"How have you been, Jerry?" Sanchez asked as we sipped tall glasses of iced lemonade.

"Fair. You?"

"Same," Sanchez said. "So what's behind this little poolside dinner date?"

"Bekker and I are heading the investigation concerning Joe DeSousa's murder," Escalante said.

"No shit. I'm in Protection, not Homicide. You want something or you wouldn't be buying me the most expensive steak on the menu," Sanchez said.

"We're looking into the possibility of someone who made death threats against Governor Ortega as a possible suspect," I said.

Sanchez looked at me. "Why?"

"DeSousa was engaged in secret meetings with Ortega to run for governor," I said. "Someone who strongly opposed Ortega might have gotten wind of this and wanted to put a stop to DeSousa before he could gain traction."

Sanchez was silent as he mulled that over. "Possible," he said.

"So how many did you arrest and take seriously?" Escalante asked.

"Maybe a dozen for making death threats, plotting to assassinate Ortega, and one I think for making a bomb," Sanchez said.

"Can your people account for them?" Escalante said.

"I'll have it on your desk in the morning."

"Any of them left-handed?" I asked.

"How the hell would I know?" Sanchez said.

"If they were arrested they had to sign for their belongings," I said. "Their handwriting would have a left-handed slant. If you could send that paperwork with the report that would be great."

"You think who killed DeSousa was left-handed?" Sanchez asked.

"I know so," I said. "I saw him. It was dark and I couldn't see his face well enough to describe details, but I saw him."

Sanchez stared at me. "I'll see what I can do," he finally said.

After dinner, we had dessert and coffee and lingered in the much cooler breeze blowing down from the mountains.

"How long were you a cop?" Sanchez asked.

"Sixteen years, the last eight as detective in special crimes," I said.

"Disability pension?" Sanchez asked.

"With early out," I said.

"After Jerry called and said you were assisting him as a private cop at the request of the DeSousa Family, I Googled you and you put away some heavy hitters," Sanchez said. "I read what happened to your wife and daughter. I'm sorry."

"It was a long time ago," I said. "My daughter is nineteen now and doing pretty well I must say."

"That's good," Sanchez said. "Jerry, I'll have those reports in the morning."

"Can you deliver them in person?" I asked. "I'll take us to breakfast."

"Sure," Sanchez said.

We shook hands and Sanchez returned to his car. Escalante and I stayed for a final cup of coffee.

"It's remote at best this will lead to anything," Escalante said.

"I know, but remote doesn't mean impossible," I said.

"What do you…?" Escalante said.

"Hold on," I said as my cell phone rang.

"Walt," I said after I hit talk.

"I'd thought I'd call you back with the monkey wrench and suggest you up the bottles of Don Q to five," Walt said.

"Go ahead," I said.

"It appears that Joe DeSousa had a long juvie record in the Bronx that was sealed and finally expunged," Walt said. "As an adult, he was arrested twice, once at the age of eighteen, the second a year later. He ran with a Portuguese street gang. Both arrests were for possession of an illegal switchblade knife."

"Name of the gang?"

"Are you ready for this? The Almighty Latin Kings."

"Catchy. Sounds like a sixties boy band."

"And all inclusive. Puerto Rican, Mexican and Portuguese. Turf included West Harlem, the Bronx and Brooklyn."

"Are they still around?"

"Most were arrested eighteen years ago for crack/cocaine and the remaining few dissolved into rival gangs or quit altogether."

"Anything new on Jane's shooter?"

"She's running down gun permits, serial numbers, and license plates," Walt said.

"I'll call you if I need you," I said.

"Don't forget the Don Q," Walt said.

"Tell Elizabeth I'll be by for a home-cooked meal as soon as I get home."

"What home and who cooks?" Walt said. "Cause it ain't gonna be her."

I hung up and looked at Escalante.

"As a kid, DeSousa ran with a street gang called the Almighty Latin Kings in the Bronx," I said. "His JD record was expunged, but he had two arrests before turning twenty for possession of an illegal switchblade."

Escalante shook his head. "Son of a bitch," he said.

"That dark side of the moon will get you every time," I said.

"I'm going home," Escalante said. "See you for breakfast."

* * *

"Where's Regan?" I asked Oz.

"She on a date with that deputy Phil kid," Oz said. "They went to the movies. That dinosaur thing everybody seeing."

"Alone?"

"No, I went with them," Oz said. "Course they alone."

"What time is it there?"

"Nine-thirty," Oz said. "Movie be over around ten-thirty, I think."

"If she's not home by…"

"In six months she be twenty," Oz said. "You can't keep her in your back pocket forever. This Price boy is a nice kid, very polite."

"Polite doesn't mean he won't…"

"What? Put the moves on her?" Oz said. "She can take care of herself. Look who her daddy is. He done put the fear of God in that boy."

"Let's hope so," I said. "If she's not home by midnight…"

"You breaking up," Oz said and hung up the phone.

* * *

"Your deputy is on a date with my daughter," I said.

"Gosh, you really do know how to sweet-talk a girl, Bekker," Jane said.

"Sorry, but it upsets me," I said.

"If you're worried Price is going to put the moves on her…"

"That upsets me even more," I said.

"Don't be. Price and I have discussed this and he knows that Regan isn't mentally ready for sex," Jane said.

"Jesus Christ," I said.

"I told him that she'll tell him when she's ready and in the meantime, he's to keep his eager little pecker in his pants," Jane said.

"That's comforting," I said.

Jane giggled. "Don't be such an old poop," she said. "She's going to grow up and do what big girls do and there's nothing you can do about it. So when are you coming home?"

"I'm staying for the funeral," I said. "We're running down some long-shot leads, so maybe five days. How is your shooter going?"

"Tomorrow I should have a list of gun owners to Honda owners," Jane said.

"If it pans out, maybe you can still join me for a long weekend?" I said.

"Sounds like someone is feeling randy," Jane said.

"If I said I just like long weekends would you believe me?"

"No, but as I'm feeling a bit randy myself, I'll see what I can do."

"About Price?" I said. "What if…?"

"Night, Bekker," Jane said.

* * *

Sleep was still hours away. I again used the time to think and try to get an understanding about what I had witnessed.

Two men show up on a deserted beach at three in the morning with bad intentions on their minds.

Maybe DeSousa had a knife with him for protection?

Maybe the smoker had the bread knife for the same reason?

Two cautious men with knives for protection.

But I doubted it.

I also doubted that DeSousa would agree to a meeting with the smoker if he felt his life was in danger. He had too much to live for to risk an early death. A successful corporation that he wanted to pass down to his kids, a loving wife, a potential run at the governorship and an impeccable reputation.

The smoker wasn't from Puerto Rico, of that I was sure. So he flew in for the meeting and didn't have time to change for the warmer climate, or…didn't bother to bring a change of clothing because he knew he wasn't staying around long enough to need them.

So DeSousa agreed to the meeting because…?

Meeting the smoker was of upmost importance. They had a deal of some kind that just couldn't wait or that they wanted to keep private.

Then why the knives? Most business executives don't bring knives to their meetings. Then again, most meetings don't take place on a deserted beach at three in the morning.

DeSousa had some dark, terrible secret that the smoker threatened to expose. Was that enough to draw him to the beach alone, armed just with a knife?

No.

DeSousa had the resources to handle the smoker in other ways. He could hire an army of investigators to deal with the smoker and an army of bodyguards for protection.

Yet he did neither.

I thought about what might put me in that type of situation.

To protect my daughter?

As a last resort only. If it came down to a knife fight to save her life, I wouldn't risk being killed, I'd bring a gun because if I were killed, she would be, too.

Blackmail?

A strong possibility.

But the question that needs to be asked is why the blackmailer would kill his victim before collecting his loot?

If you're DeSousa why risk your life in the first place? If the smoker was blackmailing him there is no evidence that says so.

The carousel in my head went round and round, and with each spin, things grew more and more confused.

I closed my eyes.

Sometimes on rare occasions I have the dream I used to have almost nightly when I was drinking. I used to drink to the point I would pass out to avoid the dream, but the drinking only seemed to heighten the frequency.

Fourteen years ago, I rushed into my home as a team of cops tried to prevent me from seeing the beaten, raped, dead body of my wife Carol. In reality, I sent four cops to the hospital before they managed to subdue me. I didn't learn Regan had witnessed her mother's rape and murder until later.

In my dream, I break free and rush into my house to the bedroom where five-year-old Regan is hiding under the bed. She sees me and comes out. Her face and hands are covered in Carol's blood. Her little face is angry. "Why weren't you here to save mommy?" she says. "Mommy needed you and you weren't here."

That's the part where I wake up drenched in sweat and fear, the kind of fear I could smell on myself.

My eyes opened and I looked at the dark ceiling.

Joe DeSousa was scared right down to his soul and that fear drove him to meet the smoker on the beach.

But afraid of what?

Chapter Fourteen

Sanchez ordered rice and beans with three fried eggs on top, a side order of bacon, toast, juice and coffee.

"I think I'll have that, too," Escalante said.

"Make it three," I said.

The waitress nodded, took the menus and replaced them with three mugs of coffee. We all took sips at the same time.

"So what do you have for us?" Escalante asked.

"Willie Salazar," Sanchez said.

"Willie?" I said.

"Real name is Wilma." Sanchez said. "Spelled with a W, pronounced with a V."

"He's a leftie?" Escalante asked.

"The only one of the bunch we arrested."

"What did Willie do?" I asked.

Sanchez had a folder and slid it across the table. I opened it and did a quick read. Wilma Salazar had been a member of a group called Puerto Ricans for Puerto Rico prior to Ortega's second election. The PR for PR was very vocal in their opposition to Ortega, making threats such as bombing voting stations, showing up at speeches to cause violent breakouts, mugging tourists inciting riots.

"They're small in numbers, but large in the pain in the ass department," Sanchez said.

"I see that," I said.

The night of Ortega's second election victory, Salazar and other members of PR for PR showed up at voting stations and blocked large numbers of people from voting that they believed were Ortega supporters.

Salazar and others were eventually arrested. He received a six-month sentence and served every day of it except one, released a day early for good behavior.

I put the folder down and took a sip of my coffee.

"So what does this Salazar do for work?" I asked.

"He's the super middleweight champion of Puerto Rico and number thirteen ranked boxer in his division in the world," Sanchez said.

The waitress arrived with our breakfast.

"This coffee is very good," I said to the waitress. "What brand is it?"

"It's local," she said. "From DeSousa."

"Thank you."

We dug into breakfast and for a few minutes the table was silent.

"We still haven't seen Hector," I said breaking the silence. "We could talk to Salazar first and then Hector. The viewing isn't until five tonight."

"I'll be there with some of my men," Sanchez said. "To protect the governor, but also because DeSousa was a good man, important to PR."

I nodded. "Where can we find Salazar?"

* * *

Wilma Salazar was skipping rope in the center ring of the boxing gym where he trained in the town of Carolina.

Carolina is home to the Luis Muñiz Airport, which I incorrectly thought was in San Juan. It's a large city by Puerto Rico's standards with a population close to two hundred thousand. It's also home to one of DeSousa's major hotels.

The gym was busy with an array of fighters engaged in various activities. Besides the center ring there were two smaller rings where fighters were sparring.

We approached the center ring and Escalante flashed his badge.

"Willie, we need a moment," he said.

Without missing a skip, Salazar said, "Fuck off." His accent was thick, but not so thick I couldn't understand him.

"I'm serious, Willie," Escalante said. "We need to talk to you."

"Where's your warrant?" Salazar asked as he continued to skip rope.

"We can get one," Escalante said. "But you can save us all some time and trouble and come down and answer a few questions."

"No speak the English," Salazar said.

"Me neither," I said.

Salazar stopped skipping rope and looked down at me.

"That's pretty funny," he said, his accent not so thick now.

"I'm a funny guy," I said.

"Tell you what," Salazar said. "If one of you got the balls to climb up here and go one round with me, I'll answer your questions."

"Deal," I said.

"Are you crazy?" Escalante said. "The man's a pro and a damn good one."

"One round," I said.

"The full three," Salazar said.

"How much do you weigh?" I asked.

"One seventy-one," Salazar said. "Three pounds over the limit. I'll make weight next fight."

"I have fifty plus pounds on you," I said.

"Weight never scared me," Salazar said. "It scare you?"

"No. Where can I get some gloves?"

"Bekker, I think you should rethink this," Escalante said.

"It's fine," I said and removed my shoes and socks.

Salazar shouted to a trainer for gloves.

I removed my shirt and tossed it on a chair.

The trainer arrived with two sets of gloves and spoke to me in Spanish.

"He wants to wrap your hands," Escalante said.

"Tell him not necessary," I said. "Lace up my gloves."

While the trainer laced up Salazar's gloves, Escalante did mine.

Then I stepped into the ring. Salazar was around six foot one and all lean muscle.

"You don't last the round; I don't got to talk to you. Take it or leave it," Salazar said.

"I'll take it," I said.

"You want headgear and a mouthpiece?"

"Do you?"

"Fuck no."

"Then let's go," I said.

Salazar looked down at the trainer. "Ring the bell and time three minutes," he said.

I walked to the center of the ring.

Salazar joined me.

"You look in good shape for an older man," he said.

"I might just fool you," I said.

Salazar grinned. "You think so?"

The bell rang.

"I'm gonna give you the bums rush," Salazar said. "It's the only way I fight."

I stepped back. "Bring it."

I knew what Salazar meant by bums rush. No jabs, no footwork, no combinations, just a charge of left and right hooks to the head the way Mike Tyson used to do in his prime when he was knocking down opponents like bowling pins.

Except that Mike Tyson weighed two thirty, not one seventy-one.

Salazar rushed forward and unleashed a barrage of left and right hooks intended for my face, but I extended my arms and let the gloves absorb the brunt of the force.

Salazar had power no doubt, but it was super middleweight power and may have been devastating against a fellow super middleweight, but I had more than fifty extra pounds on him and I handled the blows without much trouble.

"You've been in the…" Salazar said as I snapped a jab to his face.

He stepped back and grinned.

"That hurt," he said.

"It's supposed to. Want more?"

Salazar charged forward and unleashed a barrage of punches to my head, but he had to punch up and that took some of the steam out of them. I blocked what I could, but a few slipped through and landed on my nose and jaw.

I placed my glove on Salazar's chest and shoved him backward. He wasn't used to being manhandled and launched a left hook that whizzed by my face and I countered with a stiff jab that landed on the button.

"Hey, you're pretty good," he said.

"We got about ninety seconds, Willie, show me something," I said.

Salazar came in cautiously, looking for a path through my longer reach. Every time he got close, I set him back with a stiff jab to his face. With about twenty seconds, he threw caution to the wind, charged and launched a roundhouse left that whizzed by my face.

I countered with a right cross that caught him flush on the jaw. His legs buckled as he stepped backward.

The bell rang.

I lowered my gloves.

"Let's get some coffee and talk," I said.

* * *

Salazar rubbed the welt on the right side of his jaw. "Fuck, man," he said.

"It's simple engineering stress, Willie," I said. "There is more of me to absorb the stress than you."

"You been in the ring before," he said.

"It's a hobby of mine," I said. "So I went the three, let's talk."

Salazar sipped his coffee and then said, "Ask."

We were in a coffee shop not far from the gym.

"Do you still run with the PR for PR group?" I said.

"Not since I did my six months," Salazar said. "I still believe PR should dump the US and go it alone, but I gotta make a living and support my wife and three kids and rotting in jail don't get it done."

"Anybody in the group come to mind that might actually follow through on attempting to kill the governor?" Escalante asked.

"That what this about?" Salazar asked. "Somebody tried to kill Ortega?"

"No, but somebody did kill Joe Italiano," I said. "Know anything about that?"

"Should I? And who is Joe whatever?"

"Italiano," I said. "Real name Joe DeSousa."

"The rich guy killed on the beach, right?"

"Yup."

"All I know is what I saw on the news," Salazar said. "Besides, what's he got to do with PR for PR?"

"He was going to run for governor and he was a big believer in statehood," I said.

"Governor? No shit."

"No shit, Willie," I said. "So who do you know is crazy enough to pull off a stunt like that?"

"Why you asking me?" Salazar said. "I ain't run with them in years."

"Because you're a southpaw, and so is the killer," I said.

Salazar stared at me for a moment. "You think I…"

"No, but you may have some names even if you don't know it," I said. "Anybody left handed who likes the knife in your old group?"

"Best I could do is give you some names of the hotheads I used to run with," Salazar said. "I'm training for my next fight, man; I got no time to run around with those assholes no more."

"We'll check out your list, Willie, but fight or no fight, if you hold back on us, we'll come back and serve your ass," Escalante said.

* * *

"You handle yourself pretty well," Escalante said as he drove us to DeSousa's coffee plantation.

We were driving west to the Toro Negro Mountains near the town of Jayuya.

"Willie is a fighter, not a boxer," I said. "He'll take ten punches to land two. He's the type with scrambled eggs for brains by the time he's fifty."

"He gave up about thirty names," Escalante said. "I'll give the list to my detectives to run down, as if they don't have enough to do with that list of four hundred and seventeen names I gave them this morning."

We were about ninety minutes west of Old San Juan. Escalante turned onto a dirt road that elevated into the Toro Negro Mountains. After about another mile we arrived at a private road that led to the DeSousa Coffee Plantation.

At the gates, a large arch held a sign that read Hacienda DeSousa.

"Coffee plantations are often referred to as haciendas," Escalante explained.

After a ten-minute-long, very bumpy ride, we arrived at a small house where Hector lived with his family. A skinny dog was playing with a stick in the yard.

Hector came out of the house and stood on the porch. He wore a suit minus the tie and greeted us in English.

"I am going to the services for Mr. DeSousa," Hector said in decent enough English.

"Us, too," I said. "I'm John Bekker. Lieutenant Escalante and I have a few questions. It won't take long."

Hector opened the screen door and spoke in Spanish. Then he closed the door and said in English, "Please sit down in the shade there. My wife will be right out with cold drinks."

The entire porch was in the shade. We took chairs at a wicker table and a moment later, Hector's wife came out with a tray loaded with three glasses full of ice and a pitcher of lemonade. She filled the glasses, smiled at us and then returned to the house.

"Please excuse my wife," Hector said. "Her English isn't very good."

I sampled the lemonade. "Tell her it's delicious," I said.

"It should be at five dollars a carton," Hector grinned. "So Lieutenant, what questions have you for me?"

"You are one of the last people to see Mr. DeSousa alive," Escalante said.

"I suppose that is true," Hector said.

"The meeting was about coffee production?" Escalante asked.

"Yes," Hector said. "The demand for our coffee is high. We discussed purchasing the land that…what is the word for next door?"

"Adjacent," I said.

"Yes, adjacent," Hector said. "The land next to ours is perfect for growing the beans. It would increase production by twenty percent. My understanding is that Xavier will handle the details of negotiating the purchase."

"We'll speak to Xavier about that later," Escalante said. "We're more interested in how Mr. DeSousa seemed to you."

"Seemed?"

"Happy, sad, sick, like that," I said.

Hector sipped from his glass. "He said his knees hurt a bit," he said. "He said that when we first sit down to talk. He took a pill with some water."

"How did he seem otherwise?" I asked.

"He see…seem tired," Hector said. "And distracted. A few times when Xavier was talking and asked him a question, Mr. DeSousa wasn't listening. Like he was far away someplace."

"And after the meeting was over, you stayed for a few minutes?" Escalante asked.

"Yes. We talk about the crop and the production of the new land he want to purchase," Hector said. "Then I left and came home."

"Thank you Hector," Escalante said. "We'll see you later at the service."

* * *

Driving northeast on Route 52, we stopped for coffee in the small town of Beatriz so Escalante could call his detectives.

He spoke for about ten minutes in Spanish before hanging up.

"My guys have gone down half the list," he said. "Frequent visitors to first timers."

"Did you bring a tie?" I asked.

"In the glove box."

I brought a jacket and tie and left it in the back seat of Escalante's car.

I sipped some coffee and sat on the picnic table in the parking lot.

"Sounds like DeSousa had the late night meeting on his mind when he should have been talking coffee," I said.

Escalante nodded.

"He knew the meeting was going to take place, that it wasn't something that popped up at the last minute," he said.

"Appears so," I said. "Well, best put my tie on."

"Yeah," Escalante said.

Chapter Fifteen

Delgado's Funeral home in San Juan was standing room only for the five pm viewing. Cars were double-parked along the street and police were directing traffic. If we were to wait on line it would be at least an hour before we got in.

Escalante double parked across the street and flashed his badge at a rear door entrance and we skirted the line.

DeSousa was laid out in the largest room, but it wasn't large enough to hold the massive crowd that turned out to pay its respects. We got in back of a very long receiving line and it was twenty minutes before we reached Maria DeSousa. Xavier, Richard and Rose preceded her in the line. Richard didn't seem all that happy to see us.

Maria seemed a bit surprised and pleased to see us. We shook hands.

"Thank you for coming," she said.

We left the line and went to another line to view the body and when it was our turn, we knelt and said a quick prayer. In death, DeSousa appeared at peace. The makeup artist restored color to his face and as is always the case, the dead appeared sleeping and not really dead.

"I'm going outside and talk to some of the boys," Escalante said.

"Sure."

I moved to a corner of the room near a large display of flowers and studied the board of old photographs. As a young man, DeSousa was quite the dashing figure. Broad shoulders, thick black hair, slim waist.

There were some wedding photos as well. Maria, as a woman in her twenties, was quite the looker. One photo was of the bridal party, grooms to one side, maids the other with DeSousa and Maria centered.

"She was quite the looker, wasn't she?" Rose said on my left.

"Yes, she was," I said. "And you inherited her good looks."

"Not nearly, but thank you," Rose said.

"They were a great looking couple," I said.

"The bridesmaids and grooms were a mixture of Portuguese and Puerto Rican," Rose said. "And as the story goes, the tall man third to my dad's left was madly in love with mom. When dad found about it he was furious. The two almost came to blows on the streets of the Bronx."

"A long time ago," I said.

"Almost thirty-five years," Rose said. "How are you coming along with the investigation?"

"Slow and steady," I said. "We'll get there."

"I believe you will," Rose said. "Well, I have to get back in line."

"Wait, the man in love with your mom, what happened to him?"

"No idea. I doubt Mom knows either."

Rose returned to the line. I stood in the corner and watched the crowd. Most spoke in Spanish and it was difficult for me to pick up what was being said. There was no mistaking, however, the deep sorrow on their faces at having lost a boss, friend and benefactor.

I caught up with Escalante in the parking lot where he was talking to a group of cops attending the service.

"I've had enough for one day," I said.

"Office or hotel?" Escalante asked.

"Hotel. If something breaks, call me, otherwise we'll review the list in the morning," I said.

* * *

I pushed my body hard for ninety minutes in the hotel gym. Drenched in sweat, I returned to my room, put on my swim trunks and went down to the pool. The sun had just set and the pool was empty. I took advantage of having it to myself and swam twenty laps.

Odd, but I wasn't the least bit hungry when I emerged from the shower and slipped on a robe.

Hungry or not, I ordered a burger with the works from room service and called Regan while I waited for it to arrive.

"Hey, Dad, how's it going?" she asked.

"Slow and steady," I said. "Oz told me you went to the movies with what's his face."

"You know perfectly well his name is Phil," Regan said.

"Did you get home late?"

"Dad," Regan snapped.

"Just asking."

"Ask what you really want to know," Regan said. "Did we have sex? The answer is no. Phil is polite and funny and we talk a lot. Okay?"

"I didn't mean to…"

"I know. You're my dad and you can't help it, but you have to learn to trust me more," Regan said. "Because if you don't trust me, how will you ever know if I'm trustworthy?"

"Been watching Kung Fu reruns again?"

"They're showing a marathon of them all day."

"Where's Oz?"

"On a date with Louisa."

"No kidding?"

"Louisa said something about snow on the roof or something like that," Regan said. "And not to wait up. Dad, I gotta go. Molly is beating up on the dog again."

"I'll call you tomorrow," I said.

"Molly!" Regan yelled just before she hung up.

I set the phone on the table, tossed on shorts and a T-shirt and there was a knock on the door with the room service delivery.

For once the nighttime temperature was a comfortable sixty-six degrees with low humidity and I ate at the small table on the balcony.

When I was done, I called Jane on her cell phone.

"I was just thinking about you," she said. "We got a hit on the shooter and raided his apartment. Looks like he skipped, but we confiscated all kinds of crazy stuff. He's our guy alright."

"So you're free then?"

"We start a manhunt tomorrow," Jane said. "I can't exactly say tootles and leave."

"I guess not," I said. "I don't expect to be here much longer anyway."

"Don't pout, Bekker," Jane said. "You're too big, too ugly and old to pout."

"Now who's the sweet talker?" I said.

"Wait until you get home, I'll show you sweet talker," Jane said. "In the meantime, I'm still in the office."

"Your deputy and Regan are…"

"Bye, Bekker, love you," Jane said.

After Jane hung up, I sat at the table on the balcony for a while and thought.

Why did Joe DeSousa keep a meeting at three in the morning on a deserted beach?

Answer, because he knew the person he was meeting.

Through the closed sliding door, I heard the phone on the nightstand ring. I went in and grabbed it on the third ring.

"Mr. Bekker, Xavier DeSousa. I'm sorry if I woke you."

"You didn't."

"My mother would like you to attend the funeral in the morning and the luncheon afterward," Xavier said. "That's why I'm calling. Can you attend?"

"What time?"

"Funeral services are at the San Juan at eleven," Xavier said. "I'll have you picked up at ten."

"I'll be ready," I said.

Chapter Sixteen

I was dressed and waiting in the lobby of the hotel by nine-thirty. It was a warm morning and the lobby was air-conditioned, so I wouldn't be dripping with sweat when the car arrived.

Driven by a funeral home chauffeur, the car arrived on time and drove to the church in Old San Juan that was a favorite of the DeSousa family. The driver told me DeSousa donated one hundred thousand to a restoration project on the church just a few years ago.

The church was on a hill that overlooked the ocean. It was a white structure with a tall bell tower and beautiful stain-glass windows. Seating capacity was five hundred, but twice that was in attendance.

The mass was in Spanish, but I had little trouble following the Catholic service. It concluded at eleven and I filed out with the crowd and stood on the sidewalk and waited.

Xavier sought me out.

"The car will take you to our home for the luncheon," he said. "And take you back to the hotel afterward. We are keeping the burial at the cemetery closed just to family."

The procession to the DeSousa home was twenty cars long. I rode in the same car close to the rear. With traffic, the drive took about an hour.

The backyard of the DeSousa home was decked out with flowers, push-pin boards filled with photographs and long tables of food. Soft music played from a large CD player.

Gloria hired a catering service and she stumbled upon me in the backyard.

"The family will be here in about an hour," she said. "Eat and drink and make yourself at home."

I studied the photographs on the boards. The wedding photos again. The jealous old boyfriend, Xavier as a small child, Maria pushing Rose in a stroller, Richard and Xavier eating ice cream cones and dozens of family portraits.

I nibbled on some food, had a soft drink and envied the few people smoking in the garden.

Around one in the afternoon, the family arrived. They greeted guests and mingled and after a while, I managed to snare Maria.

"Can we talk privately for a few minutes?" I asked.

"Let's go to the kitchen," she said.

We found our way through the crowd to the kitchen. A fresh pot of coffee was in the large coffee-maker and she filled two mugs and set them on the table.

"Mrs. DeSousa, I feel…" I began.

"Please call me Maria," she said. "I'm not that much older than you."

I nodded. "Okay, Maria," I said. "I realize it's a tough day for you, but I feel I owe you the truth."

She sipped from her cup and waited.

"I need to be honest with you," I said. "It's my belief based upon the evidence I've reviewed that your husband's murderer is not in Puerto Rico and I doubt he will return. I don't see the need for you to waste anymore of your money on my services at this point."

Maria was silent for a moment. "Money I have plenty of," she said. "It's a husband I don't have."

I sipped some coffee.

"Lieutenant Escalante is an excellent detective," I said. "He and his staff will stay on the case for as long as it requires."

"What do you think happened?" Maria asked. "Your best theory and don't spare my feelings."

"Alright," I said. "I believe that your husband was both frightened and angry at his murderer. I believe he went to the beach at three in the morning for a showdown. I don't know why he didn't bring one of his guns for protection, but I believe that he had a knife based upon the evidence."

"What kind of knife?"

"That I don't know, but he cut the other man as there are two types of blood on his shirt," I said.

"A showdown about what?" Maria asked.

"Your husband was a wealthy man so it wasn't about money," I said. "He was well-liked, well-respected and gave generously to charity. He didn't gamble, do drugs and there were no women outside the home. It had to be about his plans to run for governor. The murderer may have been trying to blackmail him to prevent him from doing so."

"Blackmail him?" Maria said. "With what?"

"Maybe his past?" I said. "I did some checking and as a kid he ran with some pretty tough street gangs in the Bronx. He was also arrested twice before he was twenty for possession of an illegal switchblade knife. If the killer had the information and was so opposed to your husband becoming governor, he might use it as blackmail ammunition."

"I see," Maria said. "Our past has a way of catching up to us, doesn't it? I want you to know that I've known my husband since we were teenagers. He was as tough as nails back then, but never a criminal. Still, I can see how information like that could be used to hurt his political ambitions."

"You could say that for all of us," I said.

"When will you go home?"

"As soon as I help Lieutenant Escalante tie up some loose ends," I said. "A few days at least."

"I will see you before you leave?"

"Count on it."

"Where do I send payment for your work?"

"I'll leave an address. In the meantime, if you can think of someone from his past that might want to hurt him or is holding a grudge for some reason, let me or Lieutenant Escalante know right away."

Maria nodded. "More coffee?"

"Please."

* * *

The chauffeur took me back to the hotel around three. I called Escalante from my cell phone.

"I called you this morning," he said. "When you didn't answer your cell phone, I tried the desk. They said you were out."

"Last night, I was invited to the funeral," I said. "I just left."

"How is the family?"

"About what you'd expect. Anything new on the passenger list?"

"Not really. How do you determine a suspicious person just from a list," Escalante said. "Many are frequent business travelers as we suspected."

"When they're finished, have them go back and make a list of first-time visitors only," I said. "It should be a short list, but it's something to do."

"Narrow the field," Escalante said.

"When they've done that, we'll compare their locations to phone numbers on DeSousa's hard-line and cell phone," I said. "We might get lucky and get a match."

"I should have thought of that," Escalante said.

"You would have," I said. "I'm going back to my hotel. Swing by later for dinner around seven."

* * *

I left my cell phone on the bed when I went to the gym for a ninety-minute workout. A message was waiting for me when I returned. Paul Lawrence from Washington.

I used the two-cup pot in the bathroom to make some coffee and took a cup to the balcony to return Paul's call. As I punched in his number, I thought about how good a cigarette would be right about now.

After a few transfers and several minutes of listening to miserable soft rock tunes, Lawrence finally picked up.

"Well, you did it, Jack," he said. "You managed to stump the FBI."

"With?"

"Cigarette butts."

I sipped coffee. "And?"

"We identified twenty-nine of the thirty-one butts. Two are foreign and we're working on identifying them," Lawrence said. "One of them came from the street, the other the sand. The one from the sand had type B blood on it."

"That's our guy," I said. "You said foreign. Could be European?"

"I'll let you know as soon as they match it up," Lawrence said. "About the button, it's not from a common manufacture. It has a trace of B-negative blood on it. The button is probably from a custom-made shirt."

"Got to be his," I said.

"I'll let you know as soon as I know," Lawrence said.

"Thanks, Paul."

* * *

Escalante met me in the lobby around seven and we decided on the largest of three hotel dining areas for dinner because they're air-conditioned and outside was humidity so thick you could eat it with a spoon.

"My friend from the FBI called a little while ago," I said after we ordered. "He said there are two cigarette butts they haven't been able to identify as yet. One of them has type B blood on it."

"Our smoker," Escalante said. "It could be a local brand sold only in PR."

"I thought of that," I said. "Tomorrow we buy a pack of every brand made here and I overnight it to Paul. The other thing is the button. They think it came from a custom-made shirt. It had B-negative blood on it."

"There aren't that many places that make custom shirts on this rock," Escalante said. "We could send him samples of the buttons they use."

"I figured we'd do that tomorrow," I said. "So listen, I plan to go home in a few days, probably right after we finish the cigarette/button thing."

"I'm sorry to see you go, you've been a tremendous help."

"What about the passenger list?"

"Tomorrow at the earliest."

"It's out of your jurisdiction," I said. "I could ask Paul to run down the names?"

Escalante shrugged. "It's worth a shot. I owe it to the DeSousa family to do whatever it takes."

"You're not from here, are you?" I asked.

"Lawrence, Massachusetts," Escalante said.

"No kidding. How did you wind up a cop in Puerto Rico?"

"My parents are from here and they moved there to work in the mills," Escalante said. "That was back in the late forties after the war. I guess in it's time, Lawrence was quite the place. By the time I came along it was on the downswing. When I was ten, my parents sent me to spend the summer with relatives in PR to keep me out of trouble. While I was here, they were murdered in a home invasion. My aunt and uncle took me in and I've been here since. Funny, my parents insisted I speak only English, so I had to learn Spanish from my aunt and uncle or I would have been lost in school."

"Did they catch who did it?"

Escalante nodded. "A couple of junkie Puerto Ricans that fled PR for the welfare system in Lawrence. I was too young to really grasp things at the time, but they received twenty-five years by copping a plea and then were released after serving just eleven. Inside a year they had robbed and killed another family."

"That's harsh," I said. "I'm sorry."

"The police killed them both in a shootout, so they got theirs in the end."

"How much longer do you think your captain will keep the case open?" I asked.

"Hard to say without a viable suspect," Escalante said. "I'd like to think the progress we've made is enough to keep it active, but we both know how the system works."

"I do," I said.

"We have the means, the opportunity and the method," Escalante said. "What we don't have is a suspect."

"Tomorrow, what we need to do is concentrate on men leaving the morning after the murder," I said. "My guess is he was in one hell of a hurry to vacate."

"Leaving on a scheduled flight doesn't constitute a crime," Escalante said.

"True, but we have to look and see what we see," I said. "We might find a connection or a link. You never know."

"And I'm here and the suspect is there, I can't exactly go talk to him, now can I?"

"My friend at the FBI has been known to bend a rule now and then," I said.

"Hey, any friend of yours," Escalante said.

"What should we have for dessert?" I asked.

* * *

The way it works sometimes in police work when a detective is investigating a crime is you get lost in the details. You know you've missed something, but you don't know what that something is. You go over the details and clues and evidence again and again and still it eludes you.

It's happened to me many times.

It was happening to me now.

I was convinced that DeSousa was murdered by someone not from Puerto Rico. Someone who flew in to meet DeSousa and who didn't have time to buy a gun on the street and settled for a common kitchen knife he could have bought at any number of stores. He was smoker who smoked an exotic brand of cigarette and used matches probably because he didn't bring a lighter on the plane not realizing lighters

120

were off the banned list. He wore a long-sleeve shirt probably because he flew in from a colder climate, didn't bring much luggage and didn't have time to change. He left the following morning probably shortly after DeSousa's body was discovered. He's left-handed according to the evidence.

I was on the bed, staring at the white ceiling above my head.

DeSousa had a checkered past as a youth, but so did millions of others who went on to lead exemplarily and productive lives.

DeSousa owned and ran a highly successful corporation and gave millions to charity. He was well-liked, well-respected and had few if any real enemies.

He didn't gamble, drink much or run with women. On an island as small as Puerto Rico, those habits would be difficult to keep a lid on.

He planned to run for governor and stood for statehood, so that automatically made him some enemies.

Missed point: Although Puerto Rico wasn't a state, all born on the island were American citizens free to visit or move to the States at will. The smoker could be someone who moved away from Puerto Rico, or New York, knew DeSousa from the past and flew back to settle an old or new score.

In a place like New York, bad habits and enemies are easy to hide.

I made a mental note to see Maria DeSousa tomorrow at some point.

So what was I missing?

What didn't I see that I should be seeing?

I realized that I wasn't going to see it tonight and decided to sleep on it.

Chapter Seventeen

"Where can we get some decent donuts?" I asked Escalante as we ate breakfast in Juan in a Million's diner.

"Donuts?"

"And coffee for your guys."

"I assume you're not thinking double d?"

"Custom made donuts."

"I know a place."

Eduardo's in Old San Juan served donuts the size of pie plates and world-class cappuccino.

"How many men do you have working the case?" I asked.

"Eight."

"Three dozen mixed and two cappuccinos apiece," I said.

Around ten-thirty, we exchanged donuts and coffee for airline passenger reports from Escalante's detectives.

I brought two donuts and two containers of cappuccino for us and we munched and sipped as we reviewed the detective's reports at Escalante's conference table.

Three hundred and eleven males traveled to Puerto Rico without checked luggage three days prior and the day after DeSousa's murder.

Two hundred and twenty-three traveled two days prior and the day after. One hundred and ninety-three one day prior and the day after.

Four hundred and seventeen traveled from the day before to up to three days after.

Seven hundred and nineteen traveled from one to three days prior to from one to three days after.

"Quite an extensive list," I said.

"This doesn't include travelers from other countries," Escalante said.

"Are they working on first time visitors off these names?" I asked.

Biting into a donut, Escalante nodded.

"Make a copy of each list and then let's go shopping," I said.

* * *

Raphael's Tobacco Shop in San Juan carried every brand of cigarette imaginable. I bought one pack of brands grown and manufactured in Puerto Rico and brands imported from Europe, Asia, South America and even Africa. Thirty-seven brands in all.

Stuffed on breakfast and donuts, we skipped lunch and visited every tailor shop that made custom-made shirts. Most were settled in the Old San Juan area.

The button found on the beach was a pearl white color, so we concentrated on that color only. We bagged and tagged nineteen different types of buttons used on custom made shirts.

We made the Post Office by late afternoon where I mailed everything to Paul Lawrence in an overnight express box.

"I'd like to see Maria DeSousa before we head back," I said.

* * *

"Mr. Bekker, Lieutenant Escalante, I wasn't expecting to see you so soon," Maria said when Gloria escorted us to the backyard.

Richard was at the table with her. They were having afternoon coffee.

"Xavier and Rose left this morning," Maria said. "He to his office and she to school."

"What is it that you want?" Richard asked.

"Mrs. DeSousa, I'm going home tomorrow, but I'd like to stay on the case for a few more days," I said.

"Jack up the old bill, huh," Richard said.

Maria looked at her son.

"Richard, if you don't behave, I am going ask Mr. Bekker to put you over his knee and give you the spanking your father never gave you," Maria said.

Richard glared at me.

Maria looked at me. "Go on."

"Where do you live in New York?" I asked.

"Rye. A beautiful home not far from the ocean," Maria said.

"Do you have a caretaker?"

"Yes. Iris Rodriguez. She lives there year round."

"I'd like permission to visit your home and search Joe's office," I said. "There may be something there that can help. A note, a phone number, something."

"I'll call Iris and let her know you're coming," Maria said.

"Any objection to me being there?" Richard asked.

"None at all," I said.

Gloria came out with a fresh pot and two mugs.

"Please join us," Maria said. "It's such a lovely time of day. Joe and I often took coffee at this time. We would sit in the garden and not even talk sometimes."

"I won't remove anything from the house without your permission," I said.

"What exactly are you looking for?" Richard asked.

"Don't know," I said. "Something that might help us identify the man on the beach."

"I'm going home tomorrow," Richard said. "I'll give you my cell number and you can call me when you want to see the house."

"Thank you," I said. "And thank you Maria, for your kindness and your help. I know this hasn't been easy for you and your family."

Maria smiled at me with mist in her eyes.

* * *

"Ninety-seven people off the combined lists were first-timers to PR," a detective said when Escalante and I returned to his office.

"Make copies of all the lists for Mr. Bekker," Escalante said.

The detective nodded and left the office.

"I'm going home in the morning if I can catch a flight," I said. "Are you free for one last dinner?"

"I'll treat this time," Escalante said. "It's the least I can do for all your help."

* * *

"It's been a pleasure, Lieutenant," I said as I shook Escalante's hand.

We were in front of my hotel and just returned from a steak dinner we had in Old San Juan.

"Same here," Escalante said. "We wouldn't have gotten as far as we have without your help."

"I'll call you in a few days," I said "If something breaks, call me first."

I went to my room and called home.

"We just be talking bout you," Oz said.

"Who is we?"

"Me, the dog and the cat," Oz said. "The cat miss you. The dog indifferent."

"Regan?"

"She at the mall with the Phil kid."

"The mall?"

"She need new clothes for her job at the home."

"I'm flying home tomorrow. I'll let you know what time to pick me up."

"There go the peace and quiet."

"Never mind that," I said. "I'll call you with the flight info in the morning."

"Be still my heart," Oz said.

"I heard Louisa paid you a visit," I said. "How did it go?"

"She say she love me," Oz said.

"What do you say?"

"I say mind your own damn beeswax."

"You should thank me for bringing you love," I said.

"That the case, I should thank Regan," Oz said. "She the one made her feel welcome here."

"I'll call you tomorrow," I said.

I hung up, stripped down, cranked up the air conditioner and tried to sleep, but that was pretty much a useless attempt.

I kept going back to fear.

What scared Joe DeSousa enough that he risked life and limb to meet the smoker on the beach?

I read somewhere—I think in a magazine at the dentist, that Russian Tsar Peter the Great had a fear of bugs, especially roaches. The sight of one was enough to set him fleeing.

Joe DeSousa didn't run away from his fear, he ran to it.

Not knowing why was just the sort of detail to drive me buggy.

Chapter Eighteen

My time on the flight home was occupied by reading my lists and reading them again and studying copies of the passengers lists put together by Escalante's detectives.

Despite all the evidence and documentation, the passenger lists, DeSousa's background and political ambition, there wasn't a single suspect to point a finger at.

And that wasn't all that unusual. Police departments across the country had open files that went back decades. Even the FBI had hundreds of cases that went unsolved. It was just the nature of police work.

With an hour left in the air, I closed my eyes, pushed it all away and took a nap.

The seat belt announcement woke me up shortly before landing.

* * *

"You look different," I said to Oz as he started Regan's Impala.

"My tan has faded," Oz said. "My beautiful coffee-color has returned."

"That's not it," I said.

"Regan's car make me look more astute," Oz said.

"Her car is almost as old as mine," I said.

"And it smell a hell of a lot better than your heap."

Then I saw it.

"You dyed the grey out of your beard," I said.

"I do no such thing," Oz said.

"Then you plucked them out," I said.

"Wipe that grin off your face," Oz said. "For your information, Louisa do it with this little brush she have. A few strokes and grey hairs gone."

"Just for Men," I said.

"What, you think she grow a beard, of course it for men."

"No, it's…never mind," I said. "When does Regan get home?"

"Six-thirty."

"We'll go out to eat," I said. "I'll call Jane and see if she's off duty."

* * *

"Nice to see you again Deputy Price," I said.

"You too, sir," Price said.

"Order what you like, this Bekker's treat," Oz said.

Jane and Regan grinned at each other.

"Thank you, sir. I'm starving," Price said.

I was about to say something I probably shouldn't when Jane squeezed my knee under the table.

"And don't be shy about ordering dessert," Oz said.

I looked at Oz.

"That double-double dark chocolate cake look pretty good," he said.

After dinner and dessert, Price took Regan and Oz home in his car. Jane rode with me in my old Marquis.

"Mr. Bekker," Price said before I entered my car.

"Yes."

"I'd like to have a talk with you," Price said. "Sir."

"Sure, in about ten years," I said.

"It's about us. I mean Regan and me," Price said.

Sitting in my car, window rolled down, Jane said, "Phil, see that purple vein on Bekker's neck. That means he's about to stroke out. That would be bad for you. Later would be a better time."

Price nodded. "Goodnight, Mr. Bekker, Sheriff."

"Bekker, get in the car," Jane said.

I got in the car.

"Do you have firewood?"

"Should be plenty."

"Then let's go," Jane said. "You look like you could use some de-stressing."

* * *

I added several logs to the trashcan to keep the bonfire burning. It was a cool night, around fifty-two degrees, but clear and millions of stars blinked at us overhead. Jane was wrapped up in a blanket in her chair near the card table.

I took my chair next to her and filled two mugs with coffee and handed one to her.

Waves crashed on the sand about a hundred yards away.

I kept the twenty-four by twelve foot trailer I lived in for the decade when I was drinking. Since buying the house, I converted the smaller bedroom to an office and use it for my place of business, but also as a place to hang out on beautiful days and nights.

"Feeling better now?" Jane asked.

"Yes."

"Me, too."

I sipped and looked down at the dark, nearly invisible waves. To our right, about a half mile away the fringe lights of town glowed softly.

"I brought you something from Puerto Rico," I said. "I was waiting to give it to you. I'll get it."

I went inside the trailer, fished out the jewelry box and took it outside to Jane.

She looked at the box.

"Open it," I said.

She opened the lid and stared at the diamond earrings inside.

"Because diamonds are a girl's best friend," I said. "Put them on, let's see how they look."

Jane removed them from the box and put them on.

"Beautiful," I said.

Jane looked at me and started to cry.

"What?" I asked.

"It's taken us twenty years to go from a working relationship to friends to now more than friends," Jane said. "The last six months it's always been in the back of my mind that Janet was always waiting around the corner because you're not entirely over each other."

"Janet married her ex-husband three months ago as I recall," I said.

"Since when did marriage stop a cheating heart?" Jane said. "Look at the rat bastard I was married to and his dozens of tarts on the side."

I sat in my chair.

"I'm confused," I said.

"That's because you're a man," Jane said. "It wouldn't make sense if you weren't."

I took a sip of coffee. "So do or don't you like the earrings and is or isn't our relationship on solid ground?" I said.

"God you're one dumb Viking," Jane said, and stood up. She took my hand. "Let's go inside and I'll demonstrate how I feel about the earrings."

Chapter Nineteen

Jane left early for work and I sat in my chair with a mug of coffee and watched the new sun light up the ocean and beach in a glorious orange glow.

I used my cell phone to call Walt.

"I'm home," I said.

"That bit of news could have waited until I was out of bed," Walt said.

"I'll be by your office around nine-thirty if you want breakfast," I said.

"Free breakfast you mean to cover the cost of whatever favor you're going to spring on me," Walt said.

"See ya then," I said, and hung up.

After a second mug of coffee, I tossed on shorts and running shoes, and headed down to the water. I checked my watch and started at a slow jog, picking up the pace after ten minutes. I no longer ran by mileage but by time. After thirty minutes, I turned and ran hard for twenty minutes and then slowed to a quick-walk for the remaining ten.

I toweled off at the trailer and then went around to the side where I built a little gym consisting of pull-up station, an elevated push-up station, an area for jumping rope, and a one hundred and twenty pound heavy bag.

I did push-ups until my chest gave out, pull-ups until my arms gave out, and then skipped rope for fifteen minutes. Then I slipped on the bag gloves and pounded the heavy bag for thirty minutes.

By the time I was shaved, showered and dressed, it was nine o'clock and I drove to Walt's office to pick him up for breakfast.

"Who has steak and eggs for breakfast with a side order of bacon?" I asked.

"A man about to be asked a favor by a pain in the ass who doesn't know when to quit, that's who," Walt said as he sliced into his steak.

"That street gang, the Almighty Latin Kings, I'd like a list of the names and last known whereabouts," I said.

"Of course you do. Why?"

"I'm convinced Joe DeSousa knew his killer," I said. "Either from Puerto Rico, New York or his past."

Walt sighed.

"Venus has nothing to do anyway, right?"

"Off duty, I'll pay her going rate," I said.

Walt sighed again. "Follow me back to the station."

* * *

"I'd have to do this on my own time?" Venus said. "It could take a while."

"A while I got," I said. "And I'll pay your going rate for special details."

"Happy now?" Walt said. "And if you'll excuse me, I'll be napping off breakfast in my office."

After Walt left Venus's office on the first floor of the station house, Venus said, "How is that beautiful daughter of yours?"

"Has a boyfriend, a deputy of Jane's," I said.

"Oh?"

"He wants to have a talk with me."

"Uh oh," Venus said.

"Uh oh, what?"

"Sounds serious," Venus said.

"Never mind serious," I said.

"Even in this day and age, the only reason a boy asks to speak with a girl's father is he wants the girl's hand in marriage," Venus said.

I stared at Venus.

"What's that purple vein there in your neck?" Venus asked.

"Call me when you're done with the list," I said.

* * *

"I had no idea there were so many brands of cigarettes in the world," Paul Lawrence said when I called him.

"But no match?" I asked.

"Not yet, but the boys are also kind of busy right now," Lawrence said. "Terrorists threats, bank robberies, crimes across state lines, kidnappings, the usual fun array."

"I appreciate you taking the time, Paul," I said.

"I know."

"This brand must be exotic," I said.

"Appears so."

"And the button?"

"It's a button."

"I have another favor to ask."

"You wouldn't be you otherwise," Lawrence said.

"The passenger lists," I said. "If I send you the names, can you do some background info for me?"

"Send it, I'll add it to the pile," Lawrence said. "No promise on a delivery date though."

"Thanks," I said. "And fax a picture of the cigarette to Regan's computer so I can see what it looks like."

"Will do," Lawrence said.

I hung up and sat at my desk in the trailer office and thought for a while. Then I picked up the cell phone and called Regan.

"What time do you get home from work?" I asked her.

"Around six-thirty."

"Paul Lawrence from the FBI is sending me a photo to your computer," I said. "I need a printed copy."

"Nothing gross, I hope."

"No, nothing gross."

"Dad, Phil wants to have a talk with you," Regan said.

"I'm busy right now."

"Tonight, Dad. Okay?"

I sighed.

"Quit sighing and make sure you're home by seven."

"Okay, I know when I'm beat," I said.

"That will be the day," Regan said.

After hanging up with Regan, I took my notes and lists outside with a mug of coffee and sat at the card table.

I read and read again, and frustrated, I set everything aside. I dug out my wallet for Richard DeSousa's business card and punched in his number on my cell phone.

"Richard DeSousa," he said when he picked up.

"Richard, it's John Bekker calling," I said.

"Well, well," he said.

"I'm flying to New York tomorrow," I said. "You wanted to be there when I go to the house."

"What time is your flight?"

"I'll let you know in the morning."

"I'll pick you up at the airport," Richard said. "That way I know where you are at all times."

"It's nice to be trusted," I said.

"Who said I trust you," Richard said and hung up.

I called Jane, but her voice mailbox picked up and I left a message for her to call me when she could.

Then I returned to my office and made extra copies of the passenger lists, packed them into an overnight envelope, and then drove to the post office to mail them.

* * *

"This is a picture of a cigarette butt," Regan said when she handed me the copy.

"I know," I said.

"Phil will be here any minute," Regan said.

"I'll be in the backyard."

I took the copy to the backyard and grabbed a chair at the patio table.

The smoker had smoked the cigarette down to the filter and then stepped on it to extinguish it. There was a tiny fragment of white wrapper still attached to the brownish colored filter. Two gold bands wrapped around the filter. There were no other markings, no brand name or trademark symbol.

Paul Lawrence was correct in that it was an exotic, custom-made brand of cigarette.

There had to be thousands of custom-made cigarette brands from around the world, so there was little wonder identifying one brand from another was taking so long.

"You just couldn't smoke Marlboro's like every other dumb slob, could you?" I said aloud.

The kitchen door slid open and Regan said, "Jane's here."

Still in uniform, Jane approached the table and greeted me with a kiss.

"Nice cigarette butt," she said, glancing at the photo.

"I called you earlier," I said.

Jane took the chair next to me. "I know. Regan called and told me not to call you back and to show up before seven to attempt to keep you calm."

"I am calm," I said.

"When my deputy gets here I mean."

The door slid open again and Oz stepped out with a mug of coffee and joined us at the table.

"Oz, your beard," Jane said.

"Never mind my..." Oz said.

From the open door, Regan said, "Dad, Phil is here."

"This gonna be good," Oz said. "A regular picture show."

Dressed in civilian clothes, Price walked to the table.

"This gonna be real good," Oz said.

I glared at him. "He's here to talk to me, not you," I said.

"Oz, help me in the kitchen," Regan said.

Oz stood up, winked at Jane and left the table.

"Thank you for…Sheriff Morgan, are you staying for this?" Price asked.

"Do you want your head busted open like a ripe melon?" Jane asked.

"No, I don't think I do."

"Then pretend I'm not here," Jane said.

"I don't understand," Price said.

"Just keep an eye on that purple vein when you start talking," Jane said.

Price looked at my neck. "I don't see a…"

"You wanted to talk to me?" I said.

"Yes, sir. Mr. Bekker," Price said.

"For God's sake, sit down," I said.

Price sat and looked at me.

"You can start anytime," I said.

"Yes sir. Mr. Bekker," Price said and looked at me some more.

Jane sighed. "Phil, see how that vein is turning purple and starting to bulge?"

Price nodded. "I see it."

"That means to start talking," Jane said.

"I'm not sure how to start," Price said.

"Try the beginning," I said.

"Yes sir. Okay, here goes," Price said. "Regan and I…we…I mean us…we want to get engaged. I know how you feel about…are you okay, Mr. Bekker? That vein is getting…"

"You've known my daughter for six months," I said.

"I know that, sir. It was love at first sight."

"Love at…are you for…?"

Jane squeezed my knee under the table.

"How long an engagement are you figuring on?" Jane asked.

"Oh. At least two years," Price said.

Jane looked at me. "See, Jack, at least two years," she said. "That's not so bad, now is it?"

I looked at Price. "Why?"

"Why what? Sir," Price said.

"Two years."

"Oh. Well, see, Regan wants to finish her classes and that's another two years," Price said. "Also, we figure that if we save our money for the next two years we can save enough for a down payment on a house. And pay for the wedding ourselves."

"I see," I said. "Anything else?"

"Umm, well, to be honest, we plan to see that priest together a few times a week about her problems and prepare us for marriage," Price said.

"Father Thomas," I said.

"Yes, that's him."

"Did you buy a ring?" I asked.

"Not yet, no."

"You need a ring in order to ask a woman to marry you," I said.

"I know. I'll get one," Price said and stood up.

"I didn't mean right now," I said. "But as long as you're up, could you ask Regan to come out here for a moment?"

Price nodded and went inside. A moment later, Regan appeared alone.

"Dad?"

"You didn't tell him about your trust fund, did you?"

Regan's eyes went wide as she shook her head.

"Why not?"

"I want us to do this on our own," Regan said. "I'll tell him about the trust after. I think if we do this together without the trust fund, it's worth more to us than the money."

"He needs to buy a ring," I said. "If he's going to propose to my daughter."

Regan looked at me. Then she nodded and tears filled her eyes and she grabbed my neck and hugged me tightly.

"Go ask him if he's staying for dinner," I said.

Regan released my neck and raced inside. I looked at Jane and she was wiping her eyes.

"What?" I asked.

"Well," she said. "At least you didn't kill him."

"I have to go to New York tomorrow, feel like a bonfire?"

Jane gave me a quick kiss. "I feel more than that," she said.

Chapter Twenty

Richard DeSousa picked me up at Kennedy Airport around nine-thirty in the morning in a two-seater, blue sports car. He wore a suit that cost more than my entire wardrobe.

"It's a long drive to Rye," he said. "You can have coffee, but no food. I hate crumbs in the car. I called Iris and told her to expect two for lunch."

We stopped at a drive-through on the way for coffee and I watched the scenery roll by as I sipped.

"What are you looking for?" Richard asked.

"I don't know," I admitted. "Sometimes you see something and it clicks. A link, a clue, something. I'm convinced your father knew his attacker. There might be something in the house or his office that might tell us more."

"Why do you say he knew the attacker?"

"Would you meet a stranger on a deserted beach at three in the morning unarmed?" I said.

"No, I would not, but my dad had balls of steel," Richard said. "I don't."

"Maybe so, but I doubt he would have met a total stranger under those circumstances," I said. "It was also the way he approached the man without hesitation as if he knew him."

Richard nodded. "Maybe so," he said.

We were silent for most of the rest of the drive and arrived at DeSousa's Rye home close to eleven.

Set back on a tree-lined, side-street, the home was a two-story

Tudor surrounded by thick hedges in front and a large, fenced-in backyard. A path had been shoveled in the snow from the driveway to the front door. I placed the value of the home at over a million.

Iris Rodriguez greeted us at the door. She was around sixty or so, thin with streaks of grey in her otherwise dark hair.

She hugged Richard tightly.

"I am devastated," she said. "As you all must be."

"Iris, this is John Bekker, the private detective Mother hired," Richard said.

Iris gave me a quick once-over. "You look like a steak man," she said.

"I've been known to carve one every so often," I said.

"Good, because that's what I've prepared for lunch," Iris said.

"So what do you want to see first?" Richard asked.

"His office," I said.

* * *

DeSousa's Rye office was more modern than the one in Puerto Rico. A large oak desk dominated the room. There was also a bookcase full of books, a computer on a separate stand and two four-tiered file cabinets.

Dozens of framed photographs filled the walls.

I looked at the computer. "Know the sign-on password?"

"I do not," Richard said.

"Any objection to sending the hard drive to the FBI for analysis?"

"It doesn't belong to me."

"In a murder case, I don't need your permission to have the FBI remove it," I said.

"Then why did you ask?"

"I like to be polite."

I looked on the desk. A personal date book rested near the phone. "Look through this with me," I said. "See if you can identify some of his appointments."

We started with January and made a list of friends, charity events, dinner parties, doctor and dentist appointments, and fundraisers, and found nothing unusual. Nothing jumped off the page until I flipped October and the next page was December.

"When did they go to Puerto Rico for the winter?" I asked.

"Right after Thanksgiving."

"Would your father rip off one page in his personal date book and take it with him?"

"I would doubt that."

December was blank. I checked the back of the page to see if DeSousa had pressed hard enough to leave marking on the paper. He didn't.

"Is this phone a separate number than the house number?" I asked.

Richard nodded.

"Write it down for me."

"It's on his business card," Richard said. "Take one."

There was a cardholder near the phone and I grabbed several.

"Let's take a look at photos," I said. "Maybe you can name a few people for me."

"In here it's mostly Mom, Dad and us kids," Richard said.

We spent the next hour examining photos on the walls, above the fireplace, on tables and in scrapbooks Richard found in Maria's bedroom closet.

Richard was able to identify aunts and uncles from both sides of the family, old friends from the Bronx and dozens of baby pictures of himself, Rose and Xavier.

"This one is her wedding album," Richard said.

We flipped through it at the kitchen table. More aunts, uncles and friends.

One photograph was a copy of the photo I saw at the funeral home with the old flame of Maria's.

"Do you know him?" I said and pointed.

"No, but I wasn't born then."

"Your sister told me he was an old rival of your dad's for your mother's affection back in the Bronx," I said.

Richard studied the photo. "Never seen him before," he said.

"Like you said, you weren't born," I said. "Do you know when they bought this house?"

"When I was four."

"You're twenty-eight now?"

"That's right."

"When did you move out?"

"After college when I landed my first real job on Wall Street."

"Ever go back to the old neighborhood in the Bronx?"

"I was four when we moved, remember," Richard said. "It has no real memories for me."

"People from the old neighborhood did come to visit, though?"

"Sure. All the time at first, then less and less as the family spent more time in PR. I guess a lot of them have died off by now."

"Write down the names of people you remember."

"Why are you breaking my balls about that? Xavier is the one you should ask about old times," Richard said.

"Because you volunteered to be here and he didn't," I said. "Sit at the desk and write the names."

While Richard wrote, I called Paul Lawrence on my cell phone.

"Paul, Bekker," I said when he picked up.

"Got the list, Jack, but we won't get to it for days," Lawrence said.

"I know. I'm sending you a few more goodies you won't get to for a few more days after that," I said. "DeSousa's PC from his Rye home and his datebook. November has been torn off. Maybe they can microscope December for impressions from November. And a list of names to check out, and another phone number to run in/out calls on."

"Jesus, Jack," Lawrence said.

"I know, but this is an international murder case now and that makes it your territory," I said.

Lawrence sighed. "Send it."

"Thanks, Paul," I said. "Call me when you get it."

Just as I hung up, there was a knock on the door. It opened and Iris said, "I have prepared lunch."

* * *

After lunch, I left Richard at his father's desk to finish composing his list, and I spent some time with Iris.

She served us coffee in the kitchen.

"I grind the beans fresh," she said. "They are shipped from the plantation each month and I store them in the basement."

"It's very good," I said. "So you've been housekeeper for something like twenty years or more?"

"Since they buy this house."

"You must have seen a great deal," I said.

"Many things over the years," Iris said. "I watch the children grow up and grandparents pass away."

I sipped coffee and nodded.

"I'm interested in old friends from the Bronx," I said.

"I am one such old friend," Iris said. "That is how I came to work for Mr. DeSousa. I went to the same high school as he. When I needed a job, they hire me."

"Most of the old friends are gone now," I said.

"Yes. It is sad, but people die and others move away."

"Listen carefully, Iris," I said. "It's possible an old friend might have become an old enemy. I'd like you to name as many old friends as possible and maybe match up names to old photos. Can you do that?"

Iris nodded. "I'll do whatever I can to help."

We went to the living room where I had left the wedding and other albums.

"Let's look at some photos and put names to the faces," I said.

Iris nodded and after about thirty minutes we had a list of around thirty names.

"This man, do you recognize him?" I asked and pointed to a wedding photo in the album.

"Yes," Iris said. "He is from the old neighborhood. A Portuguese man I believe. I've forgotten his name over the years. Perhaps Richard would know."

"He was too young at the time," I said.

"Xavier then?"

"I'll ask him."

"Ask Xavier what?" Richard asked as he wandered into the living room.

"Old friends you were too young to remember," I said.

"I have your list," Richard said.

"Good," I said. I looked at Iris. "I need a fairly large carton."

She nodded. "I keep some in the basement from the coffee shipments."

* * *

"I'm not sure taking all this stuff sits well with me," Richard said as he drove us back to Manhattan.

"This stuff might provide a clue to the man who killed your father," I said.

"He was killed in Puerto Rico, not Rye, New York," Richard said.

"How much effort does it take to buy a plane ticket?" I said.

"If he in fact flew there from elsewhere," Richard said. "Personally, I think you and that Lieutenant are full of shit. I think he's bucking for a promotion and you're padding the bill."

I looked at Richard. Although it was barely five in the afternoon, the winter sun was down and his face was dark.

"You don't have to worry, Richard, I won't spill the beans and tell your family that you're gay," I said. "That's the source of all your hostility, isn't it?"

Richard stared straight ahead and his hands gripped the wheel so tightly the knuckles went white.

"Are you guessing or do you know for sure?" Richard asked.

"I didn't hear you deny it," I said.

Richard's knuckles relaxed as he sighed.

"My parents wouldn't understand," he said. "Rose would, but not Xavier."

"No sweat on my part," I said. "Two of my best friends are gay.

In fact, just four months ago I walked both brides down the aisle."

Richard glanced at me.

"No kidding?"

"Hundreds of straight people cheered just as loudly as if a man and woman tied the knot," I said. "And the brides worked out a funny skit where they both removed each other's garter belt."

Richard smiled. "I would have liked to have seen that."

"I don't throw stones, Richard," I said. "I'm a professional investigator and I go where the evidence takes me. No guesswork involved. That's for cop shows and the movies."

"What about the famous cop intuition and hunches?"

"Intuition without facts and evidence is worthless," I said. "And my hunches come from facts."

"So you really think my father was killed by someone he knew?"

"I do, but because that's how the evidence lines up."

"Where can I drop you off?" Richard asked.

* * *

I looked at Manhattan from the fifteenth floor window of my hotel room in Times Square. I had a good view of the Disney Store. Snow was on the ground, but Mickey, Minnie and Goofy were dancing in the streets as if it were a dry day in June.

I turned away from the window and dug out the little book from my luggage where I store phone numbers. I had the entire DeSousa array of numbers listed under D. I used my cell phone and called Rose DeSousa. Her voice mailbox picked up and I left a message.

There was a two-cup coffee machine in the bathroom. I brewed two cups and was on the second one when Rose returned my call.

"Mr. Bekker, I had a late class," she said.

"Are you free?" I asked. "I'm still working for your mother and I'm in New York and would like to talk to you. I'll spring for dinner."

"Alright," Rose said.

"Grab a cab to my hotel," I said. "The one with the revolving bar. They have a decent restaurant in the lobby. Say around seven?"

"I'll be there," Rose said.

At six forty-five, a waiter took me to a table near the window so I could watch for Rose to arrive. I had two photo albums with me and I placed them on the chair to my left. At five of seven, Rose got out of a cab. She was bundled up in a heavy coat, hat and gloves. By the time she reached my table, coat, hat and gloves were removed.

"It's a far cry from the Puerto Rican sun, isn't it," I said as she took the chair opposite me.

"It is that, Mr. Bekker," she said.

"Let's order first," I said. "We can talk while we eat."

For so small a girl, it was surprising how much food Rose could pack away.

She ordered and ate a large chicken breast with roasted potatoes and corn, a huge salad, and apple pie with coffee for desert. I had the same, but couldn't finish mine. We chatted about school, her classes and professors and some of my more interesting cases while we ate.

Over second cups of coffee, Rose smiled sheepishly as she said, "Have you figured out that Richard is gay yet?"

"From day one," I said.

"How? He isn't obvious about it. Most never pick up on it, how did you?"

"Nearly thirty years of investigative work tunes your instincts to people," I said. "You learn to spot certain things, pick up on traits, things like that."

"You told him?"

"I did. He was upset at first, but he settled down. I told him his secret was safe with me," I said.

"Xavier, Mom and the rest of the family doesn't know," Rose said. "He's afraid of being rejected by them and being outcast."

"And would he be?"

"You don't know very many old-time Latinos, do you?"

"No, not really."

Rose finished her coffee. "Is it time for business now?"

"As good a time as any," I said. "Let's take our coffee to the business section in the lobby."

We found a comfortable sofa with a coffee table in the spacious lobby and I set the albums on the table.

"I haven't seen those albums in years," Rose said.

"I'd like you to look through the photos and name as many people as possible, including the man your father was jealous of at their wedding," I said.

"I'll do my best if you think it will help, but that man, I don't know his name," Rose said. "I never did. It was sort of outlawed in our home. Besides, that happened something like thirty-five years ago."

"I know," I said. "But up to this point he's the only known enemy of your father's we've identified. I'm trying to establish old ties and links to his past that may be related to the present."

"Xavier might know, but I doubt it," Rose said. "Mom is the only one who would know for sure."

"I was hoping to give her some peace of mind for a while," I said.

"Mom is tough as nails," Rose said. "Don't worry about that."

"There's a legal pad wedged between the albums," I said. "Let's see if we can make a list of names."

Rose nodded.

An hour of so later, we had a short list of fourteen names, mostly old relatives from the Bronx.

"Do you own a car?" I asked.

"In the City?"

"Right. If I rent a car, would you take a ride with me to your old neighborhood in the Bronx?" I asked.

"I don't have any classes tomorrow until four," Rose said. "I can do it early."

"Meet me here for breakfast, say, nine," I said.

"What about Richard?"

"I'll ask him," I said.

"No, I'll do that," Rose said. "He'll say yes to me."

I walked Rose to the front lobby doors where the doorman fetched a cab for her. Light snow was falling and dusting the sidewalk white. I stood in it for a while and felt the refreshing cold, then returned to the lobby desk and used their service to reserve a rental car for the morning.

* * *

"Can you take a few days off?" I asked Jane.

"I'm the sheriff, I can do what I want," Jane said.

"I might have to return to Puerto Rico for a few days," I said. "Want to go?"

"Seeing as how my shooter is probably thousands of miles away by now and it's forty-nine degrees, if you whisper sweet nothings, I'd have to say yes."

"Consider the nothings whispered," I said. "I'll be home tomorrow sometime. I'll make the arrangements then."

"I'll dig out my summer wardrobe," Jane said. "Otherwise, how is your investigation going?"

"Like a brick in water," I said. "Still have the one piece blue racing suit you wore to the beach six months ago when we had the school outing for Regan?"

"I do."

"Pack that."

"No itsy bitsy teeny weenie bikini?"

"That one piece is about all I can stand," I said.

"What time will you be home tomorrow?"

"Late afternoon."

"Meet me at the trailer," Jane said. "I'll model it for you."

Chapter Twenty-one

I was surprised to see Richard holding Rose's hand as they walked along Broadway to my hotel.

"Mr. Bekker, good morning," Rose said. "I brought Richard."

"Morning Richard," I said. "Any favorite place for breakfast?"

"There's a diner on 23rd and Broadway," he said.

"Walk or ride?" I asked.

"Walk," Rose said. "This is Manhattan."

* * *

The diner was a neighborhood gathering point for regulars who lived there, and for tourists hoping for a glimpse of Robert De Niro, a resident of the Tribecca neighborhood. Apparently, as Richard pointed out as he ate some of his scrambled eggs, De Niro lived across the street in a penthouse apartment.

"I come here often with my…" Richard said.

"You can say it," Rose said. "With your boyfriend."

"De Niro lives around the corner," Richard said. "I've never seen him in here, but I did see him walking on the street with his wife."

"I'll keep an eye out for him while we eat," I said. "In the meantime, tell me about the Bronx neighborhood you came from."

"We were just kids when we left," Richard said. "All I know are the stories. The Portuguese from midtown started moving to the Bronx in the fifties to escape the high rents. Place called Soundview where a large population of PRs also settled."

"A lot of Portuguese also went to New Jersey," Rose said. "Newark, but I doubt many are left."

"Mom told us there used to be Portuguese restaurants all over the neighborhood," Rose said. "Mixed in with Puerto Rican restaurants. Some even served Portuguese/Spanish food to keep everybody happy."

"Dad told us one time after he bought the house in Rye that the Puerto Ricans in the Bronx thought the Portuguese spoke Spanish. Even today, many people think Brazil is Spanish instead of Portuguese," Richard said.

"I think Mr. Bekker knows that about Brazil, Richard," Rose said.

"Oh, right."

"So, take me to the Bronx," I said.

* * *

Richard guided me from Manhattan to the Bronx and onto the Cross Bronx Expressway to the Bruckner Expressway and finally to the street where he and Xavier were born.

What was once middle-class was now anything but. I parked the rental on White Plains Road and we walked around for a while. It seemed they were trying really hard to revive the area and some spots showed growth and progress, but much of it was a mess. Several buildings and storefronts were abandoned and boarded up.

"Dad told us back in the eighties and nineties, the area was full of crack houses," Richard said. "That's why he moved us out. First to Whitestone in the Bronx, and then to Rye."

"Where was your house?" I asked.

"A few blocks past White Plains Road," Richard said.

"Walk us there," I said.

The neighborhood was predominately Black with a sprinkling of Hispanic in the mix. Surprisingly, the streets were fairly empty of people, although traffic was heavy with trucks.

"Bruckner Boulevard is a major route for trucks," Richard said when I pointed that out.

"Across this street our house used to be right there," Rose said and pointed to an empty lot.

"It became a crack house and a bunch of addicts fell asleep and burned the place down about fifteen years ago," Richard said.

We crossed the street and I stopped in front of the lot where DeSousa's home once stood.

"Where did your mother grow up?" I asked.

"Across Bruckner where the large PR population was," Richard said.

"Show me," I said.

Four blocks to Bruckner, then three more blocks to a side street, we came to an entire block of abandoned buildings.

"Third one," Richard said.

The building was six flights of broken glass and empty apartments.

"So they met at a dance, romance blossomed and they got married," I said.

"Sure, I guess so," Richard said.

I studied the buildings and street for a few minutes.

"Seen enough?" Richard asked.

"For now," I said.

We returned to the rental and I drove us back to Manhattan.

"Where is Xavier's office located?" I asked as we crossed the bridge into the City.

"White Plains," Rose said.

"How do I get there?" I asked.

Richard sighed.

Seated in back, Rose said, "Turn north on 95 after we reach the other side of the bridge."

"I'm missing work," Richard said.

"I'll call Xavier and tell him to expect us," Rose said.

"I'll spring for lunch," I said. "You do go to lunch, don't you, Richard?"

* * *

The DeSousa Coffee Company had a string of offices in a modern, six-story, all glass building on Central Avenue in the city of White Plains, New York.

White Plains is a wealthy city north of Manhattan by about an hour and is home to some of the largest corporations in the country.

I parked in the visitor's lot and we walked to the palatial lobby. A security center was located just inside the lobby to the right of an elevator bank.

"Richard DeSousa to see Xavier DeSousa," Richard said to a guard.

"Sign in," the guard said. "All three of you."

* * *

DeSousa Coffee Corporation was announced by a beautifully etched, frosted glass door that opened up to a string of equally impressive offices.

"I must say I was a bit surprised when you called me, Rose," Xavier said when we entered his large and impeccably furnished office.

"My idea," I said. "We were sightseeing."

"Mr. Bekker, nice to see you again," Xavier said.

"I'm still working for your mother and I have some questions," I said. "Can we go to lunch where we can talk privately?"

"There's a nice Italian restaurant about a mile away on Route 100," Xavier said. "We'll take my car."

The restaurant was an old-fashioned, red-checkered tablecloth kind of place. It had a full menu of authentic Italian dishes and a waiter that barely spoke English. After some navigation of the menu and pointing, we managed to order lunch.

"So here's the thing, Xavier," I said. "We took a trip down memory lane in the Bronx so I could get a feel for your father's upbringing. Tough place that old neighborhood. It must have been even tougher when he was young and running around with street gangs and all."

Rose and Richard kept silent as they looked at Xavier.

"I figure that as the oldest child you can probably tell me the most," I said.

"About what?" Xavier said. "I was four or five when we moved away."

"Are you familiar with the saying you can take the boy out of the country, but you can't take the country out of the boy?" I asked.

"I may have heard it," Xavier said. "I don't see what that has to do with my father's death."

"Xavier, if you continue to play stupid with me, I will hold you upside down by your ankles and shake you like a piggy bank," I said.

Rose and Richard looked at me in amazement.

Xavier nodded softly. "What you really want to know is how was my father when he was a young man," he said.

"So tell me," I said.

"He was tough as nails," Xavier said. "He never struck me or Richard and he didn't have to. His physical presence was enough to keep us in line."

"So who did he pal around with from the old neighborhood while he was building his business?" I asked.

"You mean old gang members?" Xavier said. "By the time I was old enough to understand and remember he had removed himself from all that. Mom's influence mostly, but he also had a tremendous drive to make something of himself, and he did."

"I've seen pictures of your father's rival for your mom," I said. "What can you tell me about him?"

"Nothing," Xavier said.

"What's so important about an old boyfriend of Mom's from like thirty-five years ago?" Richard said.

"He's a link to the old days and he was an enemy of your dad," I said. "Like I said, I believe your father wasn't killed by a stranger. The old rival, if I can find him, may know other enemies from the past. Someone who resented your dad enough to murder him."

"I think the only one who can answer those questions is my mother," Xavier said.

"I was hoping to avoid that, but I don't think I can anymore," I said. "I'll have speak with her in person."

Lunch arrived and the mood lightened. We talked about college classes, the stock market and DeSousa enterprises.

"I'm leaving for PR in five days for a week," Xavier said. "I'll be commuting regularly until Rose graduates. Can you wait to see my mother until I'm there?"

"I can," I said.

"Thank you," Xavier said.

* * *

I dropped Rose off in front of NYU and Richard at his office on Wall Street. It was nearly four in the afternoon, but Richard said he often worked until eight in the evening or longer.

I suffered through rush-hour traffic and inched my way north on Broadway to the car rental place on West Fifty-ninth. After returning the car, I walked around for a while and took in some sights.

It was a warm day, almost spring-like, and the snow that was on the sidewalk yesterday had melted. I cruised east to Fifth Avenue and headed south. I had no particular destination in mind and was just using the time to clear my thoughts.

I walked past dozens of boutique shops without even seeing them. On East Fifty-third I passed a tobacco shop and it didn't register until I had crossed over to the next block. I hurried back and stood outside the tobacco store and looked in the window.

Nate Birmbaum's Tobacco Shop. Since 1885 supplying the finest in tobacco products around the world.

The windows highlighted the many brands of custom-made cigarettes, cigars and pipe tobaccos made exclusively for Nate Birmbaum.

I went in. The place was like a candy store for smokers.

A clerk wearing an expensive suit looked at me from behind a counter.

"May I help you?" he asked.

"I'm interested in a cigarette with white paper, a cork colored filter with two gold bands on it," I said.

"Yes, our Classic Blue," the clerk said.

"Can I get a pack?"

He reached under the counter and produced a beautifully wrapped box and set it on the glass counter. "Fifteen seventy-five," he said.

"For one pack?"

"And worth every penny."

"Do you have any other locations?"

"No."

"Website?"

"Yes, and catalog," he said. "Take one."

"How do customers from outside New York find out about you if this is the only location?" I asked.

"Word of mouth spread over a hundred and thirty years by discriminating clientele," he said.

"Can you buy your cigarettes in stores anywhere? Airports?"

"Heavens no," the clerk said. "That would cheapen the mystique."

I paid for the cigarettes, took a catalog and rushed back to my hotel.

In my room, I studied the cigarette box. It was gold with the words "Nate Birmbaum's Classic Blue 20 extraordinary cigarettes" on the front.

I carefully tore open the plastic wrapper and flipped open the box. It was neatly lined with twenty cork-colored, filter cigarettes. I removed one and held it under my nose. The tobacco aroma was overpowering. The filter had two gold bands that were a perfect match to the photograph.

I used my cell phone to call Paul Lawrence.

After three transfers, he picked up.

"I found the cigarette butt," I said.

"Where?"

"New York. Manhattan. A boutique store called Nate Birmbaum's. They have a website," I said. "Check a cigarette called Classic Blue. The filter is a spot-on match."

"Hold on," Lawrence said.

After five minutes or so on hold, Lawrence came back. "Son of a bitch," he said.

"Want me to send you a pack to analyze?"

"Yes."

"Our smoker is a New Yorker, or former one," I said. "They have just the one store, but a large following through the catalog and website, and they don't ship to stores including airport duty free. They don't want to cheapen the mystique."

"Heaven forbid. So maybe I'll target the passenger list to the New York Metro Area," Lawrence said. "I didn't get your package yet by the way."

"Should be tomorrow," I said. "Talk to you then."

I hung up and left the hotel and rushed back to Nate Birmbaum's. The same clerk was behind the counter.

"Back so soon?" he said.

"Let me have another pack of the Classic Blue," I said.

After rushing back to the hotel, I checked out and grabbed a cab to the airport.

Chapter Twenty-two

Jane opened the door to the bathroom in the trailer and slowly stepped out wearing the one-piece, blue bathing suit.

"Well, what do you think of the five pounds I lost?" she asked.

"I think you need to take it off," I said from my perch on the bed.

"But I just put it on."

"Want to go for a swim?"

"It's fifty-three degrees outside."

"Then take it off and save it for Puerto Rico," I said.

Jane slowly lowered the straps and wiggled out of the suit. "Oh dear," she said. "Now I guess I'll have to get dressed again."

As she turned, I grabbed her arm and pulled her to the bed.

"Get dressed later," I said.

* * *

A billion stars twinkled overhead as I tossed logs onto the trashcan bonfire in front of the trailer.

Wearing just a robe, Jane occupied a chair at the card table and sipped coffee from a mug. She was barefoot. Her toenails were painted pink and matched the nails of her fingers.

I took the chair next to Jane and reached for my coffee mug. "I had a breakthrough of sorts today," I said. "I identified the cigarette butt the smoker left behind on the beach."

"Your killer, right?"

I nodded.

Jane crossed her legs and the robe parted a bit.

"What a great pair of legs you have," I said.

"One topic at a time," Jane said. "The cigarette butts first, then my legs."

I stood up, went inside the trailer and returned with the pack of Classic Blue and handed it to Jane.

She sniffed the box.

"Smells wonderful," she said.

"They should for almost sixteen bucks a pack," I said.

"Sixteen…what, are they wrapped in real gold?"

"My smoker has expensive tastes," I said. "If this is his brand, he has means."

Jane removed one cigarette from the box and held it under her nose. "Oh good God," she sighed.

"I know."

"How long since you quit?"

"Six months and a week."

"Two months for me," Jane said and sniffed the cigarette.

"Better put it back in the box," I said.

Jane started to slide the cigarette into the box and paused to look at me. "You said your evidence is a butt and not the entire cigarette, right?"

"That's right," I said.

"And that there are two of them?"

"Also right."

"Well, these are un-smoked cigarettes," Jane said. "How are you going to get an identical match to a smoked butt with an un-smoked cigarette?"

"That's a pretty lame excuse," I said.

Jane put the cigarette between her lips, reached for the lighter on the table that I keep for bonfires and lit the cigarette. She inhaled, closed her eyes and exhaled through her nose.

"Sweet Jesus Christ but this is the best damn smoke I've ever had," she said. "Try one or I'll have to smoke two."

"Regan will…"

"Never know. I'm spending the night, remember," Jane said.

She held out the box.

I stared at it.

Jane inhaled again and closed her eyes. "You can bury my ashes in this box," she said.

"Just one," I said.

"Sure."

"I'm serious."

"Me, too."

I removed one cigarette from the box and lit it with the lighter.

One puff and I was nicotine dizzy. "God," I said.

"I know," Jane said. She inhaled and said, "This thing is the goddamn anti-Christ."

We smoked down to the filters and carefully put them out so the butts were fully intact. I went inside for the photo of the butt from the beach and when I returned, Jane had lit another.

I looked at her.

"What? You might need an extra."

It wasn't bright enough by the bonfire to see the photo clearly so I turned on the floodlight and took my seat. I unfolded the photo and set it on the table.

"What do you think?" I asked.

"I think I'm keeping this pack is what I think," Jane said.

"About the photo," I said.

Jane picked up the photo and compared it to the butts on the table. "Cork color, two rings, it's it no doubt."

"Okay, finish that one and I'll put the butts in a baggie and send them to Paul Lawrence tomorrow," I said.

"What about the other seventeen?"

"I'll pack the box in the baggie, too."

Jane snatched the box off the table. "I think I'll keep it," she said.

"Come on, Jane," I said.

"Come on nothing, I'm keeping it."

"It's evidence."

"The butts are evidence," Jane said. "You can have those when I'm done with them."

I reached for the box and Jane slipped it into the pocket of her robe. "You see this robe?" she said. "If you ever expect to see what's inside it again, you'll let me have the damn box."

"That's blackmail."

"So it is. What's it going to be, this?" Jane said and pulled out the box of Classic Blue cigarettes. "Or this," she said and parted the robe to expose her breasts.

"Dammit," I said.

"Wise man," Jane said. "Much smarter than you look."

* * *

Jane's blonde hair was spread out around her head when I left her sleeping and went for a morning run. The sun was a few minutes from rising and the beach was caught in twilight as I started to jog near the water.

The temperature was a spring-like fifty-five with the promise of mid-sixties by noon. After fifteen minutes, sweat rolled down my back. I paused for a few minutes to watch the sun come up over the ocean, then continued for another fifteen minutes before turning around.

When I reached the trailer, I toweled off, went around to the side and did a full workout of situps, push-ups and bag work that took about another hour.

Jane was seated at the card table with a mug of coffee when I was done.

"God forbid you sleep past six in the morning," she said.

A second mug of coffee was waiting for me. I sat, gave her a kiss and picked up the mug.

Jane reached into her robe pocket, produced the box of Classic Blue cigarettes and set it on the table.

"I got it out of my system," she said.

I opened the box. Fifteen cigarettes remained.

Jane looked at me.

"Okay, I had one in the middle of the night and one just now with my coffee," she said. "The rest are yours."

"I'll send the box with the butts to Lawrence this morning," I said.

Jane sipped coffee and nodded.

"Want breakfast?" I asked.

"And a shower. I'm on duty at nine."

* * *

I drove Jane to her cruiser that she left overnight in the municipal lot adjacent to the beach.

She gave me a kiss before getting out of my car because it wasn't polite for the county sheriff to be seen smooching in public. Once she was under way, I went to the post office to mail Lawrence the cigarette butts. From there I drove home.

Regan was at her job. She worked as an assistant to Sister Mary Martin, a nun at the Hope Springs Eternal compound for traumatized children. Oz was sitting in the sun in the backyard.

I made some coffee and took two mugs out to the patio table and joined him.

"Bout time we see some damn sun around here," he said.

"I made a minor breakthrough on my case," I said. "I have to go back to Puerto Rico for a few days."

Oz sipped coffee and then looked at me. "She be fine," he said.

"I know that."

"I thinking Louisa might come for a few days," Oz said.

"She's good for the both of you," I said.

"Yeah, well, I feel the fool thinking bout love at my age," Oz said.

"What's your age got to do with anything?" I said. "It's here and here that counts," I said and tapped my head and chest.

Oz sipped coffee and stared straight ahead.

"What?" I said.

He didn't answer.

"You're afraid of being hurt," I said.

Oz looked at me. "Wouldn't you be at my age?"

161

"Any age," I said. "It's all part of the process. Don't you think I worry that if Regan's first love dumps her it could be devastating to her mental state? Hurt is how it all works and if you ask me, when it does work it's all worth it."

Oz grinned. "Bekker the philosopher now, huh."

"Call Louisa, get her here while I'm away and enjoy the time together," I said. "You and Regan can double-date."

"Wouldn't that be a sight," Oz said.

"I have some plane tickets to book," I said.

I stood up and took my mug with me. "And so do you," I said at the sliding kitchen door.

Chapter Twenty-three

"I'm cross referencing arrests of The Almighty Latin Kings with background checks on its known members," Venus said. "They seem to have fallen off the map around nineteen ninety."

"How many do you have so far?" I asked.

"Twenty-three."

"Any of them Joe DeSousa?"

"Possession of a switchblade at age eighteen," Venus said.

I nodded. "How long before you're done?"

"Depends on how much bullshit Walt dumps on me," Venus said. "Don't be shy about billing me."

"Count on that, sugar," Venus said. "One thing I never am is shy."

* * *

"Nate Birmbaum's Cigarette Store?" Walt said when I showed him the catalog.

"For the particular smoker," I said.

"That lets you out," Walt said as he took the catalog and flipped pages.

"The Classic Blue," I said.

Walt's phone rang and when he answered it, he said, "Paul Lawrence, it's been a while. Yes, he's here."

"I told him I'd be here when I called earlier," I said.

Walt put the call on speaker.

"Hey, Paul," I said.

"Got the package," he said. "Did you mail the butts?"

"This morning."

"So why the conference call?" Lawrence asked.

"Yeah," Walt said. "Why the conference call?"

"Venus, Walt's data tech, is running background checks on the old Almighty Latin Kings street gangs," I said. "When she's done, I'm sending the list to you for your guys to check if any of the old gang members recently flew to Puerto Rico."

Walt looked at me.

"I should have thought of that myself," Lawrence said. "Send it when it's ready."

"Thanks, Paul," I said.

"Anything else?"

"Nope."

"Send donuts."

"Will do."

Walt hung up the phone and said, "How come you weren't this smart when you were an actual cop?"

"With age comes wisdom," I said.

"Then I must be a genius," Walt said.

* * *

"I booked two tickets to Puerto Rico and reserved a top-floor room at the hotel I stayed at last time," I said. "Our flight leaves at ten."

"I still haven't packed yet," Jane said. "I'll do that tonight."

"Bring enough summer stuff for four days," I said. "We can always pick up what you need if we have to."

"Maybe you should stay at my place?" Jane said.

"I need to talk to Regan," I said. "Come to dinner tonight. We can always leave afterward and go to the trailer. Seven-thirty okay?"

"If you think I can get home by six and be packed by seven, you're nuts," Jane said. "Jack, it's not a sin to stay at my place you know."

"I know," I said.

"But you still feel funny because my ex still owns half?"

"Maybe. A little. I'm not sure."

"Jack, if we're to have a serious relationship we can't have ghosts haunting our houses," Jane said. "I've pushed Janet out of the picture and you need to do the same with my ex."

"I know that," I said.

"So what is it then?"

"I'll tell you in Puerto Rico," I said.

Jane sighed. "By the time I'm packed it will be like ten o'clock," she said. "How about we meet at the trailer?"

"I'll be there."

"Bring food."

"I will."

"And dessert."

* * *

"I'm not sure how long I'll be gone," I said. "Three or four days at least."

Regan looked at me.

"Oz may have Louisa over while I'm gone," I said.

Regan looked at me some more.

"Dad, Phil is not going to sleep over if that's what is bothering you," she said.

"Actually, it isn't," I said.

We were alone in the backyard.

"Then what?"

"I'm a little concerned about Oz," I said.

"Oz?"

"He's seventy-two now and Louisa is a decade younger," I said. "I think she makes him feel good, but she also makes him feel old at the same time. I want you to keep an eye on him, okay?"

"I guess I've never thought of Oz as old," Regan said.

"He's not really, but if he feels that way he will be," I said. "Just keep an eye on him and Louisa when she visits."

"I will," Regan said.

"Good."

* * *

"This is dumb, Bekker and you know it," Jane said when we entered the trailer.

"I didn't say it wasn't," I said.

"What did you get for food? I haven't had a bite since lunch."

"A vat of Chinese with that cheesecake from the deli you like so much," I said.

Jane shrugged. "Well, at least you aren't totally stupid."

Chapter Twenty-four

We landed in Puerto Rico just past two in the afternoon. As we neared the island, Jane looked out her window at the mountains of the rain forest in the background and squeezed my knee.

"This is our first real trip together as a couple," she said.

"Maybe our next one will be all pleasure instead of mixed with work," I said.

We feathered a landing and after leaving the terminal, picked up our luggage and stepped outside to eighty-four degrees and bright sunshine.

The rental car was waiting and I drove from the airport to the hotel in a matter of twenty minutes.

While Jane checked out the view from the balcony, I called Escalante.

"I was wondering about you," he said.

"I'm back in town at the same hotel," I said. "Let's have dinner around seven-thirty and compare progress reports."

"I'll be there," Escalante said.

I hung up and joined Jane on the balcony.

"Is that the rain forest?" she said of the mountains in the distance.

"El Yunque," I said. "We'll get there and a few other places, but first we're having dinner with Lieutenant Gerardo Escalante. He's the investigating detective."

"What should we do between now and dinner?"

"We could hit the pool?" I said.

Jane slid open the door and entered the room. I followed her in and closed the door to keep the AC inside.

Jane opened her luggage and fished out her bathing suit. I watched as she wiggled out of her jeans and pullover sweatshirt. When she was down to nothing, she paused and looked at me.

"What?" she asked.

"God you're a sight," I said.

"Is that your way of saying you're in the mood?"

"More or less."

Jane tossed the bathing suit aside.

"It will give us a reason to cool off in the pool," she said.

"About what I was thinking," I said.

* * *

After dark, the temperature was a comfortable seventy-three degrees poolside with a nice westerly breeze from the mountains.

I sat at a table while Jane waded in the pool. If she was aware of the all-male following she had drawn, she didn't acknowledge it. A minute or so before seven-thirty, Escalante arrived.

I stood and we shook hands.

"I brought my lady friend and sometimes assistant," I said.

Jane took the ladder on the side of the pool and Escalante looked at her and said, "Holy shi…I mean, is that her? Your assistant."

"Sometimes assistant," I said.

Jane grabbed a towel off the stack, wrapped it around her shoulders and joined us.

"Jane Morgan, Lieutenant Escalante," I said.

"I've heard a lot about you," Jane said. "Jack doesn't often give praise, so you must be pretty good."

Escalante cleared his throat but nothing came out.

"Let's order some dinner before you swallow your tongue," I said.

* * *

Over dessert and coffee, we talked shop.

"This cigarette butt belongs to these cigarettes," I said, and produced the photograph of the filter and the pack of Classic Blue cigarettes and a book of matches.

Jane looked at the box of cigarettes. "You held out on me."

"Smoke one if you want so we have an actual butt to show the lieutenant," I said.

Jane snatched the box and removed a cigarette. She lit it with a match and exhaled through her nose. "You aren't always such a total dick," she said as she exhaled.

"This brand is sold at only one store in New York City," I said. "They don't export to anywhere. They have a catalog and website, but they don't advertise. Our smoker is or was a New Yorker and he didn't buy these in Puerto Rico, he brought them with him."

"Your theory holds water," Escalante said.

"I need to speak with Maria again," I said. "Tomorrow. Want to go?"

Escalante nodded.

I had my cell phone on the table and used it to call Xavier.

"Mr. Bekker," he said when he picked up.

"I'm here and would like to stop by tomorrow say around eleven," I said.

"I'll tell mother," Xavier said.

"How is she?"

"Good. A bit tired, but good. She's a strong woman."

"See you at eleven," I said.

I hung up and looked at Jane. She was nearly done with the cigarette.

"My bell is ringing," she said.

"If you're done, put it out," I said.

Jane stubbed the cigarette in the ashtray and set it on the table.

Escalante looked at the butt and then the photograph.

"It's a perfect match," he said. "No doubt."

Jane reached for the box of cigarettes and said, "He surprises you once in a while by not being as completely dumb as he looks."

She struck a match and lit another cigarette. "Wouldn't you say, Lieutenant?"

* * *

I had the AC in our room on high so Jane was hiding under the covers.

"So what is the deal with…Christ, aren't you cold? It's an igloo in here."

"I'll turn it up a bit," I said.

I got out of bed and raised the thermostat from sixty-six to seventy degrees and returned to bed.

"Better?"

"Thank you."

"What were you saying?"

"About staying at my place, why you won't do it."

"It's a guy thing."

"Every stupid, idiotic thing a guy does is a guy thing," Jane said. "That's why they're guy things."

"I can't really explain it," I said.

"Try, so maybe I can understand."

"When I was a kid, my mother had this big old tomcat," I said. "She thought the cat got lonely, so she got another male to keep it company. Do you know what happened?"

"They fought?"

"Nope," I said. "They got jealous of each other's territory and sprayed every square inch of what they thought belonged to them."

"What are you saying that you want to pee on my furniture?"

"I'm saying you can't have two males in the same house," I said. "Even if one leaves, his scent stays behind."

Jane looked at me and nodded. "I understand," she said. "My ex is in every square inch of that house and you don't like it."

"Yes."

"And maybe Mister High and Mighty Super Sleuth is a bit jealous of a ghost who no longer lives there?"

"Possible," I said. "Maybe?"

"We've had a breakthrough, but alas the session is over," Jane said. "Please pay the cashier on the way out and get under the covers because my nose is like ice."

Sometimes all a man can do is what he's told.

Chapter Twenty-five

Xavier opened the front door and looked at me, then at Escalante, and then past us to Jane. She wore a bright yellow, sleeveless sundress with blue sandals and straw hat and dark sunglasses.

She was like a lighthouse in a fog.

"Holy shi…I mean, right on time," Xavier said.

"Her name is Jane and she's my lady friend and sometimes assistant," I said.

"It's a pleasure," Xavier said. "I'm Xavier DeSousa, Maria's eldest son. Please come in and I'll get Mother."

* * *

Maria opted to talk in the garden at the large patio table. The awning was extended and we sat comfortably in the shade.

Gloria served ice-cold lemonade from a pitcher and returned to the house.

"You look well, Mr. Bekker," she said and looked at Jane. "And you look beautiful."

"Thank you," Jane said.

"Mrs. DeSousa, I'm almost certain the man responsible for your husband's death doesn't live in Puerto Rico," I said.

I dug out the pack of Classic Blue cigarettes and the photo of the filter and the filter from the cigarette Jane smoked yesterday.

"The photograph is of the cigarette butt he smoked on the beach," I said. "We know that because he first smoked one under the street light and the DNA is a match. Look at the filter from the butt here and compare the two."

Maria looked and said, "They match."

"Now look at the box and tell me if you recognize the brand," I said.

"No," Maria said. "I've never seen it before."

I opened the box to remove a cigarette and there were twelve when there should have been thirteen. I glanced at Jane and she shrugged her guilt.

"What about the actual cigarette?" I said, removed one and showed it to Maria.

She took it, inspected it carefully and handed it back to me. "I've never seen this brand before," she said. "Forty years ago, everybody smoked. I smoked Virginia Slims and Joe smoked Marlboro and sometimes Kent or Camels. We both quit when I became pregnant with Xavier."

"I never knew you smoked," Xavier said.

"Why would you?" Maria said. "We quit before you were born."

"Maria, I need to ask some personal questions," I said. "This may be nothing or it may be something, I don't know yet. I believe the man we're looking for knew your husband, possibly from the old days in the Bronx."

I paused to remove the wedding photograph from my shirt pocket and handed it to Maria.

"The man directly behind your husband, who is he?" I asked.

Maria set the photo on the table and looked at me.

"This is girl talk, Mr. Bekker," she said. "Maybe Jane and I can talk alone."

I nodded. "We'll be in the kitchen drinking some of Gloria's wonderful coffee," I said.

* * *

"What could possibly be taking them so long?" Xavier said. "It's been almost an hour."

"Are you not familiar with *girl talk*?" Escalante asked.

"They can remember what color lipstick they wore to the prom forty years later," I said.

"I don't remember what color socks I wore yesterday," Escalante said. "Or even today."

"How sure are you about this?" Xavier asked me.

"About the smoker coming from somewhere else? Pretty positive," I said. "About your father knowing his killer? Also, pretty positive."

"The man in the wedding photo?" Xavier asked.

"He's an old enemy of your father, that's all I know," I said. "He's from the Bronx and that makes him a detail, and every detail in a murder investigation needs to be accounted for one way or another."

"I understand," Xavier said. "But it's still taking a long time, don't you think?"

Escalante grinned. "When your wife starts to tell you a story, say about her day or a trip to the store, how much do you listen?"

Xavier sighed. "Not enough, I'm afraid."

"Join the club," Escalante said.

Gloria entered the kitchen.

"The ladies have asked you to join them," she said.

We went to the gardens where Jane and Maria were sipping lemonade.

"Besides this, is there anything else you require of me?" Maria asked.

"Not at the moment, but I'm sure I will in the next day or two," I said.

"I will be here," Maria said.

* * *

We went to the Kiosks for lunch. Jane picked the Peruvian restaurant. While we waited for the food to arrive, Jane told us of her conversation with Maria. She took notes in my folder and glanced at them as she spoke.

"She's quite a lady," Jane said. "The man in the photograph is Aleixo Abreu and he's from the Bronx."

"Spanish?" Escalante asked.

"Portuguese," Jane said. "He was Maria's first real boyfriend when she was fifteen. He took her to the junior prom. They broke up when she was seventeen and then she met Joe. The thing is, Joe and Aleixo knew each other from high school and were friends. The friendship soured when she started dating Joe, but not seriously. Maria went back and forth between Aleixo and Joe for years until she finally decided upon Joe for a husband."

"Was he left-handed?" I asked.

"She doesn't remember him so," Jane said.

"Odd he would attend the wedding and be in the wedding party," Escalante said.

"By the time the wedding rolled around, Aleixo was dating a cousin of Maria's and escorted her to the wedding," Jane said. "Maria said Joe was furious, but out of respect for the cousin he kept quiet."

"The cousin's name?" I asked.

"Rosa Gonzalez with a Z," Jane said. "She died five years ago from lymphoma."

"When was the last time Maria saw or heard from Aleixo?" I asked.

"Thirty years ago," Jane said. "After he broke up with the cousin, he vanished. She thinks he moved out of New York City, but she isn't sure."

"Did Aleixo run with the same people DeSousa did in the Bronx?" I asked.

"She isn't positive, but she believes so," Jane said.

"At least we know who he is now," Escalante said.

"Jack, I had the feeling she was holding something back," Jane said. "When I pressed her all she said was it was very difficult being in love with two men at the same time."

The waitress arrived with our orders and I pondered it all as we ate.

Over dessert, I called Paul Lawrence on my cell phone.

"Paul, Jack. I'm back in Puerto Rico," I said.

"Oh good, I was worried your tan might have faded."

"I don't have the list Venus is working on yet, but I do have a name," I said. "He was an old boyfriend of Maria DeSousa from the Bronx. When she dumped him and married Joe, there was bad blood between the two men. Can you run the name for me?"

"Sure. It's not like I spend all my time perusing terrorist watch lists, looking for kidnappers or man-hunting bank robbers or anything," Lawrence said.

"The name is Aleixo Abreu and he's probably around sixty years old," I said. "He's Portuguese and left New York probably around thirty years ago."

"I'll see what we got and call you whenever," Lawrence said.

"Thanks, Paul," I said.

I hung up and tucked my phone away. The waitress arrived with our food.

"How is the dessert in this place?" Jane asked.

"Don't you want your meal first?" the waitress asked.

"I like to plan ahead," Jane said.

* * *

"Why did you feel she was holding something back?" I asked Jane.

Wearing the neon blue bathing suit, her sun hat covering her face, sunglasses covering her eyes, Jane shifted her body in the lounge chair and looked at me.

"I could tell she was hesitant to reveal more than she did," Jane said. "If she were in my interrogation room and a suspect, I would have pressed the issue."

"I've seen you press an issue," I said.

"You're no slouch in that department either," Jane said.

We were about fifty feet from the shore of Luquillo Beach and the waves were breaking high and fast.

"We got an hour to sunset," I said. "Feel like riding some waves?"

"In a minute," Jane said. "I've been thinking about Maria, about what she said about loving two men at the same time. That had to be nerve-wracking for her as a young woman trying to choose."

"I can sort of relate in a way," I said.

Jane removed her sunglasses and looked at me. "Is this a confession?"

"Of sorts," I said. "When Janet and I were an item, I kept thinking about you. I felt guilty about it, but I couldn't stop it from happening. When you told me your marriage was over, I was secretly glad about it. I remember thinking what kind of a man is glad to hear that somebody's marriage is over?"

"Was that before or after you and Janet went bust?"

"Before, but I knew we weren't right for each other and it was just a matter of time," I said.

"And now?"

"I've never been so happy in all my life," I said.

Jane returned her sunglasses. "Good answer," she said. "You'll get some later."

"About the waves?" I asked.

"I'm game."

We walked down to the shore and slowly waded into the oncoming waves.

From behind me, I heard a woman say, "Keep staring, buster, and I'll poke your eyes out."

We rode the waves and got knocked around pretty good, and close to sunset we went and sat in the sand to watch Mother Nature at her finest.

As the sun touched the horizon and the ocean glowed red, Jane put her arm around my shoulder.

"What you said before about being happy," she said. "I don't think I've ever been as happy as I am right now."

"Good answer," I said. "You'll get some later."

Jane gave me a little shove. "Oh shut up," she said.

From behind me, I heard a slap and the same woman said, "You're supposed to be watching the sunset, asshole."

* * *

Around three in the morning, I woke up with the nagging feeling in the back of my mind that I'd missed something. A detail or a clue that I should have picked up on but hadn't.

It was a sticky, humid night and the AC was on high and Jane was wrapped up like a cocoon. I carefully removed the covers, got out of bed and went onto the balcony. It was around seventy-five degrees outside with humidity near ninety percent and it hit me like a steam bath.

There were two chairs and I took one. The *It* that I wasn't seeing would bug me until I solved the puzzle or someone else did for me. Either way, I was losing sleep.

The sliding door opened and a disheveled looking Jane came out, closed the door and took the vacant chair.

"What?" she grumbled.

"Thinking," I said.

"About…Christ, it's an oven out here. About what?"

"If you were a young Maria, faced with choosing between two men, how do you decide?" I asked.

Jane rubbed her blonde hair. "Are you requiring me to think at this hour of the morning?"

"Yes."

"Can I have one of those cigarettes?"

"If it will help."

Jane went inside and returned a few moments later with a lit Classic Blue cigarette and two small bottles of cold ginger ale from the fridge.

"So your question is how did she choose between two men?" Jane said as she sat and handed me a bottle.

"We need to ask her, but let's play with it," I said.

"On looks?"

"Both were young, handsome men."

"Personality?"

"Possible."

"The alpha male."

"Both seem to be alpha."

"The better lover?"

"Is that so important to a woman she would choose one man over another?"

"If I was twenty and one guy curled my toes and the other was like sleepwalking, I'd go with the toe curler."

"Possible, but couldn't a woman make a bad lover a better one if she were patient? And what if she loved the sleepwalker, but not the toe curler?"

"In women's magazines that theory works," Jane said. "In real life a selfish lover is a selfish lover and rarely does that change. I speak from being married to one for nearly twenty years. If she loved the sleepwalker and went with toe curler, she'd have one miserable marriage."

"Say that's true, what's left? How does she choose?"

Jane inhaled and happily blew smoke through her nose. "We have to look at Maria's lot in life back then," she said.

"She's young, from a poor neighborhood in the Bronx," I said. "Education is minimal, prospects for leaving the Bronx are minimal, and the future looks bleak."

Jane looked at me. "In that case, you pick the man you think has the better earning potential," she said.

"As they say in the movies, *Bingo*," I said.

"Yeah, it fits, doesn't it?" Jane said.

"Like a tailor-made suit."

"I think I need another heart-to-heart with Maria," Jane said.

"I'll arrange it tomorrow," I said.

Jane took a final hit on the cigarette and crushed it out in the ashtray on the floor between the chairs.

She stood and took my hand.

"Speaking of toe curling," she said and slid open the door.

Chapter Twenty-six

We walked around Old San Juan, visited several churches, and Pigeon Park where Jane bought a bag of corn and was bombarded by hungry pigeons. We had lunch at an oceanside café and then spent most of the afternoon walking El Moro and the historic blue cobblestone side streets.

It was close to five in the afternoon when we returned to our room. After a quick shower for two and a change into clean clothes, Escalante met us in the lobby.

"Xavier said dinner was at seven," I said.

Escalante checked his watch. "We're early," he said.

My cell phone rang and I checked the number and hit *Talk*.

"Got something interesting for you," Paul Lawrence said.

"Go ahead," I said.

"Aleixo Abreu disappeared without a trace about thirty years ago," Lawrence said. "He worked for a loan shark in the Bronx as a collector and did some other small time stuff according to old police reports. As a kid he ran with the Almighty Latin Kings for a while and get this, he and DeSousa were both arrested at a gang fight and charged with illegal possession of a switchblade. He had a Social Security number but never held a job where he paid taxes, so we couldn't do an SS check, and if he's alive and working a legitimate job, it's under a new name."

"Any death notices?"

"No. He had some relatives in the Bronx who filed a missing persons on him, but nothing ever came of it," Lawrence said.

"So he's a ghost in the system."

"More likely dead," Lawrence said. "But look how long Whitey Bulger lived as a ghost before we caught up to him, so you never know."

"Thank you, Paul," I said.

"You can thank me with a few more bottles of Don Q," Lawrence said.

"In tomorrow's mail," I said and hung up.

"What?" Escalante said.

"I'll tell you on the way," I said.

* * *

"You have more questions for me, I understand that, but can they wait until after dinner?" Maria asked.

"No hurry," I said.

"Good," Maria said. "Gloria has prepared a lovely dinner and it would be a shame to ruin everyone's appetite with questions of old boyfriends and murder."

"I agree," I said.

Gloria prepared a Puerto Rican chicken dish with rice and beans that was as good as any five star restaurant served.

"When do you return home?" Xavier asked as we ate.

"A day or two," I said.

"Mother and I are hosting a charity event in San Juan tomorrow afternoon," Xavier said. "Would you care to attend as our guests?"

I looked at Jane and she nodded.

Maria grinned.

"You may be a big tough guy, Mr. Bekker, but it's obvious to me who is the boss," Maria said.

"What is the event?" Jane asked.

"A fund raiser for the police and fire departments," Xavier said. "My father was to have been the host and MC, but I will fill that role for tomorrow and other future scheduled events."

"We'll be there," I said.

"Very good," Xavier said. "And you, Lieutenant?"

"I plan to be there with a squad of my men," Escalante said.

"Excellent," Xavier said.

"What do you wear to an event like this?" Jane asked. "I didn't bring anything formal."

"I'm afraid it is," Maria said. "But don't worry, we will fix you up. Xavier, can you call Mario in the morning and arrange for Jane to borrow a dress for the event?"

"Certainly," Xavier said.

"Now then, I believe it might be time for more girl talk," Maria said and looked at Jane. "Yes?"

* * *

Xavier served cigars from Honduras, brandy for him and Escalante, and coffee from the plantation for me.

We waited, smoked, and drank in the coolness of the evening in the garden.

"This time it's taking even longer," Xavier said.

"Women's clothes and gowns are in the mix," I said. "And that reminds me, I don't have anything formal either."

"Mario should be able to take care of that," Xavier said. "He's one of the best tailors on the island. What about you, Lieutenant?"

"I'll be wearing my dress uniform as will my squad," Escalante said.

"The governor should be there as well," Xavier said.

By the time my cigar was a nub, Jane joined us in the garden.

"Maria has gone to bed early," she said. "I'm afraid I tired her out a bit."

"She'll be fine after a night's sleep," Xavier said. "I'll see you around five at the convention center. Mario will be expecting you before noon."

* * *

It was a warm night and we sat poolside at the hotel after leaving the DeSousa home.

Jane had the legal pad where she took notes.

"A lot of painful memories for that woman," she said. "Several times we had to stop so she could compose herself. Even though it was a long time ago, the memories go deep."

"Memories of what?" Escalante asked.

"Why she chose Joe over Aleixo," Jane said. "She said Aleixo refused to grow up and leave his street gang life. Joe on the other hand, outgrew it and had ambition and drive. She chose Joe over Aleixo because of that even though, as she said, she loved Aleixo more."

"Was Joe aware of that?" Escalante asked.

"She never told him that," Jane said. "But she thinks he suspected. At the wedding, they almost came to blows. She said both had too much to drink and Joe accused Aleixo of molesting her when they were taking pictures."

"And the last time she saw Aleixo?" I asked.

"She can't remember the date, but it was soon after Xavier was born," Jane said.

"And he never contacted her after that?" I asked.

"No."

I looked at Escalante.

"Paul said Aleixo vanished around that same time," I said. "Of course Aleixo was a small-time hood and small-time hoods disappear all the time."

Jane looked at me. "What are you thinking?"

"Same thing you and the Lieutenant are thinking," I said.

"Say you're right and DeSousa did kill Abreu thirty years ago, do you really think someone from the past killed DeSousa for it three decades later?" Escalante asked.

"One of my first cases as a homicide detective was a woman we called Mary Better Late Than Never. Jane, you may remember this one," I said. "Mary married an Irishman with a drinking problem. One day he got really drunk and hit her. They had a young child at the time, so she kept it to herself. The husband got drafted into the Army and went to Korea. When he returned home he was a changed man. He hadn't had a drop in two plus years and became a devote Christian and model husband. They had three more children, the youngest being a son. Now this son had ambition and went to college and then grad school. He didn't marry until he was almost forty years old. Shortly after the wedding, Mary, now sixty-three-years-old took a gun and shot and killed her husband while he was watching a football game on TV. She called 911 and told the operator that she just killed her husband. My partner at the time was Walt Grimes. We responded, picked her up, and when we asked her why she shot her husband, she told us that he beat her. There wasn't a mark on her and in fact she appeared robust and in excellent health. We asked her when he had beaten her and she said nineteen fifty-one. I asked her why she waited forty plus years to retaliate and she said *Better late than never.*"

Escalante stared at me and then his face softened and he smiled.

"I'll admit that it's possible, but if Abreu is dead, who did the retaliation and why now?" he asked. "Mary had a reason to wait so long, she wanted to see her children raised and married before she killed her husband. What reason would the killer have to wait thirty years?"

"Maybe he didn't know where DeSousa was?" Jane said. "Maybe he just found out?"

"Possible," I said. "But DeSousa didn't try to hide his whereabouts and in fact was very visible in business and charity."

Escalante and I looked at each other.

"The governorship," we said in unison.

"Maybe we have another talk with Ortega tomorrow at the charity event?" I said.

"Maybe," Escalante said.

Jane looked at her nails. "I have a chip," she said. "I'll need to get that fixed in the morning."

* * *

I sat on the lid of the toilet and watched Jane shave her legs as she soaked in a tub full of bubble bath.

"This is becoming a very interesting case, Jack," she said. "But I have to go home in two days. I have a department to run."

"I know," I said. "I'm not sure there's much more I can do here anyway."

"But you won't quit, will you? It's not your nature to quit no matter how bad or dead-end a case may seem. It's one of the things I've always admired about you."

"Not quitting on a thing doesn't make you smart," I said.

"Being smart makes you smart and smart you are," Jane said. "Not quitting makes you tenacious and you're both."

I drifted off while watching Jane scrape her legs. The detail I couldn't put a finger on taunted me from a distance. When I thought I was close, it pulled away laughing.

I snapped out of my funk when Jane tossed her razor to the floor. "Silky smooth," she said. "Wanna feel?"

I stood up.

"Like I said, smart," Jane said.

"Don't forget tenacious," I said.

Chapter Twenty-seven

While Jane had her nails done in the hotel spa, I took a much-needed visit to the hotel gym.

I ran on a treadmill for thirty minutes, another thirty on a Stairmaster and finished off with several sets on each machine. When I returned to my room ninety minutes later, Jane was still in the spa.

I ran the AC on high and called home.

"Regan be at work," Oz said. "But that boy want to show you the ring he pick out for your approval. Louisa left this morning and she say it's a nice ring, but he could do better."

"What do you say?"

"I say tell Jane to give that boy a raise so he can buy a ring don't look like it came from a Cracker Jack box," Oz said.

"I'll be home in two days, we'll talk then," I said.

"Bring me something with coconut in it," Oz said.

I hung up and went to the bathroom and ran the shower. I didn't hear Jane enter the room, but suddenly the shower door slid open and she stepped in and held out her fingernails. They were bright red.

"What do you think?" she asked.

"I think you have very nice nails for a sheriff," I said.

* * *

A few wrong turns aside, we found Mario's Tailor Shop in San Juan in the historic section of the city.

"I'm John Bekker," I said. "Xavier DeSousa called about…"

Mario, about sixty or so, a crop of thin white hair, a pencil-thin moustache looked at Jane and said, "Jeeze. Xavier said you were ample, but I had no idea."

"I'm a fifty-two long," I said.

"Not you," Mario said. "Her."

"I need a gown for a charity event," Jane said.

"Xavier explained," Mario said. "How tall are you?"

"Five eight."

"Weight?"

Jane walked closer to Mario and whispered into his ear.

"Leave it to me, dear lady," he said.

"And my suit?" I asked.

Mario pointed to a rack at the rear of his ship. "Pick a tuxedo that fits off the rack. I got ties and shirts, too."

I went to the rack and rifled through the suits.

"Now, young lady, come with me," Mario said.

* * *

At our hotel, I shaved carefully and then took a shower. Jane was getting her hair done in the spa and didn't return until I was nearly fully dressed.

"What do you think?" she asked of her hair.

Her blonde tresses were piled into a soft bun with bangs that swept across her forehead.

"Very nice," I said. "Lovely in fact."

"Lovely is a good word. Might as well get comfortable, I gotta get dressed."

I took a seat on the sofa and watched TV for an hour. *Gilligan's Island* was hilarious in Spanish.

Finally Jane emerged from the bedroom and stood in front of me. The blue gown Mario selected was gorgeous and fit her as if tailor-made. The matching shoes brought her height up to close to six-feet-tall. She wore makeup, but it wasn't obvious to my untrained eye.

"I'm ready," she said.

"And I'm breathless," I said.

"I got a 'lovely' and a 'breathless'," Jane said. "What do I get for this?"

She turned to show me the back of the gown. There was a slit from her neck to the top of her waist that exposed much, but showed nothing.

"For that you get one very randy detective," I said.

"Sorry, big boy, I just got my hair done," Jane said.

* * *

We met Escalante and his squad of detectives at the rear entrance of the hotel reserved for VIPs.

They wore their dress uniform of the day. Escalante's chest was full of ribbons and medals to go with his lieutenant bars.

"Close your mouths, boys, before you attract flies," Escalante said to his men when I shook his hand.

Jane greeted him with a kiss on the cheek.

"At last, a real woman," Escalante said.

"Me or Bekker?" Jane asked.

"Alas, Bekker is not my type," Escalante said. "Especially in a monkey suit that doesn't fit."

"Mario said this was a perfect size fifty-two," I said.

"The suit may be perfect, but alas you are not," Escalante said. "Shall we go in?"

And with that, Escalante took Jane's arm and escorted her inside.

I sighed and followed.

* * *

We sat at the table reserved for Maria and the governor. One hundred and twenty-five of Puerto Rico's wealthiest shelled out one thousand a plate for the event. Xavier had a spot at our table, but he was backstage.

"Governor Ortega, this is Jane Morgan, my lady friend and sometimes assistant," I said.

Ortega, accompanied by his wife, stood and took Jane's hand. With her shoes on, she was a good three inches taller than him.

"Charming," he said as he shook her hand.

After twenty or so seconds of shaking Jane's hand, Ortega's wife said, "You can let go now, Santiago. She isn't a milk shake."

"Of course. Apologies," Ortega said and took his seat.

Jane sat to my left next to Maria. I heard Maria whisper to Jane, "Once a man, always a man no matter the age."

The lights flickered and Xavier appeared on the portable stage erected for the dinner.

As an MC he was surprisingly polished. After thanking us for coming, he thanked the sponsors for arranging the event, then introduced two Latin singers who sang several songs in Spanish and English while waiters served dinner.

Meatball soup with barley, followed by a thick, very tender steak, and ending with a double-double chocolate cake, wine, soft drinks, and coffee is what your thousand bucks bought for the evening.

During the dessert part of dinner, Xavier introduced a well-known, local comic who did fifteen minutes in Spanish and English. He was followed by the Police/Fireman's band with singers, and they did fifteen minutes in Spanish.

With the band silent, but still on stage, Xavier introduced Ortega and as he made his way to the stage, the band played "La Borinqueña," the territorial anthem of Puerto Rico. All stood while the song played and once we were seated again, Ortega spoke for twenty-five minutes in Spanish and English.

The main part of his speech outlined the gear needed by the police and fire departments that tonight's event would buy. He ended the speech by telling us that Maria DeSousa had matched the night's totals dollar-for-dollar, and by asking all to please stand for a moment to remember her beloved husband Joe.

The crowd stood and applauded for several minutes until Ortega asked them to sit. He then turned things back to Xavier who announced the band would play for thirty minutes if people wished to dance.

When Ortega and Xavier returned to the table, I said, "We need to talk some business, Governor. In private."

Ortega sighed. "My fee for talking business tonight is one dance with your lovely lady," he said.

Jane stood up. "With or without?" she asked looking down at him.

"With or without what?" Ortega said.

"My shoes."

"Definitely your shoes."

As Ortega led Jane to the dance floor, his wife said, "If I see your hand slip below her waist, you will go home in an ambulance, Santiago."

I turned to Xavier. "Where can we talk privately with the governor?"

* * *

"Can this be true?" Ortega asked with disbelief in his voice.

"It's plausible," I said. "Under the circumstances."

"But that would make Joe DeSousa a murderer," Ortega said.

He was sweating even with the AC blasting in the conference room. He removed his jacket and loosened his tie.

"It would if the information is true," I said. "We don't know that it is, but it is plausible as I said."

"Does Maria believe her husband murdered this old boyfriend?" Ortega asked.

"She suspects," Jane said. "But she doesn't want to believe. Who can blame her?"

"My God," Ortega said.

"We're detectives, Governor," I said. "It doesn't matter what we believe or suspect. We work on evidence and fact. It's a fact that Aleixo Abreu, an old boyfriend of Maria and rival of Joe disappeared without a trace thirty years ago. I've had the FBI search for him, and they can't find somebody if that somebody doesn't exist. Joe's murder may or may not be related to his past, but we have to look more realistically now at the possibility that he was killed to prevent him from becoming governor."

Ortega stared at me.

"Wait," he said. "Are you suggesting that somebody in my administration leaked our plans for Joe's campaign as an act of revenge?"

"Again Governor, it's plausible," I said. "And something that needs to be thoroughly investigated."

"Can that be done without destroying Maria and her family?" Ortega asked.

"I will take charge of this personally and not involve any of my staff," Escalante said. "I will share every detail with you as found and you can make the decision to go public or not on any findings."

Ortega nodded. "Thank you, Lieutenant."

Ortega turned and looked at me. "I have no authority over you, Mr. Bekker."

"I once lost everything I have in a media circus," I said. "I stand with the Lieutenant on this one."

"Very well," Ortega said. "Lieutenant, report to my office in the morning and we'll begin a review of my staff."

Escalante turned to me.

"And you and Jane?" he asked.

"We'll be there," I said. "We won't leave until the day after tomorrow."

"Well then," Ortega said and took Jane's arm. "One more dance before the band leaves."

* * *

Close to midnight, the temperature was near eighty with oven-like humidity, and Jane suggested a dip in the pool.

We lounged in the deep end away from the lights of the poolside bar.

"She knows," Jane said. "She didn't say it, but I could see the painful memory in her eyes. Maria DeSousa knows that her husband killed Aleixo Abreu thirty years ago. It was on the tip of her tongue, but she held back, afraid of the past."

"And it may have nothing to do with why he was killed now," I said. "They could be unrelated events."

"But you don't think so."

"No."

"Over the years working with you, I've learned that you have the best instincts of any cop when it comes to things like this," Jane said.

"Instinct isn't proof and we still don't have even a single suspect or a shred of evidence," I said.

"I think your hunch that someone in the governor's…he's a pretty good dancer by the way. My feet are killing me from those heels. What was I…? Oh yeah. Santiago's office is the leak."

"Santiago is it?"

"We did do the Tango together."

"Tango or not, his office is the leak."

"Looks that way," Jane said as she rubbed her right foot under water.

"Want me to massage your feet?"

Jane looked at me for a moment and then she placed both arms around my neck.

"I saw this talk show once and this doctor said the way to tell if a man really loves a woman is if he offers her a foot massage without her asking," she said.

"I thought it was diamonds," I said.

"Well, that too," Jane said.

Chapter Twenty-eight

 "We're looking for a leak in your administration," I said. "That means no stone goes unturned, no piece of paper isn't read and no staff member is immune from being looked at right down to the janitor."

Ortega looked at me from behind his desk. "I understand what you are saying, but if no one else was present at the meetings with Joe and myself, how could a staff member be involved?"

Ortega's assistant opened the office door and entered with a large tray filled with mugs and coffee. He took the tray to the conference table and after he filled each mug, he turned and said, "I'll be at my desk if you need me, Governor."

We went to the conference table and took seats.

"Let me ask you, Governor, did you take notes at the meetings with DeSousa?" I asked.

"I may have taken some on a legal pad, but probably threw them away afterward," Ortega said.

"In the trashcan under your desk?" I said.

"Yes."

"Where the cleaning crew can go through it when they clean your office," I said.

"Yes," Ortega said softly.

"Did someone come in with coffee during the meetings and maybe glance over your shoulder at your notes?" I asked.

"Possibly."

"Not to mention the fact that Joe DeSousa may have had somebody he confided in or went to for advice," I said. "And that somebody may have mentioned it to somebody else and so on."

Ortega nodded. "When I was a child we played a game called telephone tag. Are you familiar with the game?"

"Yes."

"Where do we begin?" Ortega said.

"Do you have the dates of your meetings with DeSousa?"

"I do."

"Let's start there," I said. "Get those dates and see who on your staff was working those days. The lieutenant knows what to do from there."

"You're leaving?" Escalante asked.

"We're going home tomorrow where I will continue to work with you as a consultant," I said. "Right now, I'd like to show Jane a bit more of this paradise."

Ortega stood up and shook my hand. "I hope your next visit will be under better circumstances," he said.

The he took Jane's right hand and kissed it. "And maybe we will dance the Tango one more time."

* * *

"The governor is a bit of a wolf," Jane said.

I was pulling into the parking lot of the beach in Fajardo.

"Why, did he grab a feel when you were dancing?" I asked as I found a spot and parked.

"No, but his wife saw to that," Jane said. "That she had to make sure he didn't means that he would have if he could have."

When we left the governor, we returned to the hotel to change before heading out to the beach.

Jane wore her yellow sundress over her bathing suit, her sandals, the straw hat and sunglasses.

I wore a warm-up suit over my trunks. We stuffed towels from the hotel into a bag and figured on having lunch at the beach. I rented two beach chairs at a booth entering the sand and we set up shop a hundred feet from the water under the shade of some coconut trees.

"I'm starting to burn a bit," Jane said and dug out a tube of sun block from the bag we stuffed the towels into.

"I'll do your back," I said.

Jane peeled off the sundress and I gave her back and shoulders a good going over with the sun block.

Then we sat in the chairs in the shade and watched the ocean for a bit.

After a while, Jane said, "So what are you going to do when we get home?"

"See what Paul has, work the details, see what Escalante comes up with, stir it all up and see what falls out," I said.

"You've created a big mess here, you know," Jane said. "Some good people will get hurt and embarrassed if what falls out is ugly."

"I know."

"She's been through a lot in her life," Jane said.

"Maria? I know."

"Can you end this without causing her anymore harm?"

"I don't know."

"Maybe this one stays unsolved?"

I turned and looked at Jane.

"Would you not arrest someone because it might embarrass an innocent someone else?" I asked.

Jane sighed. "No."

A thin, very dark man walking along the beach headed straight for us.

Jane said, "Jack, that man is carrying a machete."

"I see him," I said.

I went on high alert until the man walked past us and stared up at the coconut trees behind us. He selected one and then climbed it to the top with cat-like precision. Once the coconuts were within reach, he hacked at them with the machete and several fell to the sand.

Then he shimmied down to the sand and gathered up the coconuts and while we watched he hacked off the tops, dug out a pint bottle of Don Q rum, added a capful to each and stuck in a thin straw.

Then he approached us and handed one coconut to each of us.

"Jack, it has rum in it," Jane said.

"I know," I said. I dug a twenty dollar bill out of my wallet and gave it to him.

"Do you speak English?" I asked.

He nodded.

"One without the rum," I said.

"No Don Q?" he said.

"Right, no Don Q," I said.

He nodded, selected another coconut, hacked away, stuck in a straw and gave it to me. He went to make change of the twenty and I shook my head no.

"Thank you," he said and wandered away down the beach.

We sat and sipped milk from our coconuts.

"This is yummy," Jane said. "And what would make it even yummier is one of those cigarettes."

I looked at Jane.

"One a day is not going to hurt," she said. "Think of the vitamin."

"Vitamins are good for you and necessary for your physical well-being," I pointed out.

Jane dug in her bag and came up with the cigarettes and matches. "And one of these a day is good for my mental well-being," she said as she lit a match.

"When you're done uplifting your mental well-being, how about a dip?"

I had a waterproof pouch that I slipped my wallet, watch and room keys into and tied it around my waist. When Jane was done smacking her lips over the Classic Blue, we went down to the water and rode the waves for about an hour or so.

When we returned to our chairs, a thin, dark-skinned man was seated on a blanket and surrounded by long leaves from the coconut trees. He was making baskets and hats just using a thin paring knife.

We sat and watched him work for a while.

Jane said, "Can you make a basket for me?"

He paused and looked at us.

"Do you speak English?" I asked.

"Yes, English," he said.

"Those baskets on the blanket, when did you make them?" Jane asked.

He looked at the baskets and then at Jane.

"What day did you make those baskets?" Jane said.

"Day?" he said in a thick accent.

"Yes, what day?" Jane said.

"I make the day before today," he said.

"You mean yesterday?"

"Yes, yes, yes…to…day," he smiled.

"What's your name?" Jane asked.

"Name. Willie."

"Okay, Willie, make me a basket," Jane said.

"Yestoday," Willie grinned as he carved up some long palm leaves.

Within ten minutes, Willie made a large fruit basket from the palm tree leaves using just the knife, interlocking the leaves much the same as a knitter with needles would do with wool.

Proudly holding the finished basket, Willie said, "Take home like this," and squashed the basket between his hands so that it was flat. "Get home, do this," he said and removed his hand from the basket and it sprung back into shape.

"Quite a trick, Willie," Jane said. "How much for the basket?"

Willie handed Jane the basket and then held up ten fingers.

I dug out a twenty and said, "Keep the change, Willie. You're quite the artist."

Willie tucked the twenty into a pocket, sat on his blanket and went to work with the knife.

We took our chairs and a few minutes later, Willie came up behind Jane and said, "For hair for pretty lady," and tucked a beautifully constructed rose made from a palm leaf into her hair.

"Thank you, Willie, it's beautiful," Jane said.

Smiling, Willie returned to his blanket.

Jane and I watched the waves crash on the sand as the tide started to roll in.

"Hungry?" I asked Jane.

"Starved."

Inside my plastic pouch, my cell phone rang. I dug it out. It was Paul Lawrence.

"Jack, Paul. I just got a list sent to me by Walt's data officer Venus Brown," Lawrence said. "She's good. I may make her a job offer."

"Walt would have a fit if you did that," I said. "And he'd blame me."

"I know. Give my people a day or two to process all this and I'll call you back."

"Anything new on Abreu?"

"Not at the moment," Lawrence said. "I've assigned a team to dig deeper."

"I'm going home tomorrow," I said. "Last chance for some extra Don Q."

"Another four wouldn't hurt," Lawrence said. "They make nice Christmas gifts."

"So do monogrammed hankies," I said.

"I'll call you when I have something," Lawrence said.

I hung up and turned to Jane, but she was seated on the blanket next to Willie. He had a felt-tip pen and was autographing Jane's basket. I noticed he wrote left-handed.

"Thank you, Willie, you're a true gentlemen," Jane said.

Jane stood and returned to her chair.

"Where do you want to go to eat?" I asked.

"Let me have another cigarette," Jane said. "I think better when I smoke."

* * *

We decided on Italian and a trip to Luquillo where the only Italian restaurant on the island was located. It was a block away from where DeSousa was killed. The restaurant resembled a burned out storefront during the day. After dark, plywood was removed from windows and doors and the lights came on.

Inside were seven tables. A courtyard held another ten. We chose the courtyard for the ocean breeze and sounds of crashing waves.

The chef was a native Puerto Rican who happened to love Italian food and refused to serve anything else. He was a whirlwind in the kitchen, and served a chicken parm as good as any as I've had in New York.

For dessert we had chocolate cheesecake made on the premises and espresso that was very rich and creamy.

On the way to the car I said, "Want to see the crime scene?"

"Where DeSousa was murdered?"

"It's right across the street."

I took Jane's hand and we crossed over to the beach. The streetlights lit up the sidewalk and the moon was up so there was enough light to see a good ten feet onto the sand.

I stopped when we were directly across the street from the Luquillo resort where I stood on the balcony.

"I was there," I pointed. "And they were here, right where we're standing."

Jane looked at the balcony.

"And thirty feet to our right is where they found DeSousa's body," I said.

"It doesn't make sense, this whole thing, does it?" Jane said.

"No."

"Let's go back to the hotel," Jane said. "It's hot and sticky and I want to take a final dip in the pool."

* * *

Just after midnight, Jane glided the length of the pool underwater. When she popped up in the shallow end, she ran water out of her hair and stood next to me against the wall.

"We should come back here sometime when nobody is dead," she said.

The only other couple at the courtyard pool was seated in lounge chairs at the opposite end of the pool. The man was smoking a cigarette. I could see the red ember of his cigarette glow as he inhaled.

"Jane, do you still have those cigarettes?" I asked.

"In my bag."

"Could you smoke one?"

"I'd be happy to. Why?"

"Come on," I said and took the ladder out of the pool.

Jane followed and we went to our chairs where we toweled off.

"Okay, smoke," I said.

"Yes sir," Jane said and dug out the pack and happily lit up.

I picked up my watch from the chair and noted the time.

"Are you timing me?" Jane asked.

"Yes."

"Why?"

"Keep smoking," I said.

Jane shrugged and smoked the cigarette to the filter before putting it out.

"Five minutes and twenty seconds, that's how long it took to smoke one of those cigarettes," I said.

I sat in my chair. "Odd, isn't it?"

Jane sat next to me. "What?"

"The killer waited until he finished the entire cigarette before he attacked DeSousa," I said. "Five minutes and twenty seconds, that's a long time to wait before you attack, isn't it?"

"It is," Jane said.

"Why wait?" I said. "If you're there to kill DeSousa, why wait an extra five plus minutes to do it? Somebody could have happened by during that time. Even a police car on patrol. Why wait and take that risk?"

"Maybe they were talking?" Jane said.

"About what, the weather?"

"About whatever the meeting was about."

"Except that I don't think the smoker was there for the meeting," I said. "I think he was there to murder Joe DeSousa, so why risk the extra time?"

"I don't know, but maybe we can think about it for the next five minutes and twenty seconds," Jane said as she reached for another cigarette.

Chapter Twenty-nine

I wasn't all that surprised to see Escalante in the lobby when Jane and I checked out.

"Thought I'd say goodbye in case our paths never cross again," he said.

"Never say never," I said as I shook his hand.

Escalante turned to Jane and extended his right hand.

"Oh, poo to that," she said and gave him a warm hug.

He walked us to the waiting rental car curbside.

"Did you know the governor has over three hundred members of his staff?" Escalante said.

"If you get a hit on one of them call me," I said.

"And you do the same," Escalante said.

He stood on the sidewalk as I drove the rental away from the hotel.

"Good man. Good cop," Jane said.

* * *

It was sixty-two degrees and raining when our plane landed back home just before noon. After picking up our luggage, I retrieved my car from long-term parking.

"I have to go to work in the morning," Jane said.

"I know."

"Drop me off at home and I'll meet you at the trailer around ten."

By the time we reached Jane's home, the rain had stopped but the sky was still a dull grey.

I popped the trunk and carried Jane's bags to the door.

"Wanna come in?" Jane asked as she unlocked her door.

"Nope."

"Want I should get a priest to exorcise the place?"

"That's a kind offer, but no."

"See ya later then," Jane said and gave me a sweet kiss.

* * *

Oz was napping in his chair in front of the television. I used the remote to mute the sound and went to the backyard where Regan and Phil were playing on the grass with Molly the cat and Cuddles the dog.

Regan and Phil stood when I opened the glass siding doors and stepped outside.

"Dad, you're back," Regan said and greeted me with a kiss.

"Hello, sir," Phil said. "Welcome back."

"I need to run to the pet store and pick up some food for these guys," Regan said. "I won't be but twenty minutes. Phil, you wait here with Dad."

Regan dashed into the house and I took a chair at the patio table.

"There's fresh coffee, Mr. Bekker," Phil said. "Would you like a cup?"

"Actually, I would."

Phil went inside and returned with two mugs and set them on the table.

I took a sip. "Regan made this," I said.

"How can you tell?" Phil asked.

"When she makes a pot she adds one extra cup of water," I said. "When Oz makes a pot he adds one extra scoop of coffee."

Phil sampled the coffee. "I can't tell."

"What's on your mind, Phil? You look like you just drank the entire pot."

"Well, sir, it's this," Phil said.

He dug into a pocket and produced a small ring box. He flipped it open and showed me the engagement ring inside.

"I was going to take her to dinner tonight and give her the ring," Phil said nervously.

"Phil, if you give that ring to my daughter, I'll beat you with it and bury you upside down in the garden," I said.

"But you said…"

"The stone is a third the size of a Tic Tac," I said.

"It's the best I could afford right now," Phil said. "I figure to replace it down the road with something better."

"Phil, I'm going to lend you some money and you'll sign an IOU and never tell my daughter," I said. "And tomorrow when you get off work, you and I will go shopping for a new ring."

Phil looked at me.

"That wasn't a request," I said.

"I work seven to three tomorrow," Phil said.

"Perfect," I said. "Meet me at Harbinger's Jewelry Store at four."

The sliding door opened and a sleepy-eyed Oz came out with a mug of coffee.

"I see you back," he said.

"Goodbye, Phil," I said.

"Sir?" Phil said.

"He mean scoot," Oz said and sat at the table.

"I'll wait for Regan inside," Phil said.

He stood and went into the kitchen and closed the sliding doors.

"What's the matter with you?" I asked.

"Matter? Nothing. Why?"

"What's with the napping? I've never seen you this tired before."

"I never been this old before."

"That isn't it," I said.

Oz sipped from his mug, sighed and said, "It Louisa. The woman is plain wearing me out."

"Are you sure it's that and not something else?"

"Something else like what?"

"Health related maybe?"

"I feel fine otherwise."

"You're sure?"

"I sure mother hen."

The sliding doors opened and Regan and Phil came out.

"Come on you two, I got fresh food," Regan said.

At the sound of her voice, Molly and Cuddles raced inside.

"Dad, are you staying for dinner?" Regan asked.

"I have to go to the office, but let's do a barbeque at the beach tomorrow night," I said.

* * *

I ran along the water's edge for about thirty minutes. I was barefoot and wore five-pound ankle weights.

On the return trip, I ran in ankle-deep water and the canvas covering on the weights took on water and doubled in weight.

It was a fairly warm afternoon, around sixty-five degrees, and I was drenched in sweat by the time I reached the trailer.

I was freeing my thoughts during the run, hoping something I missed would suddenly show up and provide answers.

It didn't.

At the trailer, I jumped rope until my shoulders ached and my legs burned. I switched to push-ups until my chest and arms gave out and then went to work on the heavy bag.

Usually a hard workout puts my mind into a zone and allows thoughts to flow in and out until something clicks.

Today was a drought.

When I couldn't hit the bag one more time, I flopped into my chair with a cold bottle of water.

I poured half over my head and drank the rest.

Then I took a long, hot shower and slipped on a warm-up suit and sneakers. I made some coffee and took my seat and about thirty minutes before sunset, I spotted Jane's cruiser on the sand.

I met her at her cruiser when she arrived.

"I brought fruit," she said, and handed me Willie's fruit bowl. "And some stuff for the grill."

I took the bowl to the table and returned and took the overnight bag from Jane. She left her uniform in the cruiser and toted a large shopping bag from a grocery store.

"Get a fire and the grill going and I'll take care of the groceries," Jane said.

I lit the grill and then tossed a few logs into the trashcan, gave it a squirt of lighter fluid and tossed on a match.

I took my chair and waited for Jane. The fruit bowl was filled with apples and pears. Willie's handiwork held up nicely to being squished into a suitcase, tossed onto a plane and now filled with five pounds or so of fruit.

I stared at the bowl, vaguely aware that Jane had taken the seat beside me. I looked at Willie's signature.

"Bekker, are you okay?" she asked.

"What was it Willie said when you asked him when he made the bowl?"

"What?"

"He said something, what was it?"

"I don't…wait. He said something like he made it the day before today," Jane said. "Something like that. Why?"

I picked up the bowl and looked closely at his signature. It slanted the opposite of a right-handed person.

"Bekker, what is it?" Jane asked. "Is something wrong with the bowl?"

"No," I said and I set the bowl down.

"Jack, what is…?"

I grabbed my cell phone and punched in the number for Paul Lawrence's private cell number. He answered on the third ring.

"Paul, I'm home," I said. "Those reports…"

"Haven't even been looked at yet, Jack," Lawrence said. "Maybe tomorrow."

"Forget them. Toss them," I said.

"What?"

"We're looking at the wrong list," I said.

Lawrence sighed. "What list should we be looking at?"

"One way ticket buyers the day after DeSousa was killed," I said. "He probably had a round trip ticket purchased non-refundable because it's cheaper. After he killed DeSousa he couldn't take the chance and wait around, so he…"

"Purchased a one way ticket home the next day," Lawrence said.

"Exactly."

"And if he did, he signed something," I said. "And it's very easy to spot a left-handed slant in a signature."

"It is, isn't it?" Lawrence said.

"Call me when you get the info from the airlines," I said.

"How come it took you so long to figure this out?"

"I didn't, Willie did."

"Who the hell is…?"

"Later, Paul, and thanks."

I hung up and looked at Jane.

"What did you get to toss on the grill?" I asked her.

* * *

With the finger of her right hand, Jane traced a path from my shoulders to my abdomen.

"I can play connect the dots with the scars you have," she said. "Four stab wounds and three bullet holes, not to mention the broken bones. It's a wonder you can still function."

"Like the man once said, wonders never cease," I said.

"Speaking of…" Jane said as her cell phone rang.

She reached across me and picked it up from the nightstand.

"Yeah," she said. She listened for a moment and then said, "Are they extraditing him?"

She sat up. "Okay, I'll call them in the morning and make the arrangements," she said and hung up.

"They found my high school shooter in New Hampshire of all places."

"Are they sending him or is it a pickup?"

"The US Marshals will transport," Jane said. "Now speaking of functioning," she said and rolled on top of me.

Chapter Thirty

Jane left for work around seven-thirty. I lazed in my chair with a mug of coffee and watched the morning tide do its thing down at the beach for a while.

Around eight o'clock, my cell phone rang. I checked the number and said, "Morning, hon."

"Dad, do you want me to go shopping for tonight?" she asked. "I'm working a half day so I have plenty of time."

"Sure. Did you invite Phil?"

"Of course."

"Then get extra. He eats for two."

"No he…yeah, I guess he does."

"Have the gang here in time for sunset."

"Will do."

After hanging up, I went inside for a coffee refill, retook my seat and called Escalante.

"Jack, how's it going?" he said when he picked up.

"About what I was going to ask you," I said.

"Checking out the governor's staff," Escalante said. "About thirty people were working the days of the meetings with DeSousa. Not all of them the same people. About seventy-five total. What's on your end?"

"It dawned on me to look elsewhere," I said. "The smoker probably flew in on a non-refundable ticket. After he killed DeSousa, he flew out the next day on a one way. I asked Paul Lawrence to get an airline listing of passengers who flew out the next day on one way tickets."

"That was staring us in the face all along, wasn't it?" Escalante said.

"I have a favor to ask," I said. "Go to the beach in Fajardo and find a guy named Willie. He makes baskets from palm tree leaves."

"I've seen the guy. There's another guy climbs trees and makes drinks from coconuts with a machete."

"I know, I bought a couple," I said. "When you find Willie, give him one hundred dollars and tell him it's from *yesterday.* Can you do that?"

"I can. What's it all about?"

"The short version is Willie's broken English pointed me in the right direction," I said. "Call me later."

"Okay, Jack," Escalante said.

After hanging up, I went for a run along the water and then spent about an hour working out behind the trailer.

My thoughts were organized now.

Things were starting to line up and make sense.

In a panic, the smoker fled the island the next day on a one-way ticket home. Almost anybody short of a professional hit man would react the same way.

When I sat in my chair and toweled off, that nagging feeling returned that a detail I should have seen was still invisible.

After a shower, I tossed on a clean warm-up suit and drove home.

Regan was at work and Oz was taking Cuddles for a walk so I sat in the backyard and watched Molly stalk birds.

After a while the glass doors slid open and Cuddles raced out to join Molly on the lawn.

"Regan said we having a barbeque at the beach tonight," Oz said as he came out and sat beside me. "Give me a reason to wear my Hawaiian shirt you love so much."

"What about Louisa?"

"What about her?"

"When are you seeing her again?"

"She say two weeks she can fly in for a long weekend," Oz said. "Why?"

"I was thinking we could have a little backyard party next time she's here," I said.

"You done running all over the globe trying to save the world?"

"No, but I had a breakthrough today."

"I tell her next time she call," Oz said.

I looked at my watch.

"See you at the trailer around six," I said.

I left Oz in the backyard and went to my bedroom. On my dresser is a small box I used to store tie tacks, my extra watch, and trinkets. Mixed in with my junk is a small ring box. I pocketed it and returned to my car.

* * *

Phil arrived in his car a few minutes before four o'clock. He was still in uniform.

"Hello, Mr. Bekker," he said

"Okay, Phil, here's my offer," I said.

I dug out the ring box and flipped it open.

"This was Regan's mother's engagement ring," I said. "A one point nine karat diamond with the highest clarity rating. I'm giving it to you to give to Regan."

"I couldn't take that, sir. It wouldn't be right."

"Of course you can take it," I said. "You're giving it to my daughter. We'll pick out a new setting, have the stone reshaped and you can pay me back later."

"But it was your wife's," Phil said.

"Who better to have it than my daughter?"

Phil stared at me and then nodded.

We went in and spoke with a salesman at a counter.

"I'd like this stone reshaped and placed into a new setting," I said. "A raised setting with six prongs."

"How would you like the stone cut?" the salesman asked.

I looked at Phil.

"She likes the tear drop shape," he said.

The salesman examined the ring. "There will be chips leftover from reshaping, would you like them placed into the setting?"

"Yes. Phil, pick out a ring," I said.

Phil chose a raised, six prong gold band in size five that cost thirteen hundred. With the price of re-cutting and formatting the chips, the bill came to two thousand.

I paid the bill with cash. The turnaround time was one week.

"Mr. Bekker, I don't know what to say," Phil said.

"That's the point, Phil, you say nothing," I said. "Ever. See you later at the beach."

* * *

Oz was grill-master for the evening. I built a fire in the trashcan. We ate steak tips and chicken with roasted peppers and potatoes while the sun went down and the stars showed themselves before a bright, full moon dimmed them into the background.

The temperature dropped to fifty-one degrees and Jane and Regan put on windbreakers.

Molly and Cuddles huddled close to the trash can for warmth.

I had left my cell phone on the table and heard it ring. It rang four times before the call went to voicemail.

Jane looked at me.

"I'll check it later," I said.

"We're going for a walk along the beach," Regan said.

She and Phil linked hands and walked down to the water.

When they were out of range, I said, "That boy has grown on me a bit."

Jane rolled her eyes.

Oz said, "Best thing could happen is he make you a grand pappy."

I was about to fire off a snappy comeback when my cell phone rang again.

"Best answer it, Jack," Jane said. "It's not going to stop."

I went into the trailer and picked up the phone. It was Escalante.

"Jack, I've been trying to reach you," he said.

"Having a little family get together," I said. "What do you got?"

"You were right, the governor has a leak," Escalante said. "We have the guy in custody. He wants to talk but he's got a lawyer. The governor and I feel you've earned the right to be here when we have a sit down."

"When?"

"Tomorrow."

"I can catch an early flight," I said. "I'll call you in the morning."

"See you for lunch, Jack," Escalante said.

I hung up and returned to my chair.

"Well?" Jane said.

"Good thing I haven't unpacked yet," I said.

* * *

After Phil took Regan and Oz and the dog and cat home, Jane and I lingered in front of the bonfire with mugs of coffee.

"How long will you be gone?" Jane asked.

"A few days at least."

Jane stared at the bonfire.

"Want to go?"

"I can't, you know that."

"Want me to bring you back something? Another fruit bowl or hat?"

"Just yourself."

"Want more coffee?"

"Can I have one of those cigarettes?"

"How many are left?"

"Six."

"Help yourself."

Jane dug out the box and lit up. She inhaled deeply and exhaled through her nose.

"Better?" I asked.

"Yes, and you're not much good in helping me to quit you know."

"I can't follow you around like the no-smoking police," I said.

"Besides, it might put you in the mood for a little roll in the hay with an old man."

"Don't be silly, Oz left," Jane said.

"A slightly less old man."

"No problem," Jane said and inhaled. "Just as soon as I finish setting the mood," she said and exhaled through her nose.

Chapter Thirty-one

Escalante picked me up at the airport. I had one checked bag and as soon as I retrieved it, he drove us to the governor's office.

"The moment I called him into the office, he volunteered the information immediately," Escalante said. "He didn't deny going through the trash and reading the governor's notes from the meeting with DeSousa. He belongs to...you know what, why ruin the surprise."

* * *

"Your instincts for police work are extraordinary, Mr. Bekker," Ortega said.

"Nice to see you again, Governor," I said.

"Your lovely assistant didn't make the trip?"

"She had other matters that need her attention," I said.

"Well then, shall we have some lunch while we wait for the prisoner and his attorney to arrive?"

* * *

His name is Edwin Garcia. He was thirty-one-years-old and worked in the evening cleaning crew at the governor's office. He was part of a six-man crew that worked between the hours of six pm until two in the morning.

He was born in Puerto Rico, but went to high school in Miami where most of his family had moved to over the years.

"This is Mr. Garcia's attorney, Edward Fox," Escalante said.

"I would like to record this hearing," Fox said.

"No," I said.

Fox looked at me.

"Excuse me," he said.

"Why, did you burp?" I said.

"You can't…" Fox said.

"I can and I did," I said. "One leak in the governor's office is enough without having a recording floating around in lawyer-land."

"It's alright," Garcia said. "I have nothing to hide. I've done nothing wrong. All I did was look through garbage and when something is thrown in the garbage it no longer is private property."

"I grant you that," I said. "So why don't you tell me what you did with this legally acquired knowledge."

"I shared it with the movement," Garcia said. "We were quite excited to learn that Mr. DeSousa was going to run for governor."

"What movement is that, Mr. Garcia?" I asked.

Garcia looked at me for a moment as if he couldn't understand my lack of knowledge. "Why, the Natives for Puerto Rican Statehood, what did you think?"

I looked at Escalante. "NPR," I said.

"Tell Mr. Bekker what the movement is all about," Escalante said.

"Just what it sounds like," Garcia said. "Native born Puerto Ricans for statehood."

"'Native born' meaning born on the island of Puerto Rico?" I said.

"Of course," Garcia said.

"How large is this group?"

"About ten thousand or so here, but ten times that amount living in the states," Garcia said.

"Is there a leader of this group?"

"He's the first person I told," Garcia said. "It created quite a buzz in the group. We know that DeSousa would have done his best to achieve statehood."

"Mr. Garcia, you are quite articulate for a janitor," I said. "How is that so?"

"I have a degree in political science," Garcia said. "I'm going for a master's during the day. I work here nights so I can attend classes."

"The leader of this movement is?" I asked.

"I've done nothing wrong," Garcia said. "We've done nothing wrong. Can't you see that? We're the biggest supporters of DeSousa on this godforsaken rock."

"Is my client under arrest?" Fox asked.

"Mr. Fox, shut up," I said.

Garcia looked at me and then he started to cry.

"Do you think we would hurt the man who could have gotten us statehood?" he said between sobs.

"No, I don't, but somebody did," I said. "And if you leaking privileged information was the cause of DeSousa's death, then you are partially to blame for that."

Garcia composed himself and looked at me. "That doesn't make sense. Why would people who want statehood kill the man who could get it for us?"

"Maybe you had a spy for the other side?" I said. "Those opposed. It's a possibility and it's our job to find out. We'll find out who the leader is anyway, Mr. Garcia, it will just take us a bit longer is all."

Garcia looked at Fox.

Fox nodded.

"His name is Adrian Peralta," Garcia said.

"Where can we find him?" I asked.

"He…he lives in Mayaguez," Garcia said.

"One last question," I said. "When did you go through the trash and find the governor's notes?"

"Last September I believe. It may have been early October."

I nodded. "Thank you, Mr. Garcia."

"Is my client free to go?" Fox asked.

Escalante and I looked at Ortega.

Ortega nodded. "He's free to go, but may I invite you to have lunch with me? We have much to talk about."

* * *

Mayaguez is located on the southern west coast of Puerto Rico about eighty miles from San Juan. Escalante took Route 52 South to Route 2 West. The drive took over two hours and we stopped midway in Ponce for coffee and a bite to eat.

We ordered burgers and lemonade and sat at a picnic table in the shade of some tall palm trees. A soft breeze that blew north off the coast helped to soften the eighty-five degrees heat of the afternoon.

"Explain to me this movement of natives and non-native Puerto Ricans," I said.

"There is a segment of the population that feels Puerto Ricans born in the States aren't true Puerto Ricans," Escalante said.

"Even though both groups are citizens," I said.

"Citizenship has nothing to do with it," Escalante said. "Those born here feel resentment to those born in the States who call themselves Puerto Rican when they don't even speak Spanish."

"Don't you find it ironic that a group that calls itself Natives for Puerto Rican Statehood championed a man for governor who wasn't even Spanish and who they called Joe Italiano even though he was actually Portuguese?" I asked. "It's sort of like electing a Jewish Pope."

"Completely ironic," Escalante confessed. "But if they feel statehood is important enough, does it matter who leads the cause?"

"Even if DeSousa's killer is part of this group, it doesn't mean DeSousa didn't have something to do with Abreu's disappearance thirty years ago," I said.

"I know," Escalante said. "But since both are dead I see no reason to bring up DeSousa's crime if we find his murderer was a member of this group."

"Agreed. How long to Mayaguez from here?"

"About an hour."

"Want some coffee to go?"

* * *

Mayaguez was a pretty coastal town with a nice beach, lots of palm trees, churches, and rolling hills and mountains in the background. With a population just short of 90,000, it was the eighth largest city on the island.

Adrian Peralta wasn't hard to find. He had a medical clinic on PR Route 102 in the heart of town.

Doctor Peralta was seventy-three-years-old and had been practicing medicine for close to fifty years. He had a white beard, a crown of silver hair, dark eyes, and wore round John Lennon-type glasses.

We had to wait in the waiting area for an hour until he was done with his final patient of the day.

A pretty nurse dressed in white entered the waiting area and spoke to us in Spanish.

"He'll see us now," Escalante translated.

The nurse took us to an office in the rear of the clinic where Peralta waited behind an old, worn desk.

"When you called earlier, Lieutenant, I wasn't going to speak with you, but since Joe DeSousa is dead, I suppose it no longer matters," Peralta said in English.

"Mr. Peralta, it's important for you to understand that we are simply following the facts as they arise," Escalante said. "We don't think for a second that you had anything to do with Mr. DeSousa's murder."

"Then why are you here?" Peralta asked.

"Because those facts, as the Lieutenant said, led us here," I said.

"And you are?" Peralta asked.

"This is John Bekker, retired police detective now working with me as a private investigator and the only witness to the murder," Escalante said.

"Tell us about the movement you lead," I said.

"Nothing complicated about it," Peralta said. "We want statehood for this island, Mr. Bekker. If you're born here as I was, you're a citizen of the U.S., but you don't have the right to vote for the president of the country you're a citizen of if you live here. Does that make sense to you?"

I looked at Peralta and didn't respond.

"We're billions in debt, crime and drugs are everywhere, and our healthcare system is worse than Cuba's," Peralta said. "Hawaii is a state and it's half way around the world and we're a short plane ride from Florida. Becoming a state won't fix our problems overnight, but it puts us on a level playing field in Washington. I've been fighting for statehood for forty-five years and Joe DeSousa had as good a shot as any at convincing the masses on this rock to vote yes."

"You met with Mr. DeSousa?" I asked.

"At least three times," Peralta said. "Always in secret. Usually right here. When I was told the news by Garcia, I contacted Joe and he agreed to see me."

"Do you remember the last time you met with him?" I asked.

"Back in early December," Peralta said. "Joe assured me that he would run for governor and he would do his best to get statehood. We agreed not to meet again until the announcement was made official at the end of this year. I told him he would have the full support of our movement."

"And the group in the States?" I asked.

"Yes, of course," Peralta said. "There's at least 100,000 signatures on a petition to Congress and the President."

"I'm curious, Doctor," I said. "You are aware that Joe DeSousa wasn't Puerto Rican? Wasn't even Spanish."

"Yes, of course, but he believed in statehood and was willing to fight for it," Peralta said. "That is what matters most to us and the cause. Statehood, not race, religion or creed."

"Who leads the group in the States?" I asked.

"You don't really believe someone in our group would murder the man who could have helped us achieve our dream, do you?" Peralta asked.

"This is where the facts are taking us," I said. "What I think or believe doesn't matter."

Peralta sighed heavily.

"Professor Lorenzo Morales," he said.

I looked at Escalante.

"Where can we find the professor?" Escalante asked.

* * *

Driving to Fajardo to see Maria Escalante, Paul Lawrence called on my cell phone.

"Jack, Paul," Lawrence said. "The answer to the question how many people flew out of Puerto Rico the day after the murder on one-way tickets is thirty-seven."

"Can your guys get started on background info?" I asked.

"Not for a day or so," Lawrence said.

"I'm in Puerto Rico, headed to Boston tomorrow," I said. "I can fly to DC and give you a hand tomorrow night."

"What's in Boston?"

"Professor Lorenzo Morales."

"And who is he?"

"Good question," I said. "You can tell me later after you background him."

* * *

"I'm quite surprised to see you, Mr. Bekker," Maria said.

"I'm sorry for intruding on you, Mrs. DeSousa," I said. "We have some new leads and I wanted to discuss something with you."

"Can you stay for dinner?" Maria asked. "Both of you. Xavier is on his way from the office and should be here any moment."

"Sounds good," Escalante said.

* * *

"Natives for Puerto Rican Statehood?" Xavier said.

"NPR," I said.

"Joe's datebook," Maria said. "I remember you asking about it, the NPR."

"They sound like a political fringe group," Xavier said.

"They are, but they're growing," I said. "They have twice the number of signatures required to send a petition to Congress."

"I'm very confused," Maria said. "If I understand what you are saying, you think somebody in the group killed Joe. Why, if Joe could give them what they wanted?"

"All fringe groups have extremists and nut jobs," I said. "It's possible someone resented a non Puerto Rican as governor leading their cause. Stranger things have happened. A former U.S. Marine killed Kennedy. A crazy guy shot Reagan to impress an actress. When you were a teenager, a psycho went around killing couples in New York because his neighbor's dog told him to."

"I remember," Maria said. "I was quite young, but I remember."

"So what now?" Xavier asked.

"Tomorrow I go to Boston and talk to Professor Lorenzo Morales, leader of the statehood movement in the States," I said.

"Would you care for coffee and dessert?" Maria asked.

"It's getting late and I have to check into the hotel," I said.

"Nonsense," Maria said. "Stay in one of our guestrooms and tomorrow Xavier will take you to the airport."

"I'll get your bag from my car," Escalante said.

* * *

My bedroom had French doors that opened up to the backyard garden. I wasn't tired, and the breeze flowing down from the mountains was a welcome relief. Around ten in the evening, I took my cell phone to the gardens and sat on a bench that faced the mountains. A large moon illuminated the crests creating a beautiful picture.

I called home and got Regan on the phone.

"When are you coming home, Dad?" she asked.

"That's what I'm calling about," I said. "I'm flying to Boston tomorrow for at least one day, so maybe the day after. How is Oz?"

"Actually, he's good," Regan said. "He walked Cuddles three times today and even had dinner ready when I got home from work."

"Sounds like he got his second wind," I said. "I'll call you from Boston."

"Night, Dad," Regan said.

I waited a few moments and then called Jane.

"Damned U.S. Marshals," Jane said. "They let the shooter escape."

"How?"

"Son of a bitch wears glasses," Jane said. "When he was in back of the plane he broke off a stem and used it to pick his handcuffs. Then he reset them so his wrist could slide out. The Marshals never noticed the broken stem. My deputies picked him up at the airport and when he was in back of the transport van, he slipped out and took the deputy by surprise. He made the driver pull over and shot him in the chest. He might not make it."

"You at the office?"

"Where else would I be when there's a statewide manhunt?" Jane said. "Even Walt has his people out combing the woods along with the state police and National Guard."

"Jesus."

"When are you coming home, Bekker?" Jane said. "I hate to admit weakness, but I miss you."

"Few days," I said. "I'm flying to Boston tomorrow."

"Boston?"

"I'll tell you about it when you have more time," I said.

"Right," Jane said. "Bring me a crock of baked beans."

"I'll call you tomorrow," I said.

Jane sighed. "I hate missing someone," she said.

* * *

Gloria had breakfast ready by seven-thirty in the morning.

Maria and Xavier joined me at the breakfast nook in the kitchen.

"I asked Gloria to pack a three pound bag of coffee beans roasted just yesterday for you to take with you," Xavier said. "Do you have a grinder?"

"Thank you, that's very thoughtful of you," I said. "And I do have a grinder."

"And there is something else," Xavier said. "We haven't yet discussed your bill for your services."

I looked at Maria. "I'd like to continue on until we get a major break," I said. "I feel that we're close."

"You can't keep working without payment or expenses," Maria said.

"My father taught me early on that time is money, Mr. Bekker, and you have put in a lot of time," Xavier said.

"When I get home, I will send you an account of the hours worked so far, and then I'll send another when we're finished," I said. "I'll send a second account of expenses with the final total."

Maria nodded. Without makeup, she appeared to have aged a decade in the last month. Dark circles under her eyes spoke of sleepless nights despite the sleeping aids. In general, her face seemed worn out and tired.

We finished breakfast, and armed with a three-pound canvas sack of fresh roasted beans, I shook Maria's hand and told her not to worry.

Xavier drove me to the airport.

"I'm a bit confused about something," Xavier said as he drove west to the airport. "All the talk of Abreu, is that now forgotten?"

"It's entirely possible that he has nothing to do with who murdered your father," I said. "Ever see one of those follow-the-maze games where you enter a path and keep following one or more paths until you reach the end? Sometimes your path hits a wall and you have to make a detour. That's how a murder case is solved. You follow one path and hope it leads to another until it ends with a solution. The solution may have nothing to do with the first path you entered."

"My mother is tired," Xavier said. "Very tired. I hope you find that path soon."

Chapter Thirty-two

I've always held the belief that whoever designed the streets and highways of Boston was secretly insane. There is no other explanation for the one-way streets, constant rotaries and major avenues that lead to a dead end and seem to start again halfway across town.

I didn't bother to rent a car at the airport.

I went outside, found a bench near the parking garage and called Paul Lawrence.

"Professor Lorenzo Morales," Lawrence said. "Retired professor of political science at Harvard. Seventy-seven years old and lives with a housekeeper after his wife died about ten years ago. Solid reputation, a model citizen and dying of cancer."

"Shit," I said.

"Want his address?"

* * *

Morales lived in a three-story townhouse on fashionable Beacon Hill. I arrived late afternoon after a jarring, traffic-clogged ride from the airport. I toted my suitcase with me when I rang the doorbell of his home.

A female voice said, "Who is it?" over the intercom.

I pushed the talk button. "John Bekker. We spoke earlier about seeing the professor."

A buzzer sounded and I opened the glass door and stepped into a vestibule where a second, much heavier wooden door was locked. I waited and a second buzzer sounded and I entered the first floor.

"I'm Linda Carlisle, Mr. Morales's housekeeper."

She was around sixty, plump, short dark hair speckled with grey.

"Mr. Morales is in his study," she said. "I'll take you to him."

* * *

"In six to eight weeks, maybe nine at most, I will be dead," Morales said. "I will be cremated and my remains will be sent to Puerto Rico to the town where I was born and scattered in the mountains. My son died in Vietnam at the age of nineteen. I've outlived my wife by a decade. When I'm gone they will mumble a few kind words at Harvard about what a great teacher I was and that will be that. My estate is worth close to two million dollars and I have no heir or relatives worth a damn to leave it to, so what I am going to do is divide it equally three ways. A third to the NPR, a third to charity and a third to Mrs. Carlisle. She doesn't know that so please keep that under your hat."

The den was on the third floor. There was an elevator, but I took the stairs. The walls were lined with photographs. The man seated in front of me in a wheelchair was but a shell of the tall, broad-shouldered man I saw in the photographs on the way up. His back was to the window and he was framed in sunlight.

"Some would say that I have led a successful life," Morales said. "I married well, had a wonderful son who died bravely in battle, taught for forty years at a prestigious university and published six books, two of which are used in colleges across the country. I consider myself a failure and do you know why?"

"I don't, sir," I said.

"The one thing I wanted out of life was to achieve statehood for my birthplace," Morales said. "And now I am out of life and I will go to my death from this ghastly cancer and I won't live to see my dream come to pass."

There was a knock on the door and it opened and Linda entered with a cup of coffee for me, and herbal tea for Morales.

"Thank you, my dear," Morales said.

Linda nodded and left the room.

Morales tried his tea. "Horrible stuff this tea, but it's all I'm allowed to drink anymore," he said.

I sampled the coffee. It was a rich brew with bite.

"What is it you want to know, Mr. Bekker?" Morales asked.

"Ultimately, who killed Joe DeSousa?" I said.

"And you think I know?" Morales asked.

"No sir, I don't," I said. "But what I am wondering about is this, some of the people who belong to your organization. It's possible one or more in the group don't want a governor who isn't Puerto Rican even if he sides with them."

Morales looked at me. His face was gaunt and pale, his body thin and weak, but his eyes were bright and lucid.

"The last figure I had put the membership of the Natives for Puerto Rican Statehood at over 100,000," he said. "If I had to guess, I would put the number at ten of those I know by name."

"Do you have a website?" I asked.

"Yes."

"Take donations?"

"Yes."

"Can people leave comments?"

"If they choose."

"Who runs the website?"

"What are you getting at, Mr. Bekker?"

"Nut jobs and extremists are always posting junk on websites," I said. "In today's world you have to take them seriously. Someone may have been ranting against a non Puerto Rican for governor. It's a possibility that has to be checked out."

"Would you pass me the phone there on the desk?" Morales asked.

I picked up the hard-wired phone and took it to him. He dialed a three-digit number and then said, "Mrs. Carlisle, would you get Mr. Colon on the phone for me."

He hung up and held the phone on his lap.

I picked up my cup and sipped some coffee.

"Did you know Joe DeSousa?" I asked.

"Never had the pleasure," Morales said. "But his endorsement from Doctor Peralta who I know very well carried a great deal of weight with me and many others."

The phone on his lap rang and Morales answered the call.

"Yes, I called," he said. "I need you to come to my house right away. It's important."

Morales hung up and I took the phone and replaced it on the desk.

"He's ten minutes away," he said.

"Thank you, Professor," I said.

"While we wait, what is your opinion of statehood for Puerto Rico, Mr. Bekker?"

"I hadn't given it much thought until recently," I said. "I think statehood would be better for the people than remaining a holding. I think it damned foolish to attempt to become a country onto itself. It's too small with no military to prevent it from being taken over by a hostile government looking for a stronghold in the Caribbean."

"I've had those very thoughts and ideas for more than sixty years," Morales said. "I've heard all the arguments against, the higher taxes, the beholding to the federal government, the this and the that and it's all ignorance. Becoming the fifty-first state would be the best thing to ever happen to that stupid rock."

There was a knock on the door and Linda came in with a short, plump, balding man and said, "Freddy is here, Mr. Morales."

Morales nodded and Linda left the office.

"Mr. Bekker, Alfredo Colon," Morales said.

Colon looked at me.

"Mr. Bekker is a private investigator hired by the DeSousa family to look into the murder of Joe," Morales said.

Colon raised an eyebrow at me.

"And Freddie is some kind of computer genius who runs the website for NPR," Morales said. "Now if you'll excuse me, Mr. Bekker, I have to take a nap. Freddie, take Mr. Bekker to your dungeon and answer all his questions. Oh, by the way, Mr. Bekker, are you staying in town?"

"I will be as soon as I find a motel," I said.

"This house has six guest rooms," Morales said. "Pick one and leave your bag. I look forward to having dinner with you."

"Thank you," I said.

"Ask Linda to come in on the way out," Morales said.

* * *

Alfredo Colon had a small townhouse on a side street seven blocks from the Morales home.

He made a pot of coffee and took it to his office where three computers occupied three separate desks.

"I design software for various companies," he said. "That's my main source of income. I do the NPR website as a labor of love."

"You were born there?" I asked.

"I was, but my parents moved us to Manhattan when I was eight," Colon said. "I go back several times a year to visit family, usually around January when Boston is an iceberg."

"Why Boston?" I asked.

"I went to MIT and stayed after graduation."

"How did you get involved with Professor Morales?"

"After graduation, I took some of his political science classes figuring I might have to design some political websites," Colon said. "We hit it off and he opened my eyes to things in PR I was blind to. That was seven years ago. When he asked me about putting together a website I figured why not?"

"Can you show it to me?"

"Sure."

Colon took me to the desk against the wall where he sat and turned on the computer.

"Can I get you something?" he asked.

"Not right now, thanks."

"Okay, here we go," Colon said as he tapped some keys.

I watched as a webpage for the Natives for Puerto Rican Statehood appeared on the flat-screen monitor.

"This is the main page people see when they do a search," Colon said.

The page was divided into many sections below the heading. There was a section for News from Puerto Rico. Another section for Comments, and one for Contact Us. A third section was for membership and donations.

"How large is the membership?"

"Hold on, let me go to administrative," Colon said.

He tapped some keys, entered a password and a business site appeared on the monitor. He scrolled and said, "Just over a hundred thousand."

"And they've all paid dues?"

"Ten bucks a year," Colon said. "Many take it upon themselves to make donations throughout the year. Last year we had a fundraiser and offered a week in PR at a resort. That brought in over a hundred grand alone."

"What's the money used for?"

"Petitions to Congress, lobbyists for the cause, upkeep of the website and support of political candidates back home."

"We're you in support of Joe DeSousa?"

"A hundred percent," Colon said. "I was born in PR, but my father is from Cuba. If Joe DeSousa could have gotten PR statehood, I don't care if he was made of green cheese and lived on the moon."

"Did the membership know of his plans?" I asked.

"It was never announced," Colon said. "The word was to keep it secret for a while for some reason."

"Do you know Edwin Garcia?"

"Yeah, I know him," Colon said. "The little shit."

"Why do you say that?"

"Edwin is the one who found out Mr. DeSousa was planning to run for governor," Colon said. "It was supposed to be a secret until Mr. DeSousa made an official announcement, but after Edwin notified Doctor Peralta, he started posting hints about it on the website comments section. I caught them and deleted them, but I'm afraid many saw the comments. He has his own webpage where he rants and raves about politics. He made comments there as well, I'm afraid. Doctor Peralta made him take them down, but who knows who might have read them. When you factor in Facebook and Twitter accounts and things like Instagram, who knows?"

"What's Instagram?"

"Instant sharing."

I nodded. "Can those deleted posts be retrieved?"

"That would be tough, but maybe. When you delete something it's never really deleted if you are savvy enough to find it."

"Can you give it a try?"

"It will take a while. Maybe a few days."

I removed my wallet and fished out a business card. "My number. Let me get yours."

* * *

"Mr. Morales dines at six," Linda said. "He's looking forward to your company."

"Thank you, I'll be ready," I said.

My room was large, airy, with a queen-size bed and a private bathroom. I shaved, took a shower, then sat on the bed in my underwear and used my cell phone to call home.

"Hey, Dad, where are you?" Regan said.

"Boston, but I'll be going to D.C. in the morning," I said.

"You're going to miss Louisa," Regan said. "She's coming for a visit tomorrow for three days."

"I might not be in D.C. that long," I said.

"Dad, I think Oz might be thinking of getting married," Regan said.

"What makes you think so?"

"Just a feeling I get when he talks about her," Regan said. "When he told me she was coming he sounded like a kid on Christmas."

"And if he does?"

"I'll be happy for him, but…"

"Regan, I know how you feel about Oz, but if we really love him, we'd want to see him happy," I said.

"I know that. What if he moves away? What if…"

"And when you get married some day and move away, I will feel exactly the same way," I said. "But my primary focus is that I want you to have a happy life. It's no different for Oz."

"I really hate it when you make perfect sense," Regan said.

"I'll call you tomorrow and let you know how long I'll be gone," I said.

"I love you, Dad."

"I love you, too, sweetheart."

I sat on the bed thinking for a few moments, and then I called Jane.

"Where are you?" she asked when she picked up.

"Boston."

"How long?"

"Not sure. A day or two."

"I hate…hold on…what are you pansies looking at? We have a manhunt going on here. Look at me again and I'll castrate the lot of you," Jane said. "What was I saying?"

"You hate something," I said.

"Right. I hate missing you as much as I do, damn you," Jane said.

"Is that good or bad?"

"I don't know, I'm confused."

"Makes two of us," I said. "How goes the manhunt?"

"Do you know what this son of a bitch did?" Jane said. "He paid a homeless guy twenty bucks to switch clothes with him and then another twenty for the homeless guy to take a walk in the woods. The dogs followed the homeless guy for hours fooled by the scent on the shooter's clothes. They caught up with him while he was taking a piss against a tree. The guy was scared senseless and climbed the tree to the fifth branch from the top. We had to get the fire department to get him down. By that time the shooter's trail was stone cold."

"Sounds like your shooter is a thinking man," I said.

"And then some."

"You know what, I miss you, too," I said.

"Police work sucks sometimes," Jane said. "And I gotta go. The boys are looking to get de-balled. Love you."

I sat with my cell phone on my lap, sighed, and then called the airlines and reserved a morning flight to Washington.

Then I called Paul Lawrence.

"Can you pick me up at Reagan?" I asked him. "Eleven or so."

"It's the least I can do for all the extra aggravation you've given me."

"Thanks, Paul."

* * *

"Linda always dines with me, Mr. Bekker," Morales said.

On the table large enough to seat twelve was a chicken picatta dish for Linda and me and a baked fish for Morales.

"I'm on a restricted diet," Morales said. "Not even a little wine, but please help yourself, it's quite good."

"Just water for me," I said.

Linda proved an excellent cook and as I missed lunch, I had seconds.

"Are you a married man, Mr. Bekker?" Morales asked.

"I was," I said.

"Divorced?"

"She died."

"I'm sorry to hear that."

"It was a long time ago, almost fifteen years now."

"Children?" Morales asked.

"A daughter. She's nineteen."

"No thoughts of marrying again?"

I sipped some water and looked at Morales.

"I'm sorry," he said. "I have no right to pry."

"It's not that," I said. "I didn't realize it until you just asked, but yes, I am thinking about it."

Morales nodded. "That's good. And may she outlive you so you don't wind up alone and lonely like me."

Chapter Thirty-three

Paul Lawrence met me in the baggage claim area shortly after eleven in the morning. He was my age, a few inches shorter, and except for thinning hair, still possessed the youthful looks from decades ago when we first became friends.

"Had breakfast?" he asked as we left the terminal and walked to the short term parking lot.

"Nope. Just coffee."

"We could get a late breakfast or early lunch?"

"I think that's called brunch."

"I know a good place," Lawrence said. "I'll drive and you pay."

"Sounds like a good deal to me," I said.

* * *

At a pancake house on the way to the Federal Building, we ordered pancakes slathered in melted butter and syrup, as well as bacon, sausages, toast, juice, and coffee.

I brought Lawrence up to speed over seconds on the pancakes.

"Is it possible to fax that list of thirty-seven names to Alfredo Colon?" I asked.

"Sure it's possible."

"Can you do it when we get to your office?"

"I didn't say I could do it," Lawrence said. "I'm lucky if I can turn on my computer. I'll have a data tech do it."

"That's sorta what I meant," I said.

"Then sorta pay the check and let's go," Lawrence said.

* * *

Wearing a visitor's badge, I followed Lawrence into his office. The windows provided a view of the Washington Monument. His desk was situated between the two windows for the natural light.

At his desk, he made a call while I admired the view outside a window.

When he hung up, Lawrence said, "A tech will be just a moment."

"Okay to use my cell phone?" I asked.

"Sure."

I fished out Colon's number and punched in the numbers. He answered on the third ring.

"Mr. Bekker, I recognize your number," he said.

"In a few minutes, I'm going to have that list we talked about faxed to you," I said. "Can I do that?"

"Sure," Colon said. "Have it scanned to a folder and then email the folder to this email address."

I grabbed a pen off the desk and scribbled the address on a pad.

"Got it," I said. "Call my cell number when you receive the folder."

"Will do."

I hung up just as a male tech knocked on the door and then entered.

"Hey, Frank," Lawrence said. "I need you to scan this list and then email the folder to this address."

"Sure, Paul."

Lawrence handed Frank a folder and the paper I wrote Colon's email address on and said, "Call me here when it's done."

Frank nodded and left the office.

"What exactly are you hoping to find, Jack?" Lawrence asked.

"A very long shot in the dark," I said.

Lawrence's phone rang and he went to his desk to answer the call. I busied myself by studying the Washington Monument. The 554-foot tall obelisk is actually two different shades of color. Construction was halted during the Civil War around the 150-foot mark and completed afterward. I was trying to spot the exact spot where construction stopped when my cell phone rang.

"Mr. Bekker, got it," Colon said.

Lawrence was off the phone now and looked at me from behind his desk.

"Okay, so check the list of names against your membership and see if we get any matches," I said.

"That will take a while," Colon said. "A few hours."

"Time I got," I said.

"I'll call you back," Colon said.

I hung up and looked at Lawrence. "Got a spare copy of the list?"

Lawrence opened a desk drawer and produced a second file. I took a chair opposite the desk and he handed it to me.

Thirty-seven names.

Thirty-seven one-way tickets out of Puerto Rico the day after Joe DeSousa was murdered.

I read the list.

No one person jumped off the page.

Three flew to Europe.

Two went to Canada.

One went to Mexico.

The rest were scattered throughout the United States.

That cut the list down to thirty-one in the long-shot department.

"He said it would take a while," I said.

"I figured," Lawrence said.

"I think I'll take a walk and grab some fresh air while I wait," I said.

"Take your visitor's badge with you," Lawrence said. "Call me from the lobby when you get back."

* * *

It was a spring-like afternoon and the Mall was filled with people. There was lots to see and do. There was a host of famous monuments and memorials—the Smithsonian Museums and the National Zoo— but I opted to get a coffee from a sidewalk vendor and find an isolated bench to sit and drink my coffee undisturbed.

Not so long ago, a cigarette would have accompanied the coffee and the combination of caffeine and nicotine would have, in some strange way, heightened my thought process.

I thought about calling Jane, but decided to keep my cell phone line open.

After more than an hour on the bench, Colon finally called back.

"Got one name," he said.

"Stay put until I call you back," I said.

* * *

I punched in Colon's number from Lawrence's desk phone and immediately put it on speaker.

"Mr. Bekker, this is a different number," Colon said.

"I'm with the FBI," I said. "The call is on speaker. I'm with Deputy Regional Director Paul Lawrence."

"Umm, hello Mr. Lawrence," Colon said.

"Yeah, hi," Lawrence said.

"So what have you got?" I asked.

"Edgar A. Herrera," Colon said. "He's the only one on your list who is a member of the NPR and has made donations."

"How did he make donations?" I asked.

"Credit card."

"Got the number?"

"I do. Want me to read it off?"

Lawrence picked up a pen and wrote down the number on a pad as Colon recited the number.

"And posts or blogs?" I asked.

"Not that I see," Colon said.

"Any idea where he lives?"

"Nope."

"Okay, stay put in case I need to call you back," I said.

"Will do."

Lawrence hung up and looked at me.

"Let's find a tech," I said.

"I knew you were going to say that," Lawrence said as he stood up.

* * *

"This is Timothy," Lawrence said.

"Hello. Hi. I'm Timothy," Timothy said.

He was a prototype computer geek if I ever saw one. Tall, thin, beaklike features, messy, dark hair, and wide glasses.

We were in Timothy's cubicle in the data division.

"I don't really need glasses," Timothy said. "Girls like how I look wearing them."

I looked at Lawrence.

"You're kidding me," I said.

"Tim, I need you to check some things for me," Lawrence said.

"Sure, sure, just as soon as I return from my break," Timothy said. "I like to go to the water cooler on my break because the girls are thirsty and they have to bend over to drink."

"Later, Tim, this is important," Lawrence said.

"But Henrietta from…"

"Tim, focus," Lawrence said.

"Henrietta," Timothy said.

"Tim, do this for me and I will arrange for Henrietta to personally bring water to your cubical," Lawrence said.

"You mean it?"

"Promise."

"Oh gosh, oh boy, oh gosh," Timothy said.

"Tim, this is Mr. Bekker," Lawrence said. "He needs you to do a few things for us. Okay?"

"You look like a gangster," Timothy said to me.

"And you look like Dilbert," I said.

"Dilbert wears a tie, Mr. Smarty-pants," Timothy said. "Do you see a tie on me?"

"Think about Henrietta bringing you your own water right to your little cubicle here," I said. "She'll even bend over to put it on your desk."

"Oh boy," Timothy said. "Oh boy."

"Exactly," I said. "Now before you blow a gasket, here's what I need you to do. Go into your little cyber world there and find me Edgar A. Herrera. Everything about him you can find."

"There's probably thousands of Edgar Herreras," Timothy said.

"Not with this credit card number," I said.

"Henrietta will bend over?"

"As she delicately places your glass of water on your little desk," I said.

"Oh boy," Timothy said and went to work.

I looked at Lawrence who was grinning at me.

It didn't take Timothy long to locate Edgar A. Herrera. His age was listed as thirty-two. No known spouse or children. He lived in Yonkers, New York, with his fifty-five-year-old mother Inez Herrera.

"What does the A stand for?" I asked.

"Doesn't say," Timothy said.

"Pull up his driver's license."

"Okay," Timothy said.

A few seconds later, we were looking at Edgar Herrera's license.

His face was all hard angles, and his skin fairly dark. His height was listed as six-foot-one and his weight at 170.

His signature had a left-handed slant.

His name on the license was printed as Edgar A. Herrera as was the signature.

"Can you find his birth certificate?" I asked.

"I'm getting thirsty," Timothy said. "I'll need my water soon."

"Yeah, sure," I said. "Birth certificate first, then Henrietta and water."

"Okay."

Timothy went to work and up popped the birth certificate.

I stared at the monitor.

"Can I get my water now?" Timothy said. "Henrietta goes home soon."

"Jack?" Lawrence said.

My head was buzzing as if I had just downed a gallon of

Starbuck's coffee.

"What is it, Jack?" Lawrence asked.

"The middle initial," I said. "It stands for Aleixo."

"Water, water," Timothy said.

I looked at Lawrence. "Get what's her name to bring him water so he shuts up," I said.

Lawrence pulled out his cell phone.

"Tim, listen to me," I said. "Print copies of his birth certificate and driver's license and then dig up all the information on him that you can find."

"Okay," Timothy said.

"We'll be in Mr. Lawrence's office. Bring it there," I said.

"Henrietta," Timothy said.

* * *

"Jerry, you're on speaker phone," I said to Escalante. "With me is Paul Lawrence."

"How are you, Paul?" Escalante asked.

"Good," Lawrence said.

"Jerry, I'm holding a copy of a birth certificate belonging to one Edgar A. Herrera," I said. "He flew out of PR the day after DeSousa's murder to Yonkers, New York. He's a lefty. The A stands for Aleixo. On the birth certificate, his mother is listed as Inez Herrera. Father as Aleixo Abreu, both from the Bronx."

Escalante was silent. I could hear his breathing as he processed the information.

"My God," Escalante finally said.

"Keep this under wraps for now until we have a chance to check things out," I said.

"It's him, isn't it?" Escalante asked.

"It's a strong possibility," I said.

"A DNA sample would confirm it," Escalante said.

"It would."

"So what now?" Escalante asked.

"I think Paul and I will take little junket to Yonkers in the morning," I said.

"Where is this Yonkers?" Escalante asked.

"Know what a hop, skip and a jump is?"

"An expression that means close."

"That's Yonkers to the Bronx," I said.

"It's him," Escalante said. "I can feel it in my bones."

"Keep your bones warm and I'll call you tomorrow," I said.

"Jack, I…thanks, Jack."

"Sure."

Lawrence hung up and looked at me.

"Let's go see a federal judge," I said.

"Because?"

"We might need a warrant to remove DNA from the house," I said.

The phone rang and Lawrence said, "Hold that thought."

I scanned the birth certificate and driver's license while Lawrence talked on the phone.

"Timothy has some information for us," he said after he hung up. "It's on the way."

"Where's the cafeteria?" I asked. "I could use some coffee."

* * *

Inez Herrera worked as a clerk for the Post Office for twenty-seven years. She started at a small branch in the South Bronx and worked her way up the ladder to a supervisory position in sorting in the main branch in the Bronx.

Then one day about seven years ago, a fork lift operator who polished off a pint of bourbon for lunch ran her over in the warehouse and retired her to an early pension. She suffered permanent damage to her left leg and walked with a prominent limp, according to reports filed by Post Office Investigators. For her limp, she was also awarded a six-figure settlement.

She and Edgar lived alone in the house she purchased twenty years earlier.

High school records for Edgar indicate he was a decent student, but not honor roll. After graduation, he took night classes at a local college while working part-time for the Post Office. Like his mother, he worked his way up the ladder and four years ago, after graduating night school, he was placed into a supervisory position at the main branch in Manhattan, a position that paid close to six figures.

The main branch of the Post Office was a short walk to the cigarette shop where I purchased the Classic Blue cigarettes.

Timothy found a Facebook page and Twitter account for Edgar. Most of his posts were about Puerto Rico and politics. Besides the NPR, he belonged to several other sites dedicated to Puerto Rican politics.

No arrest records, a few minor traffic tickets for overdue meters and that was it.

"A Post Office worker," Lawrence said as he sipped coffee.

"Yeah, well, so was the Son of Sam," I said.

Lawrence sighed. "So tomorrow, warrant in hand we go have a chat with Mr. Herrera."

"Want to get a steak later?" I said.

"Where are you staying?"

"Wherever my suitcase winds up."

"Want to come home with me? My wife won't mind."

"Do you have a home gym where I can grab a six am workout?"

"You're completely mad, you know that?"

"I'll take that as a no," I said. "And that hotel by the airport has a decent gym."

* * *

And a lousy view of the highway from my window.

I called Jane from my cell phone as I looked out the window.

"Where are you?" Jane asked.

"A motel by Reagan Airport."

"Sounds exotic."

"Only if you like views of a dark highway."

"When are you coming home?"

"I go to Yonkers, New York, in the morning with Paul Lawrence to talk to a suspect," I said. "What about your shooter?"

"Trail is cold and dead," Jane said.

"You haven't heard the last of him," I said.

"Probably not," Jane said. "Listen, Bekker, we never really discussed us. I think when you get home we should."

"I've been thinking that very thing," I said. "I miss you like hell."

"Same here," Jane said. "Maybe we should do something about that?"

"Maybe we should."

"Think about something smart, witty and meaningful to say and we'll talk about it when you get home."

"I don't know if I can take that much pressure," I said.

"I've watched you stare down a madman with a hand cannon at point blank range and not blink," Jane said. "A few well chosen words won't kill you."

"Yeah, but I wasn't in love with the madman," I said.

Jane was silent for a moment. Then she said, "Did you mean that?"

"Yes."

"I'm going to ask you to prove it when you get home."

"What do you mean…?"

"When you get home," Jane said. "Right now I'm waiting on a call from the state police."

"Okay, "I said.

After I hung up, I tossed the cell phone on the bed and continued to watch the lousy view from my hotel window until I was tired enough and bored enough to get some sleep.

Chapter Thirty-four

The FBI jet landed at a private airport in White Plains, New York. Paul Lawrence and I were the only passengers. The pilot and co-pilot were both agents, but they stayed with the plane.

A black Ford Bronco with four agents from the Manhattan office met us on the runway.

Lawrence had ordered them up before takeoff.

"I'll brief you on the way to the suspect's home," Lawrence told the four men. "Who is driving?"

"I am, sir," one agent said.

Lawrence handed him a slip of paper. "Here's the address. If you don't know the area put it in GPS."

* * *

Once we passed through the heart of downtown Yonkers, I was surprised at how countrified the scenery had become. Woods, a flowing river called the Saw Mill, picturesque homes, and kids playing with dogs on lawns.

The Herrera home was at the end of a tree-lined block, and the backyard was wooded. The agent pulled into the driveway in front of a closed garage.

"Two stay in the car, two and Bekker come with me," Lawrence said.

It was time for business and nobody was better at it than Paul Lawrence.

We walked to the front door and Lawrence rang the bell.

It took a few moments, but finally the door opened and Inez Herrera looked at us. A cane was in her left hand.

"Yes?" she said.

Lawrence had his flap wallet at the ready. "FBI. My name is Paul Lawrence. We'd like to speak to you about your son."

Inez had been a pretty woman in youth, but that was a long time and a crippling accident ago. Her hair was mostly gray and if she had colored it she would appear ten years younger.

"What about my son?" she asked.

"May we come in?" Lawrence asked.

"No, I don't think so."

Lawrence removed the warrant from the inside pocket of his suit jacket. "This is a federal warrant issued by a federal judge. We don't need your permission to come in, but it would be a lot friendlier if I didn't have to serve it."

Inez scanned the warrant and then opened the door wide and stepped out of the way for us to pass.

"I have fresh coffee in the kitchen," she said.

"You two wait here," Lawrence told the two agents. "And keep an eye outside."

I followed Lawrence and Inez to the kitchen. We took chairs while she poured three cups of coffee.

"What is it you want to know about my son?" Inez asked as she took a chair opposite us.

Lawrence turned to me. "This is John Bekker, Mrs. Herrera," he said.

She looked at me. "How come you are not wearing a fancy suit like the others?"

"Mr. Bekker is a private investigator investigating the murder of Joseph DeSousa," Lawrence said.

There was genuine shock on her face as Inez placed both hands over her mouth. "Joe De…are you sure?"

"I'm sure," I said.

"Oh my God," Inez said. Then she regrouped and said, "I haven't seen him in thirty years. What does that have to do with Edgar?"

Sometimes blunt is the only way to go. "I believe that Edgar murdered Joe DeSousa in Puerto Rico last month," I said.

"You are insane," Inez said.

"He flew to Puerto Rico in early February, met DeSousa on a deserted beach at three in the morning and stabbed him to death with a bread knife," I said.

Inez stared at me.

"He did go away for a few days in early February, didn't he?" I said. "Where did he tell you he went?"

"To Foxwoods with some of his friends from work," Inez said.

"Inez, I know this is a long time ago, but I need you to explain the relationship between Aleixo Abreu, Joe DeSousa and yourself," I said.

Inez sighed. "We were all from the Bronx," she said. "Alex… that's what I called him. He was madly in love with Maria and so was Joe. They were friends but because of Maria they became enemies."

Inez paused to sip some coffee.

"I was also in love with Alex and he knew it," Inez said. "I think Maria loved Alex more, but Joe was the better provider, so she picked him in the end. I would have done the same. I got Alex on the rebound when she married Joe. He had a fling with her cousin, but it didn't last. I knew that and it was okay with me. We had a son, Edgar. We were going to get married, but that Maria just couldn't keep her hands off Alex and they had an affair. Joe found out about it and soon after that, Alex fell off the face of the earth. I believe that Joe killed him."

"What did the police say about it?"

"Alex was a small time hood," Inez said. "He was a decent man deep down, but the neighborhood got the better of him. What they basically said was good riddance."

"Why do you think Joe killed him?" I asked.

Inez sighed. "What would you do if an old friend had an affair with your wife and she gave birth to his son?" she said.

"Xavier is Aleixo's son?" I said.

Inez nodded. "I doubt she ever told Xavier that. What would be the point?"

"Did you ever tell Edgar this story?" I asked.

"My son lost his father when he was just two," Inez said. "He was aware that he had a dad, but he grew up without one. We still lived in the Bronx until he was ten and it was very rough on him. His grades suffered when he should have made honor roll."

"And you told him when?" I asked.

"When he was fifteen," Inez said. "He needed to know about his father. I told him everything, including that he has a half brother by Maria."

"Did you know Edgar is very active in political groups, including statehood for Puerto Rico?" I asked.

"Yes. He is very proud of his Puerto Rican heritage," Inez said. "He knows hardly anything of his Portuguese blood. Now let me ask you something, Mr. Bekker? Why do you believe it was my son who killed Joe?"

"Does he smoke cigarettes?" I asked.

"Yes. I am trying to get him to quit, but it's a hard habit to break. He didn't start until he went to work for the Post Office."

"I know all about quitting," I said. "What brand?"

"It's…wait, he keeps them in a drawer by the sink."

Inez stood and went to a drawer by the sink and returned with an unopened pack of Classic Blue cigarettes.

"Open it and remove one," I said.

While she removed the wrapper and took out once cigarette, I dug out the photo of the filter from the beach.

"We recovered two cigarettes he smoked that night on the beach," I said. "The filter is a perfect match. The recovered filter has DNA on it. Those cigarettes are only sold in one location in Manhattan and on line. You can't buy them in Puerto Rico. In addition, the man I saw light the cigarette on the beach is left-handed."

"We can match the DNA from Edgar's comb or brush and even his tooth brush," Lawrence said.

"By why?" Inez said. "I don't understand. How could he…why now after all these years?"

"I think it's…"

The two agents we left in the living room burst into the kitchen.

"It's him, the subject," one of them said.

Lawrence jumped up and they rushed to the living room.

"He gets home from work about now, doesn't he?" I asked.

Inez, tears in her eyes, nodded. "He walks from the railroad on nice days."

I stood up. "Wait here," I said and went to the living room. Lawrence and the others had gone outside.

Lawrence was on the sidewalk. I went to him and he said, "The suspect walked down the street, probably home from work and my two agents in the Bronco came out and identified themselves. He took off for the woods."

I watched as the two agents from the house entered the woods about a hundred yards away.

"They won't catch him," I said.

"Probably not."

I removed the windbreaker I had on and handed it to Lawrence.

"Want my radio?" he asked.

"Sure."

I took the small radio and clipped it to my belt. I took a deep breath and took off running after the agents. At the woods, I followed the path they took and caught sight of them about fifty yards ahead.

The woods got thick pretty quickly and it slowed the two agents down enough for me to overtake them in a matter of minutes.

I heard one of them gasp and say, "Son of a bitch."

Although it was a bright afternoon, the thick trees blocked out much of the sunlight and I had to listen for the sounds of rustling leaves to keep pace with the first two agents. They weren't far ahead.

Another hundred yards passed.

I spotted an agent hunched over with his hands on his knees. He didn't look up when I passed him.

The other agent was about twenty-five yards ahead and I watched him go down hard, but I didn't stop to pick him up as I ran by.

Edgar had too big of a lead for me to slow down or stop.

I could hear leaves rustling and twigs snap up ahead. The gap between us wasn't that far. I jumped a few fallen branches and a downed white birch tree and suddenly the woods ahead were silent.

I stopped and stayed perfectly still.

Behind me I could hear the soft gasping of an agent trying to keep up.

Nothing ahead.

Then, to my left I heard a noise.

I turned and ran. After a hundred feet or so, the thicket ended at a clearing. Several hundred feet or so ahead of me, Edgar ran hard and he was pretty damn good at it. I had at least seventy pounds on him and I knew I wouldn't catch him with speed. I would have to wear him down.

The clearing became a path and suddenly I was running alongside the Saw Mill River. It was surprisingly wide and deep with a high, rolling embankment.

I kept my eyes on Edgar. He ran with the good form of a high school track star. His lead on me had widened to about a hundred yards and I had to open my stride to keep pace with him.

Sweat glued my shirt to my back. A slight stitch developed in my side. I ignored the minor pain and kept my pace.

So did Edgar.

Until I spotted the slight deviation of his form. Edgar was beginning to weaken. The first thing that goes is the form. Legs, tired and heavy, start to give out and form becomes sloppy.

I quickly closed the gap between us to about two hundred yards.

And then Edgar hit what long distance runners call The Wall. It happens all at once, when the body is spent of fuel and the sensation is like running directly into a wall.

Disoriented, Edgar began to zigzag as he slowed his pace to that of a walk. His mind was lost now and as he zigzagged, he changed direction and now was facing me.

I closed the gap to fifty yards, close enough to see Edgar didn't know where he was anymore.

Then he slowed, stopped and stood still for a moment.

I saw his eyes close, he passed out and went over the edge and disappeared from my view.

I raced the last hundred and fifty feet to the spot where Edgar went over and he was halfway down the embankment about six feet from the river.

The embankment was steep and I had to sit and slide down to Edgar.

He was face down in the soft dirt. I rolled him over and he was breathing, but unconscious.

I removed the radio from my belt and keyed it. "Paul? Can you hear me?"

"I can. So can my men," Lawrence said.

"I'm at the Saw Mill River, maybe a mile in," I said. "I have Edgar. He's unconscious. Bring a couple of water bottles."

"You okay?"

"Yeah."

I replaced the radio, stood and took hold of Edgar under his arms. I looked down at the river. It was high from melting winter snow and cold. Cold enough to kill an unconscious man who happened to fall in.

Edgar was around one hundred and eighty pounds of dead weight. It was slow going moving to the top of the embankment, but finally we both were on safe ground.

I sat next to him and caught my breath.

To my right, about a hundred yards away, three of Lawrence's men rushed towards us.

I waited for them to arrive before I stood up.

"Water is on the way," one of them said.

Another agent said, "What happened to him?"

"He ran to the point of exhaustion and passed out," I said. "He almost went into the river."

The three agents looked down at the river.

"Jeeze," one of them said.

One of them turned around. "Here comes Dave with the water."

It took several minutes for Dave to arrive. When he did, I took a bottle of water and drank half. The other half, I poured over Edgar's face.

He slowly opened his eyes.

"Hey, Edgar, how are you doing?" I asked him.

When he was able to sit up and sip water from the second bottle, I called Lawrence on the radio.

"Paul, Edgar is awake and okay. Want to talk to him at the house or somewhere else?" I said.

Chapter Thirty-five

"Why didn't you bring me to the police station?" Edgar asked.

"Let's just say this isn't a local law enforcement situation," Lawrence said.

"That's right, you're FBI," Edgar said.

We were at the table in the kitchen of Inez's home.

He had a bottle of Gatorade and took several long swallows.

"Where's my mother?" he asked.

"In the living room," Lawrence said.

Edgar sipped more Gatorade and nodded. Then he looked at me. "You're not an FBI Agent, are you?"

"No," I said.

"I used to run track in high school," he said. "Fifteen hundred meter, the mile and sometimes the mile and a half."

"I could tell by your form," I said.

"I didn't think you would catch me," he said.

"I've done some running of my own," I said. "And those expensive cigarettes you smoke clog your lungs."

Edgar nodded.

"Alright, Edgar, let's get to it," Lawrence said.

Edgar took a sip of Gatorade and then said, "I've had enough of this. Can I have some coffee and my cigarettes?"

I went to the counter where a pot of coffee sat in the machine. I filled three cups, set them on the table and then fetched a pack of cigarettes and matches from the drawer Inez showed me earlier.

"Do you know what a pack of these costs?" Edgar asked as he opened the pack.

"Fifteen seventy-five with tax," I said.

Edgar looked at me as he lit a cigarette with a match using his left hand.

"So tell me what happened, Edgar," Lawrence said. "Why did you go all the way to Puerto Rico to kill Joe DeSousa?"

Edgar exhaled smoke and gave Lawrence a puzzled look. "You have that all wrong Agent Lawrence," he said. "I didn't go to Puerto Rico to kill Joe DeSousa. I went to stop him from running for governor."

"Why?" Lawrence asked.

Edgar inhaled on the cigarette.

"Why?" he said, exhaling. "Why? Because he killed my father and the governor of Puerto Rico shouldn't be a murderer. Wouldn't you agree?"

"So you went there to stop him from running for governor?" Lawrence asked.

"Yes."

"How?" Lawrence asked.

"Blackmail," Edgar said. "I told him I would expose the affair his wife had with my father, that his son is actually my half brother and that he murdered my father when he found out about it."

"And you met him on a deserted beach at three in the morning to discuss it?" Lawrence said.

"That was his idea," Edgar said. "He said we needed to meet in secret to work out an agreement that would satisfy both of us. I met him twice before and wanted to meet at a park or restaurant. That day, I caught up with him outside a dry cleaning store and we spoke for a while. He suggested the beach at night for the privacy. He said he couldn't risk being overheard in public."

The missing hour.

Edgar took another hit on the cigarette. "And the crazy son of a bitch pulled a knife on me," he said. "One of those big knives used for cutting bread. Could have killed me if he hadn't tripped on a coconut in the dark of all things."

I looked at the counter. Beside the coffee maker was a wood block that held eight knives in various size slots.

I closed my eyes. I saw the missing detail at last.

"He pulled a knife on you?" Lawrence said.

I opened my eyes.

Edgar stood and opened his shirt and exposed a recent ugly knife wound in his upper left chest muscle.

"I had to stitch it myself in my hotel room with a needle and thread for God's sake," he said. "The next day, I got the hell out of there."

"Joe DeSousa stabbed you and then tripped over a coconut and then…? Lawrence asked.

"I reacted without thinking," Edgar said. "He fell forward and I grabbed the knife from his hand and stabbed him twice. He was alive when I left him."

"And the knife?"

"I tossed it as I ran away," Edgar said as he sat down. "Tide probably took it."

"Paul," I said. "He's telling the truth. On the counter in Maria's DeSousa's kitchen is a block of knives like that one."

I pointed to the wood block of knives.

"One of the knives is missing," I said. "The bread knife Joe DeSousa brought with him that night to kill Edgar."

Lawrence stared at Edgar.

"We had it backwards," I said. "Edgar didn't go there to kill Joe. Joe went there to kill Edgar."

* * *

"I don't know what to say," Escalante said.

I was in Lawrence's office in Washington. We had the call on speaker phone.

"This will turn Puerto Rico on its ear," Escalante said.

"Understandable," Lawrence said. "I'm sending Edgar to Puerto Rico on a U.S. Marshal's transport plane, but not until you arrive in D.C. to escort him back."

255

"You want me to come to Washington and take him back?" Escalante said.

"Bekker's idea and for once I agree with the son of a bitch," Lawrence said.

"I guess I should go pack a bag," Escalante said.

"See you for lunch," I said.

"My treat," Escalante said.

Chapter Thirty-six

Once Edgar was safely loaded onto the transport plane, I stood next to Lawrence and looked at Escalante.

"There's enough evidence for a not guilty," I said.

"And ruin the DeSousa family in the process," Escalante said.

"Those skeletons in the closet will get you every time," Lawrence said.

"They're wealthy and will survive," I said.

Escalante looked at me.

"Jack, I…" he said.

I gave him my right hand. "Sure."

We waited until the transport plane was in the air and then walked to Lawrence's Bronco where two agents waited for us.

"Even when you're wrong, you're still pretty good at catching bad guys," Lawrence said.

I looked at the sky, at the fading transport plane.

"If you even think about saying, Louie, this could be the start of a beautiful friendship, I swear Paul, I'll never ask you for another favor," I said.

"Oh no, not that, Jack," Lawrence said. "How could I possibly go on without doing you favors?"

"Speaking of favors," I said.

"Let me guess, you want me to take you home in our jet," Lawrence said.

"Think of the headlines, the publicity," I said. "FBI solves murder from thousands of miles away. They will write a book about it, maybe even a movie. Brad Pitt or Matt Damon will play you. A ride home is a small price for such glowing headlines."

Lawrence sighed.

"When?" he asked.

"I have to go shopping first," I said.

Chapter Thirty-seven

I took my car from the airport directly to Jane's house. She was still on duty, so I sat on her front steps and waited.

Around six in the afternoon, just as it was getting dark, her cruiser pulled into the driveway and parked behind my car.

I stood up.

Jane exited the cruiser and walked to me.

"What favor?" I asked.

"Stay over at my house. Sleep in my bed. Prove to me there are no ghosts between us," Jane said.

"I can do better than that," I said.

I dug the box of Classic Blue cigarettes out of a pocket and gave it to Jane.

"While they are great cigarettes, the gesture is a distant second to…"

"Just open the box," I said.

Jane flipped open the lid and looked at the engagement ring in the otherwise empty box.

"Is this for real?" she asked.

"Never more real," I said.

Holding the box, Jane engulfed me in a tight hug.

"What took you so goddamn long?" she said.

And then her cell phone rang. She glanced at the incoming number.

"It's Regan," she said, and answered the call.

She listened for a moment and then said, "He's here with me. We're on the way."

Jane hung up. "It's Oz, he's had a heart attack. We'll take the cruiser."

* * *

Regan, Jane, and I stood up when the doctor entered the waiting room in the emergency ward.

"He had eighty percent blockage in two arteries," the doctor said. "He's probably felt tired for a while. Anyway, we've cleared the blockage and inserted a stent. Damage to his heart is minimal. Your daughter saved his life, Mr. Bekker."

I looked at Regan.

"She somehow got an aspirin in him and gave him CPR until the ambulance arrived," the doctor said. "She wouldn't take no for an answer when she was told she couldn't ride in the ambulance."

"How…?" I said to my daughter.

Regan shrugged. "The nuns taught me," she said.

"He can go home by the end of the week, but he will need some tender loving care for a while," the doctor said.

I heard footsteps behind us.

"I can do that," Louisa said as she walked past me. She looked at the doctor. "Well," she said. "Take me to him."

About The Author

Al Lamanda is a native of New York City. His mystery novels include *Dunston Falls, Walking Homeless, Running Homeless, Sunset, Sunrise, First Light, This Side of Midnight*, and *With Six You Get Wally*. He has been nominated for the Edgar Award and the Nero Award for his mysteries, and was selected as the 2017 Nero Award winner for his John Bekker crime novel, *With Six You Get Wally*.